A SHADOWED EVIL

A SHADOWED EVIL

A Hawkenlye Mystery

Alys Clare

This first world edition published 2015
in Great Britain and the USA by
SEVERN HOUSE PUBLISHERS LTD of
19 Cedar Road, Sutton, Surrey, England, SM2 5DA.
Trade paperback edition first published
in Great Britain and the USA 2015 by
SEVERN HOUSE PUBLISHERS LTD.

British Library Cataloguing in Publication Data

Clare, Alys author.
  A Shadowed Evil. – (A Hawkenlye mystery)
  1. D'Acquin, Josse (Fictitious character)–Fiction.
  2. Helewise, Abbess (Fictitious character)–Fiction.
  3. England–Social life and customs–1066-1485–Fiction.
  4. Detective and mystery stories.
  I. Title II. Series
  823.9'2-dc23

ISBN-13: 978-0-7278-8520-3 (cased)
ISBN-13: 978-1-84751-620-6 (trade paper)
ISBN-13: 978-1-78010-673-1 (e-book)

All Severn House titles are printed on acid-free paper.

Severn House Publishers support the Forest Stewardship Council™ [FSC™],
the leading international forest certification organisation. All our titles that
are printed on FSC certified paper carry the FSC logo.

Typeset by Palimpsest Book Production Ltd.,
Falkirk, Stirlingshire, Scotland.
Printed and bound in Great Britain by
TJ International, Padstow, Cornwall.

In memory of my parents, together again –

always in my heart.

Iosse's Maternal Family Tree

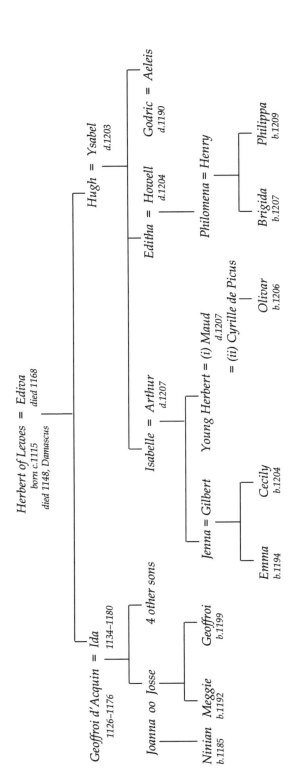

PROLOGUE

February 1212

He lay in his lonely little bed, curled up into the smallest shape he could contrive. He was six years old, and so scared that he was quite sure he was going to wet himself. *She* would be so angry if he did. She would probably do what she did last time and push his face into the stinky sheets, as if he was a puppy that had made a mess on the floor. He must get up and reach under the bed for the piss pot. He *knew* he had to. But he also knew there was a monster under the bed.

He hadn't really seen the monster. All the same, he could describe it. It had a big, long snout and a thick, ropy neck that sort of spread out into its shoulders. It had spiky bits on the top of its head and all down its neck and backbone. It was hairless, and its skin was hard and scaly. It made a rustling, rattling noise when it moved. It moved *oh so slowly*, like a snake sliding across the ground. It had huge gaping jaws and its breath smelt foul, like old meat. And its teeth—

NO. Don't think about its teeth, don't, don't, *don't* . . .

The little boy gave a soft moan, quickly stuffing his fist in his mouth to muffle it. He mustn't make a noise. *She* had told him that, so many times. He must be a big brave boy because he wasn't a baby any more. He was a Person of Importance. He must behave like a little lordling.

He didn't want to be a little lordling. It meant things he didn't like. It meant wearing stiff, uncomfortable clothes that had to be kept very clean all the time. It meant having to have nice manners at table. It meant he wasn't allowed to play with the other boys because they were servants' children. *She* had caught him playing tag-and-run with the groom's little lad, and she had pulled him away, that horrible expression on her face when her lips seemed to fold in on themselves and her eyes went cold and empty, and then, inside the house where nobody could see, she'd boxed his ears so hard that his head rang and he couldn't hear properly for quite a long time.

That had been quite a lot of days ago. His ears still hurt, sometimes.

He thought for a while. He realized she hadn't punished him since then. Well, not by hitting him, anyway, although she still kept sending him to his room when he'd done something naughty. Often he never knew exactly how he'd been bad or which one of her many rules he had broken. She had so many rules. It seemed to him that the more people did what she said – and it was funny how they usually did – the more rules she came up with.

Being sent to his room such a lot was good in one way, and that was he didn't have to see so much of Her. It was almost as if, having worked so hard at trying to make him the sort of boy she appeared to want – a *little lordling* – now she had stopped trying. Perhaps he *was* a little lordling now, and that was why she'd stopped, but he didn't really think so. Much more likely was that he was so bad at being it that she had despaired of him and given up.

It was all right in his room, but it was very lonely.

I wish my daddy was here.

He wasn't sure if he'd whispered the words out loud or just thought them. They were true, either way. But his father was dead: he knew that. He had a new father now. The new father was quite nice, and he had a kind face. But he didn't seem to know about boys.

Don't think about my daddy.

The other thing he didn't like about having to be a lordling and a Person of Importance was that he was no longer allowed to sleep in a safe, cosy, warm bundle with lots of other people. *She* said that Important People demanded and received their own beds. They slept in what she called *splendid isolation*, although he didn't really understand the words. He knew what they meant, though. They meant *being all by myself in the pitch-dark with nobody to hold my hand and nobody to snuggle up to not even a dog and so desperate to wee that it was going to come out and so afraid so so so afraid of the monster that I don't even dare put one foot out of bed.*

He lay very still. Perhaps if he didn't move at all the need to wee would go away. He could hear the house. It made soft, gentle sounds as if it was murmuring. As if, now that everybody was in bed and it was silent and dark, the house got a bit of peace and took the opportunity to have a little chat to itself. *Hello, house, have you had a nice day?* That was a bit silly, and the little boy grinned to himself in the darkness.

It was a good house. A friendly sort of house. It was very, very old – somehow he knew that, although he couldn't remember if anybody had actually told him – and he thought that a lot of good, kind people had lived in it and left something of themselves in its stones. The boy liked living there, and, had it not been for the monster, and Her, he would have been happy. Well, quite happy.

He felt that the house liked him, too. It felt as if its darkness wrapped itself round him, comforting him. He had sensed that there was a big, strong presence looking out for him. Once when he'd screamed out loud because of the monster, and *She* had come and shushed him, pinching and punching and pushing at him and telling him to behave himself, he'd thought that, just for the blink of an eye, a big, strong man had come out of the shadows and told her to go away. The man cared about him. The man had defended him from Her.

He really, *really* hoped the man would come again.

Desperate, his bladder bursting, suddenly he threw himself out of bed, scrabbled beneath it for the pot, directed a long, strong stream into it, shoved it under the bed again and then scrambled back under the covers, pulling them right up over his head.

He screwed his eyes tight shut. The monster was there. He had caught a glimpse of it as he pushed the piss pot back under the bed. A horrible, dark, thick, curled-up forelimb, like a huge coil of rope, only it ended in long, curved, wickedly pointed talons. The little boy gave a whimper.

Was that snaky forelimb even now uncurling? Blindly pushing forward across the dusty floor, sensing for him, snuffling for his smell, the terrible talons extending as the monster prepared to strike?

He listened, straining so hard that it made his ears hurt.

Nothing. Not a sound.

Ah, but monsters were very clever. Perhaps it was just pretending not to be coming for him . . .

He lay still as stone for an eternity. Still no sound.

He wondered how long he would have to endure the darkness and his bone-deep fear before morning came.

ONE

Josse d'Acquin looked up at the sky with anxious eyes. This morning, setting out from the House in the Woods, the weather had been mild, misty and damp. But the month was February: too early in the sun's year for unseasonal warmth to be reliable. Now the wind had changed, going round to the east, the clouds were clearing and the temperature was falling. Despite having made an early start, there were many hours of the journey still ahead.

He turned round in the saddle, looking back at Helewise, riding behind him. 'It's getting colder,' he said, despite himself unable to keep the worry out of his voice. 'Are you warm enough?'

'I am, Josse,' Helewise said with a smile, nudging her heels into her grey mare and coming to ride beside him. 'Thanks to you and your sensible precautions, I am wearing several layers of good wool, and my travelling cloak is sufficiently thick and heavy to keep out worse weather than this.' But he noticed that she, too, gave a swift glance up at the sky. 'How far have we to go?'

Only someone who knew her as well as Josse did would have detected the faint note of concern in her voice. Bracingly he said, 'We're well over halfway now; more like three-quarters, I'd say. We'll go through the gap in the downs, turn westwards for a few miles, and then we'll see the town ahead of us.'

She nodded. 'Let's get on, then.' She kicked Daisy, and for some time they went at a steady canter, eating up the miles.

Emerging from a winding track on to a wider road where there was room to ride abreast, Helewise broke the companionable silence. Perhaps, he thought, she was growing more concerned about the steadily increasing cold, and trying to take their minds off it . . . 'Tell me about the house and its inhabitants, Josse,' she said. 'You used to visit when you were a boy?'

Eager to play his part, Josse replied, 'Aye, that's right, I did.' He broke off to rein in his horse, letting Helewise pass and then taking up a position on her other side – the eastern side, from which direction the wind was blowing with growing strength – in the hope that Alfred's big body would afford her some protection. 'Although my mother moved to northern France after she married my father, she never forgot that her roots and her kin were in England, and she dispatched me regularly to stay with her brother Hugh and his wife Ysabel.'

'And their children – your cousins – were all girls, you told me?'

'Aye. Three of them, Isabelle, Editha and Aeleis, and, although Isabelle was nearest to me in age, Aeleis was my favourite.' He smiled at the memory. 'She was the tomboy, the leader into mischief, and wherever she went, I willingly followed.'

'And what of the house?' Helewise's teeth were chattering, and Josse only just made out her words. He pressed his heels to Arthur's sides, subtly increasing their pace.

'Southfire Hall has been in my mother's family for many generations,' he began. 'The house is ancient, and they say there's been a dwelling on that spot, on the top of the rise of the downs to the south-west of Lewes, since time out of mind. The first time I went there, Uncle Hugh was having an extension built, which, as you'll imagine, made the most exciting playground for my cousins and me.' He glanced at her, then wished he hadn't, for her lips were blue with cold. 'We had the run of the place,' he went on in a tone which, even to his own ears, sounded far too hearty, 'exploring into all the strictly forbidden places, because everyone was much too busy and harassed to watch over us.' He smiled briefly. 'Aeleis always took it as a personal challenge when someone told her somewhere was not safe for children and strictly out of bounds.' His smile widened as the images formed in his memory: grubby faces and hands, cut knees, and his boyhood self trying to help a small girl restore a ripped and filthy gown before her nursemaid discovered the damage. 'The old undercroft – beneath the original building – was the best place,' he went on. 'It was vast and creepy, spooky with long-forgotten things and low, half-blocked doorways to subterranean passages and little rooms that nobody had seen in decades, if not more. It was as if –' he paused, thinking how to put a fleeting childhood impression into words – 'as if the whole site bore an imprint of every dwelling that preceded the present one, like old footprints half-obliterated by later ones. We once found what looked like an ancient hearth,' he added, the memory suddenly surfacing, 'and Aeleis pinched a flint and tinder from the kitchens so that we could light a fire.'

'And did you?' Helewise managed to sound as if, despite the increasingly uncomfortable and worrying conditions, she was enjoying the tale.

'No,' he admitted with a grin. 'There was no draught, since whatever hole had once provided for the flow of air had long been blocked up.' He chuckled, a sudden picture in his mind of Aeleis cursing and swearing as she rubbed her streaming eyes. 'We choked ourselves on the smoke.'

They had come to a place where the road descended a long, steep slope, and they turned their attention to their mounts, picking their careful way down. On level ground again, Helewise said with a sigh, 'And now it seems that your Uncle Hugh is seriously ill.'

'He's dying, Helewise,' Josse said gently. 'My cousin Isabelle would not have sent word to come had it not been so, given the season and all that it carries with it.' Bad weather, winter-damaged tracks, short daylight, he reflected morosely.

'You cannot be sure he is dying!' Helewise protested. 'All the message said was that he was sick, and wandering in his mind.'

'He is an old man,' Josse said, struggling with a sudden, unexpected surge of emotion. 'Old men die.'

She let that go without comment. 'When did you last visit?' she demanded.

'A while back, now.' He tried to work it out. 'It was at Christmastide, and, even then, Uncle Hugh was grown stout and balding. It was just before we had that business with the heretics.[1] Must be all of ten years.'

He heard her laugh softly. 'Dear Josse, that was twenty years ago.'

Twenty years? He spun round to look at her, aghast. Had so much time gone by, then? He studied her – the clear grey eyes, the wide mouth always so ready to smile, the modest headdress of spotless white linen beneath the hood of her heavy cloak, the straight back and square shoulders that did not bend under heavy

[1] See *A Dark Night Hidden*.

loads. *I do not believe it*, he thought, although in truth he did. *You look exactly the same as you did when first I set eyes on you, and I believe I have loved you every day since.*

It was not a sentiment for expressing aloud; not when they needed more than anything to press on to Southfire Hall as fast as they could. So he just smiled and murmured, 'Is it really so long?' and they rode on.

Presently they came to the town of Lewes, and made their way across the bridge over the river Ouse that linked the two parts of the settlement. The waterfront was lined with warehouses and taverns, and several craft were tied up along the quays. The river was vital to the town, for it was the means by which the many businesses transported their produce and their goods to the rest of the world. Now, however, the port lay quiet and there were few signs of activity, for the rapidly falling temperature had driven most folk indoors.

They passed the castle, up on its imposing rise to their right. Then, descending to ride for a while beside another, smaller, waterway, they saw the great spread of the priory over to the left. Josse, watching Helewise, observed her close attention to the network of buildings, gardens, stables, streamlets and ponds. Her eyes were wide with awe, for it made Hawkenlye Abbey look like a small rural convent.

Leaving the priory behind, they headed towards the higher land to the south-west of the town. 'This area is known as Southover,' said Josse. Helewise nodded. Reaching the steeply rising track that wound its way up Southfire Hill, they began the long, weary ascent. 'And now,' he said encouragingly, 'we are very nearly there! The place where my father Geoffroi first met my mother is perhaps half a mile ahead. He—'

'He had returned from crusade,' Helewise interrupted, 'and made his way to the household of his good friend, Herbert of Lewes, to break the news of Herbert's death in Damascus to his family.'

Whilst he was gratified that she remembered the tale, nevertheless Josse felt it was his role to tell it. 'Geoffroi found a compact stone house up on the ridge of the downland,' he went on, 'for this was many years before the extension was built, and the dwelling was modest. He saw a courtyard wall decorated

with bisected flint stones, and, within, shallow steps leading up
to the stout door of the house. And, once inside, he met Herbert's
widow, her son Hugh and her daughter Ida, who, quite soon
afterwards, became his wife and my mother. Although,' he added
hastily, 'naturally there was quite a long gap between the two
events.'

'Naturally, Josse,' Helewise said primly, although there was
laughter in her eyes. 'As if I would imagine any different.'

They were at the top of the track now, and the house stood
before them. The flints in the courtyard wall glistened with a
light frost, and the reddish-gold stonework looked bleached by
the cold. From somewhere within the large and inviting bulk
of the house, smoke rose. Candlelight glittered through a narrow
window. Josse led the way through the gate and into the yard
and, just as a young lad and a wiry, older man hurried out from
a low stable block to the left of the entrance to take their horses,
the first snowflakes began to fall.

The cold and the long ride had stiffened Josse's joints, and for
several moments as, with brisk efficiency, the man and the lad
set about their task, all he could do was mutter his thanks while
he tried to rub the deep ache out of his hips and knees. Helewise,
unsurprisingly, had remembered her manners, and was responding
politely to the old man – a head groom, perhaps – as he enquired
about their journey.

'Lady Isabelle said to notify her the moment you arrived,' he
was saying, 'and I've already sent one of the stable boys to do
just that.' He turned to Josse, a sympathetic smile on his face.
'She'll soon have you warm and snug, with good, hot food inside
you.'

He led the way across the courtyard. Josse stared about him,
trying to reconcile memory with actuality. There was the original
building, and there, to the left, the first extension. But now the
dwelling had been extended again: on the opposite side, a tall,
graceful wing rose up, set against the original hall and projecting
out in front of it.

He was just wondering how large the family had grown, to
require so much space, and, indeed, how prosperous his kinsmen
must be to be able to afford so much new construction, when,
at the top of a flight of shallow stone steps, the main door of the

house was opened. A tall, deep-bosomed and wide-shouldered woman stood in the doorway, her comely face creased by a happy smile. 'Josse!' she cried, flinging her arms wide and flying down the steps. 'Dear Josse, you're here!'

Then she enveloped him in a tight, warm hug, kissing him resoundingly on each cheek. Filled with affection, his head flooding with happy memories, he hugged her in return. 'Oh,' he said softly, 'you haven't changed at all!'

He disentangled himself and, holding out a hand to Helewise, drew her forward. For a brief moment he looked right into her eyes, feeling as he always did the familiar upsurge of love. 'This,' he said, 'is my Helewise. Helewise, this is my cousin Isabelle.'

Isabelle took Helewise's hands in hers, and her smile disappeared into a look of horror. 'Oh, but your hands are *icy*!' she exclaimed, squeezing all the harder as if she would comfort Helewise with her own warmth. 'Didn't you have any gloves?'

'Yes!' Helewise replied with a laugh. 'Here.' She held up the thick, fur-lined gauntlets. 'The worsening cold proved too much for them.'

'Come inside at once!' Isabelle commanded, ushering them up the steps in front of her. 'I have prepared a private room for you –' there was a definite note of pride in her voice, for such an arrangement was a luxury afforded by only the best households – 'and now you shall get warm, refresh yourselves with a little food and drink – not too much, for there is to be a welcoming feast for you tonight – and then you must rest.'

She reached round Josse to push the heavy, iron-studded oak door wide open, and side by side he and Helewise entered Southfire Hall. The door opened into the first extension, but little could be seen of it just then, for daylight was fast fading and few lamps had yet been lit. Josse had an impression of passages winding away, arched stone doorways leading off them. Isabelle turned to her right, going under an archway in a thick stone wall, and now the original hall that Josse recalled spread out before him.

It was an old structure, rectangular in shape, long and low. A row of stout pillars ran down each of the longer sides, and it was oriented east–west, with the north side facing the courtyard and the gates. Down the middle of the floor ran a deep, stone-lined hearth, in which a bright fire burned. Josse had an impression of quite a lot of people over on the far side of the hearth. Some were seated on an arrangement of benches and settles; one or two sat apart. A trio of children played with their dolls on the stone-flagged floor.

Isabelle cast a quick look across to the little gathering, but hurried Josse and Helewise on down the length of the hall, keeping to the near side of the fire. 'No need just now for introductions,' she said with kindly tact, 'for you are exhausted and chilled to the bone; in no mood, I'm sure, for courtesies and the effort of remembering a dozen names. There will be time later for—'

Suddenly one of the children leapt up and ran around the end of the hearth, turning back on herself to skid to a stop in front of Isabelle. She planted her feet firmly and stared up at the newcomers. She was about eight, Josse thought, and enchantingly pretty.

'May not even one of us be allowed to say hello and welcome, Grandmamma?' she whispered, with a knowing smile up at the newcomers as if she knew perfectly well whispering wouldn't prevent them overhearing.

Isabelle crouched down before the child, her wide skirts fanning out round her. She brushed the child's fair hair off her broad forehead with a gentle hand, then briefly held the little face in tender hands and kissed it. 'Be *very* swift, then, Cecily, for our guests have endured a long ride in the cold and have more need of peace and quiet than grand speeches of welcome,' she whispered back.

The girl grinned up at Josse and Helewise. 'Sorry,' she said, 'I should have realized. Welcome! I'll save the rest for later.'

She turned and skipped away. His eyes following her, Josse now noticed that another of the group had also come towards them. She was a short, round-faced woman, and she took very small, precise steps, moving with an odd, jerky action. 'I tried to stop her, Isabelle,' she said with an edge of self-righteousness, 'but, as usual, she had her own ideas.'

All the affection that had warmed Isabelle's expression as she greeted Josse and Helewise, and crouched to pet her granddaughter, abruptly vanished. 'Thank you, Cyrille,' she said neutrally. 'No harm done.'

Then, her shoulders stiff, she strode on down the hall and led Josse and Helewise out beneath a second arched entrance at the far end. This gave on to a stone-walled passage that extended to right and left, with one or two elongated slit windows and several doors opening off it. Isabelle walked on to the furthest doorway, and, going on inside, stooped by the lively fire burning in the small hearth to light a taper, with which she set a flame in two lamps. 'Now,' she said, 'please, relax and make yourselves comfortable.'

Josse stared round the room. It was generously sized, yet its spaciousness was dwarfed by the huge bed set against the far wall. The bed had a carved wooden head and foot, and was piled with pillows, crisp linen, soft, fluffy wool blankets and glossy pelts. Beside it, a small table held a brass tray on which there was an earthenware jug of some steaming liquid smelling of spices, a wooden platter of bread, cold meats and cheese, and a jug of hot water beside a bowl which had a clean white cloth neatly folded over it. Helewise, standing right beside him, let out a quiet moan of pleasure. Turning to Isabelle, she said, with fervent sincerity, 'Oh, *thank* you!'

Isabelle smiled. 'It's a pleasure to receive you both,' she replied. Then, looking straight at Helewise, she added, 'Josse's wife is as welcome beneath this roof as Josse has always been.'

Josse opened his mouth to speak, but Helewise's sharp elbow in his ribs stopped him.

'I'll leave you,' Isabelle was saying, already moving towards the doorway. 'If you need anything, please call.'

Josse hurried after her. 'Helewise will, I'm sure, make immediate use of your kind hospitality,' he said, 'but, before I do likewise, will you take me to see your father? He is, after all, the reason for our visit.'

Isabelle turned back, her face full of contrition. 'Of course, Josse! I'm sorry – I should have thought. Come with me.'

With a quick enquiring glance at Helewise, who nodded her encouragement, he followed his cousin along the passage.

Isabelle led him back through the central hall, walking swiftly and keeping to the shadows. They entered the extension through a different archway; this one was set further away from the main door. They strode on, along successive corridors, until, right over on the east side, they came to a low doorway set deep within the wall. Isabelle tapped gently and called out, 'Father? Are you awake?'

There was the mumble of a reply. Isabelle opened the door, and then stepped aside to let Josse go past, following him into the room.

Lying in a narrow little bed beside which a small brazier burned lay the still figure of a very old man. At first, had Josse not known that this was his Uncle Hugh, he would not have recognized him. The last time he had seen him – twenty years ago, as Helewise had so recently reminded him – Hugh had been a loud, stout man with quite a lot remaining of his curly, auburn hair. Warm-hearted, generous, demonstrative, quick to anger but far quicker to laugh, Josse had many happy memories of him. In his own mind, Uncle Hugh had been undisputedly the lord of his own household; everyone else had known full well (although nobody ever let on to Hugh) that, in reality, it had been his wife Ysabel who was in charge. But Ysabel had been dead nearly ten years now, and already Josse had felt her absence. Plump and breathless, yet exuding always an air of calm, quiet competence, Ysabel had been a strong woman.

Now, Josse looked with sad, shocked eyes at the husband Ysabel had left to carry on without her. He was diminished: shrunken from the big barrel-bodied man he had once been into a skeletal figure who barely raised the heavy bedding. Josse knelt down beside the bed, reaching out to take hold of one of the bony white hands. 'Uncle Hugh?' he said gently. 'It's me, Josse.'

The waxy lids peeled apart, opened, and Hugh's eyes met Josse's. For a moment he did not speak, and his unaltered expression suggested he hadn't understood. 'I'm your nephew, Josse,' Josse repeated, 'Ida's son.'

'No need for long-winded explanations,' came Hugh's thin, reedy voice. 'I had but the one sister, so any nephew must be one of her sons.' Then the hand inside Josse's suddenly contracted into a squeeze – a surprisingly strong one – and Hugh said, 'Good to see you, Josse.' He closed his eyes again, still holding Josse's hand, and presently there came a small snore.

'He knows who I am!' Josse said softly after a while; he

wanted to make sure Hugh was asleep before starting to talk about him. 'I wasn't really expecting that.'

Isabelle came to crouch beside him, looking at her father with loving eyes. 'He has good days and bad days,' she said. 'Well, not days, really – he can change very quickly from recognizing us, and conversing perfectly logically, to crying out and protesting wildly about things that quite clearly disturb him profoundly. We cannot understand what distresses him so, for his words make no sense.'

'And you cannot hazard a guess?'

Isabelle frowned in thought. 'He seems to think there is some evil here,' she said after a moment. 'Within this dear old house, which all of us – and Father in particular – have always found to be such a protective, safe, *good* place, he seems to fear that there is a hidden danger that none but he perceives.'

'A hidden danger,' Josse repeated softly. He hoped very much that his uncle's fear signified no more than the fuddling of the mind that so often accompanied old age; the idea of evil and peril being present here, in this warm-hearted household, was quite abhorrent. 'Do you think he could be right?'

'Oh, *I* don't know, Josse!' Isabelle's frustration and distress were apparent in her tone. 'He believes it, anyway. At times he tries to sit up, staring wildly round the room, and he says something that sounds like "Marte", or perhaps it's "Maria"; I can't tell, since only the *Mar* sound is clear.'

'Martyr? Or the blessed Virgin Mary?' Josse suggested. 'Had he become very devout in old age?'

Isabelle grinned. 'Not particularly. I think that in truth he only went to church as often as he did because of Father Edgar. You remember him?'

'The chess-playing priest!' Josse exclaimed, memory surging back. 'Aye, indeed I do.'

Isabelle laughed. 'You always were an awful chess player,' she observed. 'And you took forever to make your moves.'

'Especially when I played Father Edgar,' Josse agreed. 'Mind you, he was very good.'

'So he ought to be,' Isabelle said with spirit, 'seeing as he never let anyone he found beneath our roof get away without playing him at least once. Why, I recall how, one day, he . . .'

Her quiet voice went on with the reminiscence, but Josse barely heard. *Southfire Hall, chess*, he was thinking. There was some connection; and it was a strong one, powerful enough to reach out to him down the long corridor of the years. But he could not bring to mind what it was.

Josse became aware that Isabelle had fallen silent. Hugh was sleeping deeply now, and the fingers twined with Josse's had gone slack. Gently Josse tucked his uncle's hand beneath the bedclothes, then he got to his feet.

'Goodbye for now, dear uncle,' he murmured. 'I'll come back soon.'

Treading softly, he and his cousin left the room, and she quietly closed the door.

TWO

Helewise opened her eyes and, still dazed with sleep, looked around the room. She hadn't meant to nod off. When Josse had gone off with his cousin to visit his uncle, Helewise had merely thought to stretch out on the luxuriously dressed bed for a short while and rest her tired body. But the rigours of the long day, and the hard ride in increasingly cold and progressively more alarming weather, had taken more out of her than she realized. She had drawn a thick, warm, soft blanket over herself, snuggled a hollow for her head in the wonderfully soft pillows, and before she had time to finish warning herself to stay awake, had fallen asleep.

She had dreamed vividly. She saw a small boy standing in the doorway, peering at her round the edge of the door. *Be careful*, whispered this dream boy. *There are monsters here. There's one under my bed, and there is probably one under yours, too.* She had heard her own voice whisper back. *I will be on my guard*, she promised. *I will take a big stick and thrust it furiously into the space beneath the bed, and it will poke the monster very hard in his eye, and he will run away.* The dream boy had giggled, but the laughter had not quite extinguished the fear in his blue eyes. He had a mop of thick, fair hair, and, as he smiled, she saw that he had a gap between his two front teeth. They were the big teeth; the child seemed to be about six. Then, in the way of dreams, the boy changed, features, colouring and clothing morphing until Helewise knew, somehow, that she was looking at the boy version of Josse. He was frowning – angry about something – and he had a big stick in his hand. A hand reached out and smoothed her hair, and the adult Josse – her own beloved Josse – bent down over her and said softly, 'Sleep, dear heart.' She had been vaguely aware of the big bed rippling as he lay down beside her, and then slumber had reclaimed her.

Now she sat up, propped by the mound of pillows and rubbing the drowse from her eyes. Her dream was still vivid, and she smiled at the memory of the handsome little boy, and of the image of the child that Josse had once been. He was no longer beside her on the bed, although the rumpled covers and dented pillows confirmed that he had been there. Helewise's smile widened. Josse had very nearly protested when Isabelle had referred to Helewise as his wife, and only her timely dig in his ribs had stopped him. *For I am his wife*, Helewise thought. Did not the wise and devout monk Gratian state that the only thing necessary to make a binding bond was the spoken willingness of each partner to take the other as their spouse? *And so we have done, my Josse and I*, Helewise reflected. She had said to him, *I receive you as mine, so that you become my husband and I your wife*, and then he had repeated the vow to her. In Gratian's view – and Helewise's – that made her and Josse married, even if the vow had been made alone, in a place apart, and without witnesses. In any case, until the endless quarrel between King John and the Pope came to an end – if it ever did – and the interdict was at last lifted, the absence of priests in England meant that Helewise and Josse's solemn and sincere vows to one another were the best they could do.

Helewise stretched extravagantly, enjoying the sensation of being warm right to the tips of her toes. This brief, restorative period of privacy wouldn't go on much longer, and soon now she must get up and set about tidying herself, in preparation for meeting the family and attending the feast that they had kindly prepared. There seemed to be rather a lot of people to meet, and it had been a thoughtful gesture on Josse's cousin's part to hold back from making the introductions the moment Helewise and Josse had arrived.

Helewise lay back again, thinking about Isabelle. There was no mistaking the fact that she and Josse were kin. Both were big-boned, strongly made people, and of similar height: Isabelle was tall for a woman. There was something in her features, too, that strongly resembled Josse. Their colouring was different, however. Josse's hair was grey-flecked brown and what could be seen of Isabelle's, beneath the white bands of her headdress and the light indoor veil, was fair turning to silvery white. Also, Josse's eyes were brown where Isabelle's were sea-green, the bright colour surrounded by a band of indigo. Yet the shape of both pairs was the same, as were the golden lights that shone in the irises. And the cousins both had that indefinable air of strength and firm resolve that had first drawn Helewise to Josse, recognizing in him a man to depend on, and in whom to discover a true, loyal friend. A man, in short, to love.

Isabelle, Helewise was sure, would prove to be out of the same mould. Josse had told her that Isabelle's husband had died five years ago, but whatever the magnitude of that grief had been, she seemed to have learned to cope without him. She would no doubt—

The door to the bedchamber opened a crack, and Josse's head appeared round it. 'You're awake!' he said, smiling as he pushed the door fully open and came into the room. 'I'm glad, for I've been sent to tell you that the meal will shortly be ready, and invite you to come and meet the household.'

'Gladly,' she replied, hastening to get up and straightening the rumpled bed. She washed her hands and face – some time while she slept, the hot water had been replenished – and then she smoothed back her hair and tucked it under her wimple, arranging her soft, silky veil over it. Then she smoothed the creases out of her gown and stood before Josse for his inspection. 'Do I look all right?'

He grinned. 'Aye, you'll do.' Then he held out his arm to her, and she put her hand on it. Side by side, they left the room and set off along the corridor.

'This house is a veritable warren!' she said quietly to him. 'I'm sure it is going to take me a while to find my way around.'

'Aye, it's been extended even since my last visit, and they've built a new chapel, within the house.' Josse pointed ahead. 'That's it, in there.'

'A chapel!' Helewise exclaimed. 'May I see it?'

'Well, not just now, because the family await us, but later, of course. I'll explain the layout of the whole house.'

'You've been taken on a tour, then?' she said with a smile.

'Aye. Young Herbert – he's Isabelle's son, and my Uncle Hugh's grandson – showed me around while you slept. I've also met the family, which has grown considerably since I was last here, and I begin to understand the need for more living space. The big building where you and I first entered is the original extension, built when I was a lad, like I told you. That's where most of the family have their own rooms. Beyond it, stretching away to the south towards the higher ground, there are the kitchens, the servants' quarters, the ovens and bakehouse, and a series of workshops. The long, low room with the hearth is the original hall – always referred to as the Old Hall – and the building we're in now houses guest quarters and a solar.'

'First a chapel, now a solar! How lovely,' Helewise said wistfully.

'Maybe one day,' Josse murmured. He was well aware of her long-held desire for both, in the House in the Woods.

'What's it like?' she asked.

'The solar? Very fine,' Josse acknowledged. 'There's plenty of space for those wishing to get away from the bustle of family life. There are comfortably padded settles, some groups of stools and benches for those wanting to sit together to sew, or draw, and arched windows facing out to the west to catch the afternoon and evening light. Oh, and a small opening facing out to the north, too, looking out over the valley.' He gave a mock-shudder. 'Too high for me,' he said with a grin. 'Herbert invited me to lean out and see just how long and steep the drop is, but one swift glance was more than enough. The ground falls away like the side of a mountain.'

'And now,' Helewise said, for, even strolling slowly, they had almost reached the Old Hall, 'it's time to meet the family.' For a moment, she tightened her grip on Josse's arm. Then, hand in hand, they walked on into the hall. A series of trestles topped with long boards had been put up, set with knives and platters, benches set along one side and five fine oak chairs opposite.

Isabelle was looking out for them, and came hurrying to the doorway to greet them. 'You are refreshed, I see,' she said, taking hold of Helewise's hand. Then, leaning close, she added in a voice just for Helewise, 'I will keep the introductions brief, then we can get down to eating and drinking.'

Helewise suppressed a smile.

'Now,' Isabelle said, 'here is my sister Editha, also, of course, cousin to Josse.' She led Helewise before a fine, carved chair in which sat a frail-looking woman, thin, a little bent. She looked up at Helewise with eyes as brown as Josse's. 'Forgive my not getting up,' she said, holding out her hand. 'Welcome, Lady Helewise. I am very happy to meet you.'

Lady Helewise! It was not a form of address she had expected. 'And I you,' she replied. 'But, please, just Helewise. We are, after all, kinswomen.'

Editha bowed her head in acknowledgement, and a swift smile crossed her lined face. Helewise had the strong impression that she had just passed a small test.

'Editha is, like me, a widow,' Isabelle was saying, 'and here is her daughter, Philomena, and her husband, Henry.' A blonde-haired woman, beautifully dressed, and a pleasant-looking man whose reluctance to meet Helewise's eye suggested shyness. 'These are their children, Brigida and Philippa –' Helewise recognized the youngest pair of the trio who had earlier been playing with their dolls – 'and they will just say a *very* quick good night before their nurse takes them off to bed.' She frowned in mock ferocity, and the two little girls collapsed into giggles.

'This is my daughter Jenna.' Now Isabelle drew forward a strong-faced woman whose face, although not beautiful, was undoubtedly striking. 'Her husband, Gilbert, is away from home, involved with business affairs that have taken him down to the coast, where we fear he may now be stranded if the threatened deterioration in the weather comes about. Here are my grand-daughters, Emma' – a calm-faced, fair young woman of perhaps eighteen, who made Helewise a graceful courtesy, 'and my little Cecily, whom you have already met.' The impish little girl who had earlier hurried to welcome the guests skipped up to Helewise, tried to copy her sister's curtsey, and fell over. Helping her up – there had come a sharp hiss of disapproval from someone, and the child had blushed and scowled furiously – Helewise whispered, 'I did that once. It's not easy to master a decent curtsey but, if you like, I'll show you how I taught myself to stay on my feet.'

Cecily looked up at her and gave her a look of such gratitude that Helewise knew she had found an ally. Quite why she might need one, she did not know.

'And, finally,' Isabelle said, 'may I present my son, Herbert.' As a man in perhaps the early thirties came to kiss her hand, Helewise thought, *Isabelle is a woman who loves her son very dearly, for I heard something different in her voice when she spoke his name.* Herbert straightened up and looked right into Helewise's eyes. 'Welcome to our house, Cousin Helewise,' he said with grave courtesy. Helewise opened her mouth to respond, but Herbert had already turned away. He had grasped the hand of a stocky figure standing right behind him – crowding him, almost – and now he drew her forward. 'This is the lady Cyrille de Picus,' he said. His tone reflecting his pride, he added, 'My wife.'

The woman had edged in front of Herbert, and now stood up close to Helewise, the protuberant light-blue eyes staring at her with a particular piercing intensity, as if they habitually peered into private corners and personal concerns. 'Good evening, my *dear* Lady Helewise,' Cyrille said effusively, and she leaned forward to kiss Helewise's cheek. Up close, her skin was pale, and the plump cheeks shone with a light film of grease. She was dressed in a gown of dove-grey, the fabric fine and costly. Her white headdress and gorget fitted quite loosely, allowing strings of thin, gingery hair threaded with grey to escape and straggle across her forehead. She was short, yet gave the impression of being taller than she was because of the stiff and upright manner in which she held herself. Her thick neck stretched taut above sloping shoulders, and she stuck her jaw in the air as if hoping to disguise a double chin.

'Good evening to you, too,' Helewise said politely. 'How good it is to—'

But Cyrille had already turned away. 'I must check the board,' she muttered, 'since those empty-headed serving girls never listen to orders and undoubtedly will have failed to set out the right knives and forgotten they were told to polish the best glassware.' She looked briefly back at Helewise. 'Please excuse me,' she said, her face falling into lines of resignation and exaggerated distress. 'But you know how it is in a big household. Unless one sees to things oneself, standards inevitably slip.'

She hurried away towards the table, and her short, flat feet in their soft leather house slippers made a flapping noise on the stone flags of the floor.

There was a brief and slightly awkward silence, and then, as if by pre-arrangement, several people all began talking at once. Herbert – surely with a slight flush staining his cheeks? – asked Helewise about her journey. Isabelle cornered Josse and suggested he accompany her to their seats at table. Editha called out to her niece Jenna's husband to help her get up out of her chair. The two smallest girls were ushered away, with wails of protest, by their nurse. Cecily, after a brief, furious and unsuccessful protest to her mother, went with them.

And Helewise, making herself concentrate on the small talk of her conversation with Herbert, was at the same time wondering why, when without doubt Isabelle was the senior woman here, it had been Cyrille de Picus who had taken it upon herself to go and check – surely unnecessarily – on the final arrangements of the table setting.

The welcoming feast went on for some time, as dish after dish was set on the long boards. Although there was not a huge amount of anything – the family, like every other one in the land with the exception of those in the topmost echelons, was suffering from the King's never-ending demands for more and more taxes – someone, probably Isabelle, had gone to a lot of trouble to do the very best with what was obtainable, and many of the dishes clearly included costly ingredients in the recipe: a tray of little honey cakes were coloured the unmistakable yellow of saffron, and the dark, rich gravy for the meats was flavoured with brandy. The wine was excellent. Helewise, savouring a mouthful, recalled Josse telling her that one of the many commodities his merchant uncle Hugh traded was wine. Presumably, she reflected, glancing down the table towards Young Herbert, he was now in charge of affairs. Judging from the extensive additions to the house and the quality of tonight's fare, he was making a good job of it.

Isabelle sat in the head of the household's place, on a high-backed, beautifully-carved chair midway down the table. On her right sat Josse, her cousin and her honoured guest, and Helewise was on her left, with Herbert next to her. Beside Josse sat Cyrille. On the opposite side, Helewise faced the invalid Editha, who, she noticed, had been helped to her place on the bench and provided with a couple of small pillows. Helewise wondered why Editha had not been allocated one of the oak chairs, which were surely more appropriate for someone so obviously frail and perhaps in pain. Was the careful assigning of places in accordance with position so important that it overrode consideration and simple kindness?

Henry sat opposite Isabelle, and Philomena, Jenna and Emma took up the remainder of the bench. Emma, Helewise observed, was putting herself out to help her great-aunt, reaching for the dishes that seemed to be Editha's favourites, retrieving a fallen cushion, and frequently asking, in a softly pitched tone, whether she was comfortable. Perhaps she, too, Helewise mused, sensed the injustice of poor Editha having to sit on the bench. She and Josse, she knew, had no choice but to accept the places either side of Isabelle; for tonight, at least. But it would have been a generous gesture on Cyrille's part to suggest quietly to Editha that they swap places.

Helewise's reverie was interrupted by Herbert, asking politely if he might refill her glass.

The long meal went on, and the noise level increased as the wine was consumed. Helewise, trying to gain an impression of both the individuals and of the family as a whole, managed a fair stab at both. She spoke at length to those nearest to her, tentatively concluding that Henry, while indeed very shy, was possessed of an observant eye, a thoughtful mind and a quiet, delightful wit. Editha bore whatever affliction ailed her with courage, and, although Helewise quite often saw her wince with pain, not once did she hear her utter a word of complaint. Emma was modest in her demeanour and preferred to listen than to talk; she must have overheard Josse speaking about the sanctuary that Helewise and the household at the House in the Woods had founded, where the poor, the sick and the desperate came for succour, for, taking advantage of a moment when Helewise was not engaged in conversation elsewhere, she leaned across the table and asked Helewise to tell her all about it.

At the other end of the table, Helewise observed that the two women sitting opposite Cyrille spoke mostly to each other. Sometimes one or other addressed a remark to Josse, but each time Cyrille interposed, deflecting the question as if implying that Josse ought not to be bothered. *She is trying to show him consideration*, Helewise thought charitably. *Perhaps she believes him to be tired by the journey, preferring to eat and drink without interruption.* But that wasn't really very likely; anyone with eyes and ears could see that dear Josse, far from being exhausted, was having a wonderful time, talking, laughing, raising his glass to this person and that as he tried to compensate for twenty years' absence in one evening.

At last empty platters outnumbered full ones, and even Josse admitted he'd had quite enough wine. The conversation became sporadic, and then, led by Editha, one by one the family members rose and made their good nights. Soon, only Isabelle, Josse and Helewise, Herbert and Cyrille remained at the table. Helewise noticed that Cyrille kept shooting glances at her mother-in-law, as if waiting for some action or signal; was she, Helewise wondered, expecting Isabelle to be the next to leave? Surely it didn't matter, here in this friendly, informal home, in what order people retired for the night?

She was not to find out. As if Isabelle too had noticed, and was irritated, abruptly she turned to Cyrille and said, 'Go to bed, Cyrille. I wish to go on talking to Josse and Helewise, if they are happy to stay up a little longer?'

'Aye,' Josse said, at the same time as Helewise murmured, 'Of course.'

Cyrille stood up. Her expression was disapproving, as if Isabelle's remark had displeased her. She lifted her chin, straightened her back, and, with the barest of nods, turned and strode away. Herbert got up to follow her. 'Stay, if you wish, son,' Isabelle said.

But he shook his head. Briefly resting a hand on his mother's shoulder, he smiled down at her and muttered, 'Best not.' Then, bowing low to the three of them who remained, he hurried off after his wife.

The last sounds of their footsteps faded and died. Isabelle gave a sigh. Then, after quite a long pause, she said, 'It is good to have you to myself at last, Cousin Josse.' Turning to Helewise, she added courteously, 'And you too, my lady, naturally.'

Helewise said, 'Isabelle, please, if you would like the chance to speak privately to Josse, truly I don't mind! I am more than happy to return to that very comfortable bed and—'

But Isabelle put out a detaining hand. 'No, Helewise – there is, in truth, nothing private about what I want to say, for the

situation is known to every person in this house, except one.'
Again, she sighed.

After another, longer, pause, Josse said, 'Won't you share your
thoughts with us? We should be glad to hear whatever is on
your mind.'

Isabelle flashed a very brief smile. Then, without preamble,
she said, 'My son Herbert was previously wed to Maud, as you
probably recall, Josse.'

'Er – aye.'

Helewise hid a smile. She was quite sure that Josse had no
more memory of Herbert's first wife than she had.

'Poor Maud wasn't robust,' Isabelle went on, with the faint
note of condescension so often heard in the strong when
speaking of their feebler kin, 'and she died after only eight
years of marriage. They had no children.' Her sigh this time
was even deeper. 'Herbert, of course, is Hugh's heir, and it
has always been desired that he – or, indeed, his sister or his
cousin Philomena – should produce a male child to inherit in
his turn. But we in this family have but the one male of the
bloodline, and, for the rest, a surfeit of girls.' She gave a
rueful laugh. Then, hastily, less some angry deity might be
listening and have some appalling nemesis in mind, she added,
'Not that I don't love my Jenna, and Philomena, and Emma,
Cecily, Brigida and little Philippa dearly, and not one would
I exchange for a boy.' She gave a firm nod, as if to emphasize
her words.

'What – er, what of the future?' Josse said. Helewise, knowing
him so well, guessed what he was trying to say, although he was
employing such careful delicacy that she was quite sure Isabelle
didn't.

'What do you mean, Josse?' Isabelle said.

'I was simply wondering whether – um – whether boy children
might still be born.' Josse, Helewise observed, had flushed
slightly, although it might have been from the wine.

Isabelle gave a snort. 'Emma's eighteen, and it might be reasonable to look to her to marry and reproduce,' she said with a touch
of anger, 'but she is not interested in men and does not want to
be a wife. She thinks the whole male-centredness of society is
wrong and, in her own words, has "no wish to perpetuate an

unfair system". Instead, she intends to give her life to God and enter a convent.'

For the second time that day, Josse was about to speak when Helewise stopped him. This time, too far away to nudge him, she spoke over him. 'What of her mother, your daughter Jenna? She is surely still of childbearing age?'

Isabelle turned to her, and there was relief in her face, as if she welcomed someone who spoke without awkwardness about delicate matters. 'There is a gap of ten years between Emma and her little sister,' she said matter-of-factly. 'Jenna is not a very fertile woman, and, in addition, Cecily's birth damaged her, so that the risk of future pregnancies must be avoided.'

'There are others,' Josse put in. 'Your other granddaughter, and Philomena, and her little girls.'

'Yes, Josse, *little girls* is exactly what they are!' Isabelle flashed back. 'Cecily is eight, Brigida is five, and Philippa – dear God, the child's very name reveals how we yearn for a boy child! – is but three.' For a moment, she dropped her face in her hands, kneading her temples as if her head pained her. 'And Philomena is disinclined to go through another pregnancy. "Undoubtedly it would be another girl," she says, not without justification, "and heaven knows we've got enough already."'

Silence fell. It was, Helewise thought, a distressed, resentful silence. She was about to make some mollifying comment, for she had taken to Josse's cousin Isabelle and found herself wishing to comfort and to help, when Isabelle spoke again.

'Forgive me,' she said, reaching out to take their hands. 'Here you are on your first evening, distressed, I dare say, about Father, wanting to relax and no doubt ready for your bed, after the journey you had, and all I can do is moan!'

'You've done a lot more than that,' Josse protested. 'You have welcomed us with a kind and open heart, and provided the sort of feast we haven't seen in a long time.'

'Indeed,' Helewise agreed. Then – for, even as she spoke she had been thinking – she said, 'Why, Isabelle, does this absence of a male heir to come after Herbert disturb you so deeply just now?'

Isabelle turned shrewd eyes to her, then muttered over her shoulder, 'This one doesn't miss much, Josse.' A smile creasing her face, she said, turning back to Helewise, 'Having posed the

question, would you care to suggest an answer?' Helewise hesitated. 'Go on,' Isabelle urged, 'you won't distress me or anger
me, I assure you.'

'In that case,' Helewise began – it was Josse's turn, she noticed
with a private smile, to try to stop her going on; he was making
frantic throat-cutting gestures at her behind Isabelle's back, but
she ignored him – 'in that case, I would suggest that your concern
has somehow to do with your new daughter-in-law.'

'Your arrow strikes right in the gold,' Isabelle murmured. 'Not
that new a daughter-in-law, for she married my son last year.'
Her hand went up to her forehead again, and she closed her eyes.
'Cyrille is but thirty-two,' she said – *As young as that?* Helewise
thought, for she had judged the woman to be nearer forty than
thirty, if not older – 'and, in all likelihood, she will give my son
children; boys, perhaps.'

'And that is not a welcome thought?' Helewise prompted
gently.

Wordlessly, Isabelle shook her head. 'I cannot warm to her,'
she said, dropping her voice to a barely audible whisper as if
she feared Cyrille had got out of bed and crept back up the
passage to listen.

'Perhaps she won't get pregnant,' Josse said bluntly.

Isabelle met Helewise's eyes, and both of them grinned. 'Dear
old Josse,' Isabelle said. 'Straight to the essence of the matter.
But, in any case,' she went on, her smile fading, 'Cyrille already
has a son, whose every thought, comment and moment she controls
with rigid care, for she is determined he shall be a *credit* to her.'
She made a small sound eloquent of her disapproval. 'Cyrille was
married before, to a boyhood friend of Herbert's named William
Crowburgh, and when William died two years ago and Herbert
went to pay his respects and give his commiserations to the widow,
that meeting led to friendship, love, and, eventually, marriage.'
She paused. 'Herbert is, for now, young Olivar's stepfather. He
is, however, in the process of adopting him as his heir.'

Josse was looking mystified. 'Then wherein lies the difficulty?'

Again, Isabelle and Helewise exchanged a glance. *Because
the boy is hers*, Helewise thought. She thought it diplomatic to
leave Isabelle to say it.

Isabelle again took Josse's hand. 'Don't misunderstand me,'

she said softly, 'I like Olivar very much; he's only six, he's lost the father he adored and is utterly bewildered, and he's a very sweet, lovable child. I know he can't change who gave birth to him, but, all the same . . .' She didn't finish the sentence. Helewise didn't think she needed to.

'What exactly—' Josse began.

He was interrupted by sudden noises from outside. A voice crying out; heavy thumps, as if a fist wielding something hard were banging it against the gates; the sound of running feet within the house; a door opening.

Josse was already out of his chair. 'I will go and investigate,' he said, striding away towards the door.

'Josse, no, the servants will attend to it!' Isabelle called after him. He ignored her.

'He prefers,' Helewise remarked tonelessly, 'to see to things himself.' Isabelle looked at her. Both women laughed.

Quite soon, Josse was back, accompanied by the older man who had earlier taken their horses, a man in the livery of a senior indoor servant – a steward? – and a goggle-eyed boy almost breathless with the excitement of the moment. Addressing Isabelle, Josse said, 'There's been an accident. A man and his horse have had a bad fall. It seems he was trying to make for Lewes, along the track that runs on the top of the downs, but in the worsening weather, his horse missed its footing. Both are badly injured, and, in addition, they have been out in the severe weather for some time. It's been snowing,' he added.

Isabelle was already on her feet. 'Nicholas,' she said, addressing the servant, 'fetch Willum, Matthew and Tab and a hazel hurdle, go out and *very carefully* bring the injured man inside. Take him to the guest chamber beside the chapel.' The steward hurried off. Isabelle turned to the old groom. 'Garth, you must do what you can for the horse.'

'Aye, my lady.' The groom touched his fingers to his forelock, then hurried off in the steward's wake.

'Now,' Isabelle said, apparently talking to herself, 'I need hot water, cloths for washing wounds, blankets to warm the poor soul, a fire in his room—'

Gently Helewise touched her arm. 'Josse and I will help,' she said softly.

Isabelle gave a curt nod. 'Thank you. It's a pity this had to happen on your first night with us, but there it is. Follow me.'

Then, already giving instructions about where to find blankets and kindling, she hurried out of the hall with Josse and Helewise trotting along behind.

THREE

He must have fallen face-down, slightly to the left. He had dislocated his left shoulder and he had a huge bump in the middle of his forehead. The impact appeared to have broken his nose, which had bled freely, drenching his lower face, throat and the front of his chemise with scarlet. Pain and possibly concussion were making his mind wander: when Josse asked him his name, he began to say 'Pa—', then a dazed look came into his eyes and he stopped.

'Where am I?' he demanded, his wide eyes skittering wildly around the room and the faces looming over him. 'What house is this?'

'It is Southfire Hall,' Isabelle said soothingly, as with swift, assessing hands she felt up and down his left arm and around the damaged shoulder, 'and you are welcome here. We will take care of you.'

He murmured his thanks.

'Can you tell us your name, and where you are bound?' Josse persisted.

Isabelle caught his eye, carefully miming an instruction, raising her eyebrows in silent query. Josse swallowed, nodded, and flexed his hands. '*Keep him talking!*' she hissed.

'Whoever is expecting you, your kin or friends,' Josse improvised, 'will surely be worrying, and we will send word, if you will say where to send it.'

There was a long pause. The man was young – perhaps in the mid-twenties, Josse thought, staring down at him – and his blond hair was thick and wavy, reaching to his shoulders. Beneath the dirt and the blood, the structure of his face was good, with well-defined cheekbones and a firm jaw. He tried to speak, swallowed, and tried again. 'Peter,' he managed.

'Peter, aye, very good. Go on,' Josse said chattily. He braced himself.

'My name's Peter Southey,' the young man said, his voice stronger now, 'and no concerned soul awaits me, for I was bound for some inn in Lewes, if any would have opened its doors to one arriving so late on a night such as this. I – *aaaaagh!*'

His scream split the air. Josse, with Isabelle watching him hawk-eyed as if to reassure herself he really did know what he was doing, had taken advantage of the young man's temporary distraction, as he answered the questions, to thrust his knee into the man's armpit and reduce the dislocation.

For a moment, Peter continued to sob softly. Then he fainted.

'Well done,' Isabelle said. 'If you warn them what you're about to do, they tense up and the job becomes twice as difficult. It's good that he's unconscious,' she went on, staring down critically at the patient, 'for now we can get on with tending him without him yelling out and waking the whole household; not that they're likely to hear, since they're all over in the original extension.' She was gently palpating the grossly swollen nose. 'I'm sure it's broken,' she observed. 'What do you think, Helewise?'

For some time the three of them worked over the insensate form of Peter Southey. Leaving the two women to discuss and treat his wounds, Josse concentrated on removing the clothing. The heavy, padded tunic was wet with melted snow, and would need drying. The chemise would have to be soaked to get the blood out. As, with great care, he eased the sleeve off the left arm and finally got the chemise free, Josse noticed that the young man wore something around his neck, hanging on a fine leather thong. He sponged the pooled blood off the chest – quite a hairy chest, he observed – and then reached down to pick up whatever hung from the thong.

Not a crucifix, or a medal bearing the image of the Virgin or a favourite saint, but a small, soft suede bag, tightly tied closed with fine thread wound in an intricate knot. Josse held the little bag in his hand. It was roughly as long and as broad as the top joint of his thumb, and it contained something hard. A precious stone? A piece of gold jewellery? 'None of my business,' Josse muttered, and he laid it gently back on the young man's chest.

When there was nothing further that could be done for Peter Southey, Isabelle politely but firmly sent Josse and Helewise off to bed. 'I will stay with him,' she said, in the sort of voice you didn't argue with, 'so that, when he wakes, I shall be able to reassure him that he's all right. Go!'

They went.

Quite a short time later, they lay side by side in the luxurious bed, trying to get warm. They had kept most of their clothes on; the thought of icy sheets on bare skin was not to be contemplated.

Josse tried to lie still, for he knew Helewise was worn out and needed to sleep, but he was restless. There was a question he had been burning to ask almost since he and Helewise had arrived at Southfire Hall, but, somehow, the occasion to do so just hadn't presented itself. Now, unless he was prepared to get out of bed and return to Isabelle in her vigil, he was going to have to wait till morning.

'Hell and damnation!' he muttered softly.

Not softly enough: 'What's the matter, Josse?' came Helewise's drowsy voice in the darkness. 'Can't you sleep? Are you too cold?'

'I'm warm enough, sweeting,' he said, hugging her close. 'It's not that which keeps me awake.'

'What, then?' There was a rustle of crisp linen as she propped herself up. He had detected a note of resignation in her voice, as if she knew quite well she wasn't going to get any sleep either until he had shared what was on his mind.

'I have been wondering since we got here about Aeleis,' he said. 'She's the third of my cousins, Hugh and Ysabel's youngest daughter, and she was—'

'The tomboy, the mischief-maker and your constant companion,' Helewise finished. 'Yes, you told me. And you're right; she's not here, obviously, and I haven't heard anybody mention her name.'

'Neither have I,' Josse agreed. 'It worries me. If she was dead, surely they'd have said so? They'd have sent word to us at the House in the Woods, wouldn't they?'

'I don't know, Josse.' There was a pause, then Helewise went on, 'What do you remember about her? Tell me all you can, and then perhaps we may hazard a guess at what has become of her.'

Josse stretched out his arm, and Helewise moved so that she could rest her head on his chest, held warmly against him. 'Although I was always very fond of Isabelle, and Editha too,

Aeleis was my favourite,' he began. 'When I first came here I was very homesick, although I dared not admit it, and Aeleis understood. I thought she would scoff at me for being such a baby, but instead she decided to distract me.' He grinned in the darkness, remembering. 'And her idea of distraction was to take me exploring with her.'

'Was she still at Southfire Hall when you visited for that Yule season?'

'Aye, she was.' An image of Aeleis's laughing face came into his head. She was such a pretty, vivacious woman . . . 'She'd been widowed a year or so previously.'

'How tragic!' Helewise exclaimed softly. 'She must have been young, to have lost a husband, and the husband young to die.'

'Aye, you'd think so,' Josse agreed. 'But she gave no sign of grief. Editha told me it was a blessing, in some ways, that Godric – Aeleis's husband – had gone, for he had been twelve years Aeleis's senior, and, according to Editha, so elderly and pernickety in his ways that he might have been older by twenty years or more. He used to wear himself out, apparently, fussing and fretting about his lively young wife.' He paused, thinking back. 'Editha also said Aeleis was better off without him,' he added. 'She said Aeleis could breathe again, once he was dead.'

They lay together in quiet companionship for a while. Then Helewise said, 'I might be very wrong, and please don't think I am in any way disparaging your cousin, but do you think it possible that she left to find some excitement?' Josse drew breath to reply, but she hadn't finished. 'You said she always sought adventure – danger, even – as a child. She was married, at a young age, I'd surmise, to a fussy old man who must surely have seemed very dull to her, and who constantly tried to restrict her freedom. When he died, might she not have come to the conclusion that, if there was any chance of her having the excitement she craved, she would have to seek it for herself, outside the family home? Why, they might have come up with another dull old man for her if she stayed, especially if her exploits threatened to embarrass her kin.'

Suppressing his instant reaction to leap to Aeleis's defence, Josse thought about it and realized he didn't really need to. Helewise hadn't been criticizing her; what she had just said showed both understanding and compassion. And she was right: kicking up her heels in some sort of wild, romantic fling, yearning for thrills and not stopping to consider her family's reaction, sounded exactly like Aeleis.

He gave a huge, jaw-cracking yawn. 'Let's ask Isabelle,' he said. 'We'll find a private moment tomorrow – maybe visit her at her patient's bedside – and I'll ask her to tell me what's happened to Aeleis.' He drew the bedding more closely up around his ears. 'Sleep now?'

'Sleep now.'

It was apparent the next morning that the household had been informed about the unexpected guest. As the family convened, the injured man was the sole topic of conversation. Helewise observed Isabelle, looking somewhat harassed, trying to deal with several people's questions all at once.

'Thank you, Jenna, yes, I'd be most grateful if you'd see to having his garments laundered, and no, Editha, there's no need to offer him your specially soft blanket because he is already as comfortable as we can make him. As far as I know, Cecily, his horse is not going to die, but if you wish to reassure yourself fully, I suggest you go out to the stables and ask.' Finally, Isabelle turned to the short figure standing right beside her. Watching closely, Helewise thought she saw Isabelle make an attempt at a kindly smile. 'Now, Cyrille, what were you saying?'

'I was offering to sit with the patient and attend to him,' Cyrille said grandly. 'I am, as you know, experienced in caring for the elderly and the sick, and I have my own little ways and methods of making people cosy.' Something in her tone made it plain that she was quite sure nobody else could possibly possess such skills.

'What a kind thought,' Isabelle murmured. 'However,' she went on, as Cyrille began to speak, 'I have already made the necessary arrangements for the nursing of our guest, and I myself will be in charge.'

'Oh, is that wise, when you always say how busy you are, and how there are never quite enough hours in the day?' Cyrille asked, an expression on her round face that contrived to be both pitying and vaguely critical. 'Why not relinquish this task to me?'

'I don't—' Isabelle began. Helewise caught her eye; Isabelle's good temper seemed rapidly to be running out.

'Isabelle has already asked me to help her,' Helewise said. She hoped she had interpreted Isabelle's look correctly; Isabelle's expression of relief suggested she had. 'After all, as a guest, I have nothing else to do. Besides, Josse and I were with Isabelle when the injured man was brought in,' she went on, improvising swiftly, 'and he knows my face. Better, we think, not to have too many unfamiliar people going into his room.'

Cyrille had turned to glare at her. 'Are *you* experienced in nursing the sick and the dying?' she demanded rudely. Helewise heard Josse give an indignant snort, but, to her relief, he didn't speak. 'It's a particular talent, you know, to make a patient feel reassured and at their ease. Only a *very* few of us possess it,' she added self-importantly; in her own eyes she was clearly one of the foremost in this select group.

Isabelle had heard enough. 'Our guest is not sick, neither is he elderly, and I sincerely hope and pray that he isn't dying,' she said with asperity. 'Now, if you will all excuse us, Helewise and I will be about our duties. Come, Helewise.'

With a quick glance at Josse – who, she observed, still seemed to be fuming at anyone having the temerity to question her nursing skills – Helewise followed Isabelle out of the hall.

'Thank you for that,' Isabelle said. 'Will you really help me?'

'Of course. I know you didn't actually ask me, so I apologize for having involved you in an untruth, but I could see that you didn't welcome Cyrille's offer.'

'Really? That was observant,' Isabelle said.

Again, Helewise suppressed a smile. Isabelle, she reflected, couldn't have made her antipathy plainer had she stood up on the table, stamped both feet and shouted.

Quietly, Isabelle opened the door to the room where the injured man lay. A grey-haired servant in a white headdress and plain dark gown was seated on a stool beside the bed, and, seeing her mistress, she stood up and came over to the doorway. 'He's been sleeping, my lady,' she said softly. 'Restlessly, at times, and moaning. His injuries pain him, I'll warrant.'

'No doubt,' Isabelle agreed. 'Thank you, Agnes – you are relieved.'

With a bob of a curtsey, the servant disappeared along the passage. Helewise and Isabelle, moving to opposite sides of the bed, stared down at the man in their care.

'The fall hasn't improved his good looks,' Isabelle remarked after a while.

'No, indeed,' Helewise agreed. This morning, the lump on his forehead was even bigger, and the broken nose was grossly swollen and purple with bruising. Peter had two black eyes, and the puffed-up lids were shiny, bright scarlet. He was bare-chested, and the white linen bandage supporting the dislocated shoulder looked pale against his skin.

Perhaps sensing their close scrutiny, Peter tried to open his eyes. 'Ouch,' he murmured. 'What's happened to my face?' He put up an exploratory hand; his left one. He gave a cry of pain.

Gently Helewise took hold of his wrist, laying the hand back against his bandaged chest. 'Best not to move that arm,' she advised. 'You injured your shoulder when you fell, and you need to rest it while it heals.'

Peter gave a brief nod of understanding. 'And my face?' he repeated, now investigating with his right hand. 'Dear Jesus,' he cried in panic as his fingers found the grotesquely enlarged nose, 'what's happened to me?'

'Hush, now,' Helewise said soothingly. 'You appear to have fallen on your face and left shoulder, and your face took much of the impact. Your nose is broken, and you have a bump on your forehead.'

He peered up at her, trying to see through the slits between his eyelids. 'Will I mend?'

'You'll mend. Now, rest, lie back, and Lady Isabelle and I will look after you.'

He turned his head to look at Isabelle. 'Where is this place?' he asked. He had, it seemed, forgotten asking the same question the previous night.

'Southfire Hall,' Isabelle said, exchanging a glance with Helewise. 'We told you—'

'You told me last night; yes, of course, so you did,' Peter said. 'I had forgotten. Is this place near Lewes?' He opened his eyes more widely, staring innocently up at Isabelle.

'Nearby, yes,' she replied. 'The road descends from the

downland a short distance further on, and Lewes lies in the valley.'

'I fell,' Peter said, sounding amazed. 'Yes, it's coming back to me now. My horse's feet slid from under him, and – *my horse!*' He tried to sit up, but slumped back with a moan.

It was Isabelle's turn to soothe him. 'Your horse is being well cared for,' she said calmly. 'My head groom is very experienced, and he told me this morning that your horse has suffered no serious damage. Bruising and some cuts, but rest in a warm stable under my groom's care will soon put him right.'

'It seems,' Peter said, 'that I have much to thank you for.'

Isabelle inclined her head in acknowledgement.

Helewise, watching, was struck by the odd thought that, for some reason, Peter resented having to be grateful. She told herself not to be silly.

The cold, overcast day slowly passed. For long spells, Isabelle left Helewise alone with the injured man, and Helewise, admitting guiltily to herself that it was a relief to have a worthy reason to absent herself from the bustle of family life, sat contentedly watching over him. It was warm in the little room; the grey-haired servant returned from time to time to mend the fire in the small hearth, and brought food for Helewise. The patient needed little attention, sleeping for much of the day. Once or twice Helewise offered food, but he declined, although she persuaded him to drink some water. Periodically she put a hand on his forehead, testing for fever, and, whenever he stirred, she would speak to him to make sure he remembered who and where he was. If he had suffered concussion last night, then it was possible he might descend into that frightening, mind-wandering state which usually implied some injury within the skull.

As she sat there beside him, Helewise prayed that that would not happen.

Some time in the afternoon, Isabelle's daughter Jenna came to keep Helewise company. Tall and strongly built though she was, she moved with quiet grace, and Peter did not wake as she pulled up a stool and sat down beside Helewise. 'How is he?' she asked softly.

'Sleeping more peacefully now. The pain is subsiding, perhaps.'

Jenna nodded. There was a brief but not uncomfortable pause, then she said, 'It was good of you to come to my mother's rescue this morning. She finds Cyrille trying, and it would have been hard for her if she'd had to accept her help.'

'Yes, I saw as much,' Helewise replied. She wanted to find out more about Isabelle's antipathy towards Cyrille, but hesitated to ask what might be seen as intrusive questions. 'I'm sure Cyrille meant well, and was thinking only of the well-being of the wounded man,' she said mildly.

Jenna's response was surprising. 'That is a generous remark but, if I may say so, one that only a stranger to this household would make.' She paused. Helewise was about to prompt her, but then, as if she had tried but found she couldn't keep her emotions to herself, Jenna said in a furious hiss, 'Cyrille de Picus very rarely means well, and the only person whose well-being concerns her is herself.'

'Oh. I see,' Helewise murmured.

'My lady, I very much doubt that you do,' Jenna flashed back. 'Oh, she dresses it up very prettily, always pretending that she acts only for the good of others, but she's a mean-spirited, cold-hearted woman with an extremely high opinion of herself that she believes everyone else should share, she is a know-all who thinks she is always right about absolutely everything and an expert in so many skills it'd make your head spin, and *nobody* in this house is safe from her intense scrutiny and her rigid judgement.'

The echo of her angry words died away. Helewise said, 'You don't seem to like her much.' Jenna spun round to glare at her, saw the smile hovering on her lips, and, to Helewise's relief – for the remark had slipped out – first grinned and then began to laugh.

Quickly, glancing at the sleeping man, she stopped. 'I'm sorry, Lady Helewise,' she said. 'It is no concern of yours if we suffer difficulties with her, and wrong of me to involve you.'

'I don't mind,' Helewise said. She waited, hoping very much that, having begun to open her heart, Jenna would go on.

She did. 'It's her pernickety, fussy ways that really annoy me,' she said. 'She never stops picking on the three little girls – my Cecily, and my cousin's two, Brigida and Philippa. Oh, I know they can be a handful, and very often they do indeed need correction and sometimes punishment, but, for one thing, it's been a long, hard winter, and they're full of high spirits and sick of being cooped up indoors. For another – and this is my main argument with Cyrille – it's not up to her to discipline them. She makes the children ten times worse, following them around, spying on them, as if she's just *waiting* for one of them to misbehave. And, since those naughty children know quite well what she's up to and that the rest of us don't approve, sooner or later one of them – usually my Cecily, I'm afraid – provokes Cyrille by some act of mischief performed right under her nose.'

'What sort of—' Helewise began, but Jenna, well into her stride, needed no prompting.

'She's always telling them to be careful they don't dirty their gowns, or to make quite sure they don't kick the wall when they take their boots off, and she looms over them when they're eating as if she's just waiting for food to be spilt or a mug to be dropped,' she said, her voice tight with anger. 'In truth, the matters with which she concerns herself are so petty that anybody else would ignore them. Oh, but not Cyrille, for she watches, she remembers and she insists the girls must be brought to account and made to answer her accusations. Very often, of course, the children deny them, and then Cyrille says they're lying.' Jenna paused. 'She has the habit of creeping around when nobody's about, checking whether the house is neat and tidy, as if the responsibility is hers.' Again, she hesitated, brows drawn down in a frown. 'It's not so much what she does,' she said eventually, 'since, in fairness, most people prefer a well-run, clean household to the alternative. It's the way she does it, as if it's all such a trial and she's being heroic to take on such a grave responsibility.'

'Perhaps,' Helewise suggested, 'she hasn't got enough to do?'

Jenna snorted. 'That's true, my lady, for my mother runs the house with great efficiency. We all have our duties, and the servants are well trained and long practised in their daily routine. Cyrille has precious little to occupy her but her needlework and her devotions. She is *very* devout, and an example to us all,' she added, as if, aware that her remarks had been uncharitable, she had hurriedly cast around for something complimentary to say. She looked down at her hands, folded in her lap, and muttered something that Helewise didn't catch: it sounded like *The house doesn't like her*, but it must surely have been *The household doesn't like her . . .*

Helewise thought for a moment. 'Why do you think she acts in this way?'

'Because she believes she's the most important person in the house,' Jenna replied. 'She's Herbert's wife, and he'll inherit from my grandfather Hugh when Hugh dies, and already she sees herself as the lady of the manor. God alone knows what she'll be like when she really is,' she added with grim intensity.

'Does she perhaps feel insecure?' Helewise wondered aloud. 'Anxious, perhaps, in case she may not be up to the role when the time comes?'

'Huh!' The abrupt sound eloquently expressed what Jenna thought of that. 'Feelings of insecurity and anxiety are utterly foreign to her, my lady.'

Silence fell, but Helewise felt the aftermath of Jenna's furious remarks still rebounding in the close-shuttered room. 'I am sorry for you all,' she said eventually. 'I cannot see a solution, unless perhaps your brother might be persuaded to speak to her, and suggest to her that she moderates her behaviour a little.'

'Herbert loves her, and I will not ask that of him,' Jenna said firmly. 'He lost his first wife, and has been lonely without her. Somehow he has succeeded in finding happiness with Cyrille, and I for one am reluctant to spoil it for him.' She got to her feet, slowly, as if the movement cost her great effort. Then, looking Helewise in the eye, she said, 'It is our problem, and we will have to find our own answers. I apologize once more for my outburst. It won't happen again.' Then, with a curt nod, she let herself out of the room and quietly closed the door.

Helewise's next visitor was Josse. He perched himself on the stool Jenna had vacated and, holding both her hands, said, 'You have done Isabelle a good turn by sitting with our patient here, for she has been busy all day and would have been hard put to find the time to care for him herself, as, indeed, would the other women.'

'It has hardly been arduous!' she replied. 'I've really rather enjoyed it.'

'How is he? Has he been rambling?'

'No, he's been quiet. I think we can soon conclude he has suffered no worse injury than those we already know about.'

'Thank God,' Josse breathed.

'Amen. Now, tell me about your day – what have you been doing?'

'I spent quite a long time with Uncle Hugh this morning, but he didn't make a lot of sense.'

'I'm sorry to hear that.'

'He's distressed about something,' Josse went on, his brow furrowed, 'and I had the feeling he was looking round for someone he expected to see.'

'You, perhaps?'

Josse smiled. 'No, sweeting. I don't think he knew I was there most of the time, although he did once say with perfect clarity, "We'll have a game of chess, young Josse, as soon as I think I'm up to beating you like I always do."'

'What else did you get up to?' Leaning closer to him, she added in a whisper, 'Did you have some nice, cosy chats with the lovely Cyrille?'

He laughed, swiftly suppressing it. 'No, I've managed to avoid her for much of the time, although she did corner me in the solar this afternoon, when the sun shone briefly and we all scurried in there to enjoy it.'

'What did she say?'

He shook his head, as if in disbelief. 'You'd hardly credit it, but she said I must go with her and sit with Editha – and this was in Editha's hearing, mind – because Editha was ailing and had to spend too much time resting while everyone else was out and about, and it was up to us – by which Cyrille clearly meant it was up to *her* – to tend to Editha and organize constant company and entertainment for her.'

'Wasn't that kind and considerate?'

Again, Josse frowned in puzzlement. 'It ought to have been, aye,' he agreed, 'and had anyone else done it – you, or Isabelle – that's just what it would have been.' The frown deepened as he went on thinking it out. 'It was the way she did it,' he said finally. 'Clearly, Cousin Editha is frail, and, from what I observed and was told, she's forced to spend far too much time in Cyrille's company, as Cyrille keeps insisting she's the only one who can look after her properly. Why, I heard her myself! She said to Editha, not even bothering to lower her voice – perhaps she thinks she's deaf as well as frail – "I know what older, weaker people need, the poor, dear souls, and it is my duty to take care of you."' He grinned suddenly. 'I had the impression that Editha had to fight the urge to get up and thump her.'

He had forgotten the need to speak softly. The man in the bed stirred, opened his swollen eyes – both they and his nose looked even worse this evening – and said, 'I think I'm hungry.'

Josse insisted on taking Helewise off for a short break while the grey-haired woman and another servant brought a light meal for Peter Southey and helped him eat it, and after that, Isabelle said she would stay with him for an hour or so. Later, however, once Helewise and Josse had eaten with the family, she crept back to the patient over whom she had sat all day.

'He's just gone to sleep again,' Isabelle whispered as she went into the room, finger to her lips in warning.

'Good,' Helewise whispered back. 'He ate a little?'

'Quite a lot,' Isabelle said with a smile. 'It'll be a few days yet before he's up and about, but I think he's out of danger.'

'I am happy to hear it.'

The two women sat quietly for some time. Helewise felt a sense of calm descend. Presently Isabelle said, 'Do you mind if I leave you? I have a dozen things to do before bed.'

'Not at all.'

'I'll send one of the servants along later,' Isabelle said as she got up, 'although I'm not sure he really needs watching tonight.'

Helewise heard her footsteps fade away along the passage. All was very quiet. Time passed. In the pleasant warmth, comfortably full after a tasty supper, Helewise felt her eyes begin to close . . .

She was back in her dream. The small blond-haired boy was back, opening a door into a room that looked remarkably similar to the one in which Helewise sat. Seeing her, he smiled and came shyly to stand beside her. *Did you find any monsters?* he whispered.

Not one, she whispered back.

The boy stood on tiptoe to peer down at the man in the bed. In a strange fusion of dream and reality, Helewise became aware that, although she had undoubtedly fallen asleep, now she was awake.

And there really was a little boy in the room with her.

She reached out a hand and gently took hold of his arm. 'Careful,' she said softly. 'This poor man dislocated his shoulder last night, and, although he's been mended, it would hurt him a lot if someone jogged him.'

The boy turned solemn blue eyes to hers. 'I'll be careful,' he said. 'You shouldn't hurt people, should you?'

'Not if you can possibly avoid it,' she agreed.

The boy gave a sad little sigh. 'I'm not supposed to be here,' he confided. '*She* told me I have to keep myself to myself, and not go talking to people, and she'll be very cross if she finds out I've come to see you, but I wanted to see the man who fell, and it gets very boring on my own.'

Her heart went out to him. She had guessed who he was, and what he had just said seemed to confirm she was right. 'You're Olivar, aren't you?' Even as she spoke, she thought: *Why has he not been introduced?*

He stood up straight and made her a courteous bow. 'Yes, I am, and you are the lady Helewise, wife of Sir Josse d'Acquin, who is here to see his Uncle Hugh because he's not very well. Sir Hugh, I mean, not Sir Josse,' he added, his small face falling into anxiety. 'I am sure he is very well indeed.'

She took hold of his hand. 'Yes, I know what you meant,' she assured him.

She was torn: she wanted very much to keep this lonely little boy with her for a while, for he was surely in sore need of some kindness and some company, but if by so doing she got him into trouble, then her impulse to help him would misfire.

'Will they—' she began. But she didn't complete the remark, for footsteps came hurrying along the passage, the door was flung open and Cyrille de Picus stood there, her plump face flushed and working with anger.

She paused to compose herself, then, pale blue eyes fixed on her son, said in a cold, flat voice, 'I am not aware of having given my permission for you to leave your room, Olivar. Two days, I believe I said, and the time is not yet up.' She paused, glaring at him as if she despised him. 'Another day's confinement, I think, to drive home the lesson of obedience to my wishes.' A sob, quickly stifled, broke out of the boy, and he fled.

Helewise fought hard to hold back the instinctive protest. *It is not your business*, she told herself firmly. *For all you know, Olivar did something very naughty, and deserves his punishment. Keep quiet!*

When she believed she could speak without revealing her inner turmoil, she said politely, 'Our injured man is recovering, we believe. He has slept for most of the day, which is, as I'm sure you'll agree, the best way for the body to heal.'

'Hmm,' Cyrille said, craning round Helewise to look at the patient. 'What is his name? They told me, but I forget.'

'Peter Southey.'

'Ah, yes.' She was leaning over him now, peering at the bruised and battered face. 'He's going to wish he'd been a bit more careful, when he looks into a glass and sees what he's done to himself.'

'The swelling and discolouration will subside, in time,' Helewise said quickly; it was scarcely a tactful remark to make over a badly injured man, even if he was asleep.

Cyrille sniffed. 'Perhaps.' She stared down at Helewise, one gingery eyebrow raised as if she thought full recovery unlikely. 'Good night.'

Then she turned on her heel and strode away.

After a moment, Peter Southey said softly and without opening his eyes, 'Who was that?'

'Oh! I thought you were asleep!'

He opened his eyes and grinned at her. 'Unfortunately not.'

'You *will* heal,' Helewise said earnestly. 'Your face probably feels quite unlike your own just now, but soon you will look like yourself again.'

'You are kind, my lady. Who did you say our forthright visitor was?'

'I didn't. Her name is Cyrille de Picus, or it was, for now she is the wife of Herbert, the son and heir of this house.'

'I see,' Peter murmured vaguely. Then he closed his eyes, eased his damaged shoulder and went back to sleep.

FOUR

Josse lay in bed, aware that, beside him, Helewise was already asleep. He did not want to disturb her, but his mind was too active for sleep. His head kept filling with random images and scenes from the past; his own past, in this very house.

Even as a child, somehow he had recognized that there was something very special – unique – about Southfire Hall. He had come, he supposed, to take it for granted during those successive visits before he had grown to manhood. When he had returned in later years – that Yule visit spent with the family was a good example – the days had usually been too full of chatter, song, laughter, good food and drink, and the celebrations of reunited kinsmen glad to be together again to allow much time for meditative introspection. Not, Josse reflected ruefully, that that was really one of his strong points, anyway.

This time, this sad time, when he had been summoned because his dear Uncle Hugh was in all likelihood dying, was different. Yesterday's welcoming feast had been generous, and his cousins and their families were clearly relieved that Josse had made the effort and come to stay, but, despite the generous fare and the levity, the shadow of sick Uncle Hugh had hung over them all. Now that the injured man – Peter Southey – was also under Southfire's capacious roof, the mood had become even more sombre, as if, without actually saying so, the inhabitants all felt that it was not seemly under the circumstances to indulge in cheerful gossip, laughter and boisterous fun.

And the resulting atmosphere – quiet, considerate, contemplative – had allowed the house's own voice to be heard.

I am becoming whimsical, Josse told himself. *Houses do not have voices!*

But, from somewhere so close as to be perhaps within him, the soft response came: *This one does.*

He smiled, letting his eyes close. *I'm falling asleep, after all*, he thought. *I am in that state in which waking and dreaming mingle.* He let himself relax, surrendering to it, and almost at once, as if the house had simply been waiting for the chance, his mind filled with memory after memory; no longer small, scattered vignettes, as they had earlier been, but now joined into a cohesive whole, the scenes so vivid that it was as if he had been flung back through time and once more walked where his childhood self had walked . . .

'If you ruin another gown, Aeleis,' Isabelle says in a voice exactly like her mother's, 'I shall not help you mend or restore it, and you shall answer for the consequences.'

'Don't care,' Aeleis retorts. She is four years old, a boy in a girl's body, strong and mature for her years and scornful of her older sister's ladylike ways. She grins at Josse, who is watching the scene anxiously. He knows he ought to support Isabelle, for she and he are the oldest children and it is ceaselessly impressed on them that they must control the younger ones – Isabelle's little sisters and Josse's younger brother Yves – and always Set A Good Example. So often is that phrase repeated, and in such severe tones, that, to Josse, its words have acquired capital letters. Not that he is very good at distinguishing capital letters; he can only do so in the beautiful bible in the parish church, with its gorgeously coloured illuminated initials at the start of each section.

But Josse doesn't want Aeleis to start acting like a modest little girl. He wants her to go on being his companion-in-exploration and, indeed, his guide, for she knows her way around Southfire Hall much better than he does. In his defence, he has only been here three days, and has had little opportunity to creep off alone. He is nearly nine years old, big and well grown; soon he will become a squire, and what small part of his life remains his own will also be taken away.

This brief summer at Southfire is his last chance of freedom before the adult world claims him. He will go on coming here – his mother has told him so, and she is always right – but, otherwise, for so far into the future that it doesn't bear thinking about he will be at someone else's beck and call, under someone's orders (probably several someones), and every single moment of every single day will be spent doing what he's told.

No wonder, then, that, no matter what the consequences in terms of punishment, he is quite determined to enjoy himself while he can. Now, today, as soon as Isabelle has finished her lecturing, and provided Josse can evade his little brother (Yves is homesick and a bit clingy), Josse and Aeleis are planning to make their unobtrusive way beneath the house towards the entrance to the undercroft, where they will wait until the builders' backs are turned and then slip inside. Assuming it hasn't been discovered and blocked up since yesterday evening, they will then crawl behind a certain huge pillar and through the tiny space they found yesterday afternoon.

They have no idea what they will find there. They know it is so profoundly dark that you can't even see your hand in front of your face, that it has a strange smell – 'Like being deep in a mole's hole with your nose right in the earth,' Aeleis says – and that it's so well hidden that nobody can have set foot in there for hundreds and thousands of years.

Josse says *hundreds*; Aeleis says *thousands*, but she always exaggerates.

Today Aeleis is carrying beneath her skirts a small stone oil lamp which she pinched from the kitchen. Some of the oil has slopped on to her hem, but she was careful to fill it so there should be plenty left for the rush wick to soak up. Josse has flint and steel to make a spark. They are determined to shed light on whatever it is they have discovered.

They reach the entrance to the undercroft. Nobody is looking their way; nobody is even in sight, although they can hear the master mason arguing with the master carpenter, loud voices raised in the still, warm air. They hurry into the cool, dim space. Rows of short, stubby pillars stride off into the darkness in front of them, their sturdy strength holding up that wide, vaulted roof and the unimaginable weight above it. Josse doesn't like thinking about that.

He feels Aeleis's small hand creep into his. He grasps it, glad of her touch. They hurry on, for the workmen may resolve their quarrel any moment and return to their tasks, and there is no time to lose.

They reach the pillar which conceals their secret. Josse has been thinking, and concludes that it is roughly in the spot where the house's main entrance used to be, over on the south side of the main hall. He and Aeleis crouch down on hands and knees, preparing to go through the narrow little tunnel. Josse, being quite a lot bigger, has to crawl on his stomach. Again, he is uneasily aware of the colossal weight of earth and stone above him. He feels his heart beat faster, and it is hard to breathe. He forces himself to go on. He is close to panic. Was the tunnel as long as this yesterday? Have they come to the wrong place? Will he get stuck and die here? Should he somehow tell Aeleis, scrabbling along right behind him, to retreat so he can go back? What if he *can't* go back?

But then abruptly he is out of the tunnel. Leaping to his feet, he stands upright in the pitch-black space. Aeleis's voice, very close and horribly loud in the dead silence, says, 'Here's the lamp. Light it, Josse,' and he obeys.

They stand in awe of the place they have found.

Is it a cellar? If so, it was a rich man who had it built, for, as they discover when they scrape away the earth, debris and dust of countless years, inset into the cracked and worn flags of the floor is a mosaic. It is made of tiny glazed stone tiles which, when Aeleis spits on them and rubs at them with her skirt, are revealed to be of many colours and placed so as to make up a picture. It is a strange picture: a very tall figure in a long pale robe stands before what is obviously a fire – orange and yellow flames like tongues – set in what looks like a round hearth. Out of nowhere a name flashes into Josse's head: *Hestia*. He says it out loud, his voice soft, almost chanting the word.

'She's a goddess,' Aeleis says knowingly. 'She tended the sacred fire.'

There is a silence. Josse feels a chill down his back, as if someone had dribbled cold water on him. 'We found a hearth,' he whispers. 'A real hearth. Remember?'

Aeleis nods. 'We tried to make a fire but it just smoked.'

'Aye,' Josse agrees. 'There was probably once a hole to make a draught, but it'd have got blocked up.'

'The extension's being built over where the hearth is,' Aeleis says. 'They'd have had to fill up the holes.'

'Aye, they would,' Josse says absently. He is thinking. An ancient hearth. A mosaic, probably far, far older. Fire. Tending the sacred fire.

And his Uncle Hugh's house, where Josse's maternal line have lived since memories began, stands above an area called Southover, and the house is called . . .

As if she reads his mind, or shares the process of his thoughts, or perhaps both, Aeleis whispers, 'Southfire. Southfire Hall.'

The shudder comes again. Josse holds his breath, expecting the onset of deep, atavistic fear. It doesn't come.

Aeleis, very close beside him, says confidingly, 'It's not a scary place, is it, Josse? It's very, very old, and it's dark, and it's forgotten, but I'm not frightened.'

'Nor am I,' he quickly agrees. 'This house is never frightening.' It is as if he is at last putting into words something he has always known. 'It's – it's a friendly house.'

Aeleis is nodding eagerly, her long, heavy golden-brown hair already half out of its tight braids and bouncing round her pretty, animated face in time with her nods. 'I'm *never* scared,' she says proudly. Then, with strict honesty, she amends the statement: 'Well, I *do* get frightened when I have bad dreams, or there's a big storm with bangs of thunder, but then it's as if the house comes and comforts me, and I'm not scared any more.' She pauses, then, sounding almost embarrassed, as if this is a whimsy too far, adds quickly, 'If anything evil came, I reckon the house would kick it out.'

'Mmm,' Josse says absently. He's sure she's right, but he's thinking of something else. *The spirit of the house.* This phrase, like the name Hestia, has just popped into his mind.

Is that what they've noticed, he and his little cousin? The presence of a friendly, protective spirit? Like her, he has often sensed a – a *kindliness*, is the best description he can come up with, within the old walls of Southfire Hall. Spirit of the house . . . Who said that?

He remembers. It was his mother, Ida; Uncle Hugh's elder sister. When Josse was not much more than Aeleis's age and being sent on his first visit to his mother's kin so far away in the land called England, he had been so upset, the night before departure, and she had come to comfort him. 'I don't want to go away from you and I'm scared about going over the sea and what if they don't like me and suppose I cry because I'm home-sick and what if I get scared in the night and you're not there?'

he had sobbed. And she had hugged him, and he had breathed
in her loved, familiar scent of lavender and spices, and she had
said softly, 'You'll be all right. The people are kind, and if ever
for a moment you are frightened or unhappy, the spirit of the
house will comfort you.' He must have shown his doubt in his
face, for, kissing him, laughing gently, she added, 'I grew up
there, and I know. You'll see!'

He is jerked back to the present. Aeleis, with the short span
of attention of a child not quite five, has got bored with the
mosaic, and wandered off to explore a dark corner. She is digging
in the dust and the dirt, and Josse thinks she is doing what she
always does, and hunting for treasure. He has told her often that
she's unlikely to find anything, but her faith remains strong. He
hopes very much it will prove justified. He is very fond of his
little cousin.

He follows her to her corner. 'I think there's another gap here,'
he says, pushing at a roughly shaped stone that seems to be lying
at an angle. Sure enough, it moves a little, and he increases his
efforts. Aeleis, distracted from her digging, hurries to help. They
work the stone loose, and presently crawl off along a long, dark,
stone-lined tunnel that seems to be part of a whole network of
similar tunnels. All of them are roughly square . . .

The sun is low in the sky when they finally remember that
there is a world up there above the tunnels, the ancient cellar,
the forgotten crypts and the old undercroft. In that world, people
are probably wondering where they are and getting ready to be
very cross when they find out what the two of them have been
up to. 'They mustn't find out,' states Aeleis firmly, 'or else they'll
try to stop us coming back down here again.'

Try to stop us, Josse notes with a grin, not just *stop us*; Aeleis
is not a child who willingly gives up on something she really
wants, and she has virtually no respect for authority. They are
back in the undercroft now – thankfully it is deserted – and, in
the light that seems bright after the darkness of the older underground places, he can see that Aeleis is filthy, as is he. 'We'll
have to be clever, and sneak into the house without being seen,'
he says. 'First, though, we'll make our way under cover to the
area behind the kitchens, and get the worst of the dirt off.'

Their luck holds. They wash hands, faces and feet – both are barefoot – and Aeleis beats as much dirt as she can out of her skirt, then makes a pretty good attempt at re-braiding her hair. 'Don't go too far!' Josse says with a smile. 'You usually come in looking sweaty and bedraggled, and if you're too tidy, your nursemaid will wonder what's wrong with you. She might even,' he adds, because he likes to tease her, 'decide you must be unwell, and insist you go straight to bed and stay there.'

'*NO!*' yells Aeleis in protest. She sees Josse laughing, launches a flying fist at him, misses, and races after him as he flees for the sanctuary of the hall.

Later, still thinking about ancient fires, Josse seeks out Uncle Hugh. Hugh has just returned steaming and sweaty from doing whatever it is he does all day, and, his boots off and lying on their sides on the floor, he has pressed the soles of his bare feet on to the cold stone flags. There is a look of bliss on his ruddy, plump face.

Josse goes to sit on the floor beside Uncle Hugh's bench. 'Please may I ask you something, Uncle?' he says politely.

'Of course, my dear boy!' Uncle Hugh replies with a big smile. 'Questions are free!'

Not entirely sure what that means, Josse says, 'It's about this house. Is it very, *very* old?'

Uncle Hugh looks vaguely surprised, as if he had expected something rather more mundane. 'Er – yes, yes it is,' he says. The deep furrows in his brow suggest he is thinking hard. 'Southfire Hall has been in the family for many generations,' he says after a moment. 'My mother Ediva's great-grandmother built the original hall when she brought her new husband here. She was a big, strong woman, they say, like so many of our kin, both male *and* female.' He smiles. 'They made their dwelling in the old manner, which was a long house with a fire pit and aisles down each side separated by lines of pillars. Its door faced south. It was a wooden structure, and, in time, as the family began to prosper, wood was replaced with stone, and the hall in which we now sit was erected. More years went by, and now we have outgrown our hall and, as you see, we are building an extension, so that the members of the family no longer have to sleep all together with the servants and the animals.'

Josse, thinking it was a joke – his uncle's grand house is no peasant dwelling – laughs politely.

Uncle Hugh regards him, his eyes kindly. 'Oh, it's true, young Josse,' he murmurs. 'Not many years ago, even a man such as I thought nothing of bedding down only a few paces away from his animals, and, indeed, the great majority of people still live like that, and will go on doing so.'

'Oh,' Josse says. Then, in case Uncle Hugh is about to begin one of those you-don't-know-how-lucky-you-are lectures beloved of grown-ups, he heads him off. 'And was there a house here before your mother's great-grandmother built her hall?' he prompts.

Uncle Hugh's eyes have gone sort of soft. 'Ah, now, here we leave the world of fact and enter into the realm of legend,' he says mysteriously. Leaning closer to Josse, he says softly, 'When I was a lad, a few years younger than you, young Josse, my nursemaid would tell me stories. She was old – Lord, she was so old!' His face twists into an expression of wonder, as if, even now, he can scarcely credit what he is saying. 'She had been nurse to Sithe's children – Sithe it was who built the hall – and she claimed that, when she was a girl, she knew Sithe's mother, Aeda.' Uncle Hugh is staring at Josse with round eyes, as if he expects Josse to be deeply impressed. Since Josse has no idea who Aeda was, or why Uncle Hugh's old nursemaid having known her should be so impressive, Josse is at a loss.

'Oh, my!' he says inadequately.

But he doesn't think Uncle Hugh has heard. 'They used to have fires on the downs,' he is saying, his voice sounding strange; sort of *distant*, Josse thinks. 'They were tended by special people, for to look after the wildfire was a great honour.'

'Were they beacon fires?' Josse asks. He has heard of beacon fires, and knows they have long been used as a means of passing a signal very rapidly over long distances.

'Hm? Beacon fires? Yes, I suppose they served that function,' Uncle Hugh says. 'But it wasn't their original, true purpose. The fires on the Caburn, and here at Southfire, were sacred fires, and they—'

But just then, at the very point where it's getting really interesting, Uncle Hugh stops. Glancing down at Josse, a sheepish expression on his face, he mutters something like, 'Not meant to speak of that in front of the youngsters.'

'Was there a building here before Sithe built her hall?' Josse asks again, forcing himself to sound very patient and polite. He really wants to know, for he is thinking of those mysterious tunnels that open off the dark crypt. It's surely not likely that Sithe excavated so extensively beneath her wooden dwelling, so if she didn't make the floor and the hearth, who did?

Uncle Hugh looks relieved, as if glad that Josse has asked him about something he *is* prepared to discuss. 'Well, young Josse, I can't swear it's true, but old Nena – that's my nursemaid I was telling you about – had a great fund of tales, and she used to say that, once upon a time, when this land was occupied by the invader who came from the south, wonderful dwellings called villas were built on the places where conditions were most favourable. Now these villas, Nena said, were so luxurious and so comfortable that each one, even if belonged only to an ordinary man, was fit for a king. She said one such villa was built up here, where Southfire Hall now stands, because the people from the south knew this was a good place, and that any dwelling constructed here would have a nourishing, protective spirit.' Josse is about to question this rather extraordinary and totally fascinating statement, ask his uncle to elaborate, but Uncle Hugh is in full flow. 'She said that once, when she was a girl, she had discovered old tunnels and passages that she said had been excavated back then. Of course –' he smiles indulgently – 'Nena was a great one for stories, and I expect she made it up. She said,' he adds, again leaning close and lowering his voice, 'that those old villas were heated by means of narrow, brick-sided trenches that ran beneath the floor, and that fires were lit so that the warm air ran down all the little tunnels! She said –' now he was whispering – 'that they used to send small boys crawling down the tunnels to light the fires and to clear away obstructions, and quite often the boys got badly burned, even killed, and that, if you listened very carefully on a still, dark night, sometimes you could hear their terrible screams.'

Josse feels sick. He remembers those little tunnels that he and Aeleis crawled along only today. He imagines a fire suddenly erupting, a blast of hot air, flames, smoke, trying to fight his way back and out to safety and getting stuck. Burning. Dying in agony. Nausea rises in his throat, and he swallows hard.

'My dear boy, I'm sorry!' Uncle Hugh's concerned voice brings him back to the safety of the present. He is looking anxiously at Josse. 'Dear Lord, but you've gone quite white! I *am* sorry,' he repeats, 'I had no idea that old tale would upset you!' Uncle Hugh is a kind man.

'It's quite all right,' Josse assures him. He has no intention of telling his uncle about his and Aeleis's discoveries down beneath the house. Since he isn't going to explain, however, there is a danger that Uncle Hugh will think his nephew a bit of a girl, frightened by an old nursemaid's horror story. 'I *loved* the story,' he adds. 'It didn't upset me at all – it was just that I . . .' He thinks frantically. 'Just that I'm getting quite hungry, and for a moment I felt a bit faint.'

Uncle Hugh, who seems to know all about the prodigious appetite of growing boys, takes Josse at his word. He pats him on the shoulder, chuckling, and says, 'Ah, what it is to be young, and have the day revolve around meal times!' He struggles to his feet, reaching to pick up his boots. 'I will see you at supper, young Josse,' he says, and he strolls away.

Josse stretched, carefully so as not to disturb Helewise. He was sleepy at last, for the long excursion into the past had been almost hypnotic; as if he was already half in a dream. He thought back over all the memories that had just come pushing and shoving into his mind. How Aeleis had said she was never scared. How his mother had said that the spirit of the house would comfort him if he was sad or upset. How his Uncle Hugh had said the ancient people knew it was a good place to build, for it had a nourishing, protective spirit. How his own forebears had lived here, in this spot, for so long. It was no wonder, he reflected, that he felt so welcome here. The place was his ancient home; the very stones called out to him.

There was something else right on the edge of his thoughts; another memory, but a more recent one, and not of his uncle, or indeed any of his kinsmen on his mother's side. He frowned in the quiet darkness, trying to bring it to mind. Something to do with tending the sacred fire . . .

As if in response to his attempts, suddenly the violent image exploded in his head. Without understanding how, he *knew* without a doubt that it was a vision he had experienced before. He saw immense flames searing up into the night, in vivid shades of violet, purple and gold, brilliant against the night sky. He saw a woman, very tall, dressed in a pale robe and with a circlet of silver around her head, set on thick hair woven in complicated braids. She cried aloud, a sound that sounded like singing, but he did not understand the words.

He seemed to hear a voice – his own voice – say, *There is no magic in my family.* Another voice – a beloved voice, that of Joanna, his lost love – replied gently, *There is, Josse.*

He stirred restlessly, disturbed by his thoughts. What was happening to him? Why, suddenly, was all this coming back to him, and with such vividness, such force? Was it somehow important that he remember these things? But why?

Drowsiness was overcoming him at last. He didn't fight it, for he knew he was weary. He made himself relax, glad of Helewise's warm presence next to him.

He closed his eyes. Yawned. Felt the pleasure of surrendering to sleep. And, just as consciousness faded, he thought – perhaps he dreamt – that someone said, *The house is making it happen.*

He smiled, already barely awake. His last thought was, *How absurd!*

FIVE

In the morning, before they went to join the family and break their fast, Helewise and Josse sat side by side on the bed discussing Olivar. Helewise had briefly explained last night about how the little boy had come to the room where she had sat with the injured man, and how his mother had come and sent him back to his room.

'I did wonder why he wasn't presented to us that first evening,' she said now. 'Everyone else was, yet his absence wasn't explained. He wasn't even mentioned till later, when Isabelle told us about him. Wasn't that rather odd? Especially since he'll inherit in his turn from Herbert, now that he is to be adopted as Herbert's ward.'

Josse frowned. 'It is odd, aye, but it's not really any of our business.'

'I know, but—'

He put his arm round her, holding her close. 'You told me that Cyrille had sent him to his room for two days because he'd been naughty, so, presumably, she must have decided that being allowed out to meet us would have been a treat, and therefore not in keeping with being punished,' he said.

'But she's his *mother*!' Helewise protested. 'I agree that it wouldn't have been right to curtail the punishment – although, in my view, two days is a little excessive for someone only six years old – but why didn't she at least tell us about him? When Herbert presented her to us, why didn't she say, "I look forward to introducing my son to you, but it will have to wait because he's been sent to his room for throwing stones at the cat," or whatever it was he did.'

Josse chuckled, but then, apparently noticing her expression, straightened his face. 'It's what you or I would have done, my love,' he said. 'But there are as many different styles of being a parent as there are parents, and perhaps Cyrille has found she has to be strict with her son in order to make him obey her.'

'He didn't seem like the sort of child who would cheek his mother, constantly rebel against her and perpetually get into scrapes,' she persisted. 'He struck me as a very sweet, rather timid little boy.'

'And you spoke to him for how long?'

She had to concede the point. 'Yes, all right, it wasn't very long. But it was enough for me to form quite a strong impression, nevertheless.'

He went on hugging her. 'What should we do?'

She loved him for that: although she could tell he thought she was worrying needlessly, still he was prepared to do what he could to help.

Hugging him back, she said, 'There isn't much we *can* do. As you rightly said, it's none of our business. But—'

'But you feel sorry for the lad,' Josse finished for her.

'Yes.'

'In that case, we'll wait till he's allowed to rejoin the rest of the family, and then see if we can get to know him, and judge if you're right about him being timid. How's that for a start?'

She smiled up at him. 'For a start, dear Josse,' she echoed, 'it will do very well.'

But Olivar didn't appear. Cyrille, it seemed, had kept her word, and made her son stay isolated in his room for another day as punishment for having left it the previous evening to go and investigate the injured man.

Helewise tried, without making it obvious, to study Cyrille de Picus. She, too, however, was absent for the first part of the day. Helewise heard Isabelle ask where she was, and Herbert reply that she was feeling a little tired, and had decided to spend the morning resting. 'Is there anything she needs?' Isabelle asked. 'Would she like someone to sit with her?'

'No, thank you,' Herbert replied. 'She has her needlepoint and her book of devotions, and is content with that.'

Since it was agreed that, Peter Southey being out of danger, there was no more need for him to be constantly tended, Helewise found herself at a loose end. Used to being so busy that frequently the days seemed to come to an end almost as soon as they had begun, she had little idea what to do with her unaccustomed leisure. Josse must have noticed that she was restless, and he invited her join him on his daily visit to his uncle.

Accepting with alacrity, she followed him into the extension, and along a labyrinth of passages to the old man's room. Josse tapped on the door, and a soft female voice said, 'Come in.'

Editha sat beside the bed, holding one of her father's hands. Hugh was propped up on a bank of pillows, but his eyes were closed and he appeared to be asleep.

Editha greeted Josse and Helewise with a smile. She started to get up, reaching out to draw forward a padded settle set against the wall, but Josse forestalled her. Editha sank back in her chair, a slight frown on her face.

'Kind of you, Josse,' she said, quite sharply, 'but I am perfectly capable of moving a settle, whatever others may say.'

Helewise caught Josse's eye. It was clearly a reference to Cyrille. 'I'm sorry,' Josse said as he and Helewise sat down. 'I thought that—'

Editha smiled tightly. 'No, *I* am sorry, Josse. I shouldn't have barked at you.' The smile vanished, and she sighed. 'I am not as strong as I once was, it is true, and my joints stiffen in this cold weather so that at times I can barely move, but I am not in my dotage yet, and I resent being treated as if I'm standing on the edge of the grave, and have lost my wits as well as my mobility.' Her voice had risen in anger and now, with a glance at her father, she made an obvious effort to bring herself under control.

'Cyrille perhaps thinks only of your comfort,' Josse began hesitantly – unwisely, in Helewise's opinion, watching Editha's flashing eyes – 'and—'

'Cyrille thinks only of Cyrille,' Editha interrupted him. 'She desires to portray herself as wiser and more experienced, in every single area of life, than everyone else. Furthermore, she believes that perpetually telling us all what a fine nurse she is demonstrates her loving, compassionate nature.'

'Does it not?' Josse asked innocently.

Editha regarded him for a long moment. Then she said curtly, 'No.'

The three of them sat in a rather awkward silence for a while.

Then Editha said, 'Again, I apologize; you have come to see how Father is, and I have yelled at you concerning my own problems and haven't said a word about him.' She looked tenderly at Hugh, whose eyes were slowly opening. 'He has slept long, and sometimes, when that happens, he wakes up and has one of his good days.' Leaning forward, she said gently, 'Father? Are you awake? Would you like something to eat?'

Now Hugh's eyes were fully open, and he was looking at the three people at his bedside. 'Dear Editha,' he murmured. 'Yes, I am indeed awake, and I would very much like some food. And one of your sister's herbal concoctions, if she would be so kind.' Editha raised his hand to her lips, kissed it, then got up and hurried out of the room.

Hugh now turned to Josse. 'Still here, nephew?' he asked with a smile, which spread as he went on, 'I take it as a bad sign, that my family seem to be gathering around me. Anyone would think I was dying.'

'Uncle Hugh, I'm sure—'

But Hugh stopped him. 'Now, Josse, we all have to die, and I do not fear it,' he said quietly. 'But let us speak of more cheerful matters.' He was staring at Helewise, a roguish gleam in his eyes. 'You have brought a beautiful woman to see me, and you haven't even had the courtesy to tell me who she is.'

Josse looked straight at her. Unable to resist the temptation, she half-closed one eye in a tiny wink. Then, grinning, he turned back to Hugh and said, 'This is Helewise, Uncle.'

Hugh stretched out his thin hands, and Helewise took them. 'I am delighted to meet you,' he said. 'Josse always was choosy, even as a lad, and I can see now why he waited so long to take a wife. You are most welcome, my dear.'

'Thank you, Uncle Hugh. May I call you that?'

'I should be happy if you did. Now,' he said, with the air of someone getting down to business after the completion of the pleasantries, 'how do you find my household? Is my grandson's new wife still managing to get up everyone's nose?'

'She – er, she does have a slightly unfortunate manner,' Josse said.

Uncle Hugh burst out laughing; a happy, spontaneous sound, that brought colour and vitality to his thin, pale face. 'You have clearly spent too much of your life with great lords and ladies, young Josse, for you speak like a diplomatic courtier. Let us have plain speech; I no longer have time for the luxury of circumlocution.' He eyed them, one after another, then said in a low voice, 'I do not trust her.'

Not *trust* her? Helewise was surprised at the remark. Even after so short a time at Southfire Hall, she could understand that getting along with Cyrille wasn't easy, to say the least, but surely that was only because the poor woman was still finding her feet amid her new family, and hadn't yet learned the benefits of tact and perception. For Uncle Hugh to call her untrustworthy was a lot more serious, and, watching Josse, Helewise could see he wasn't sure what to make of it. 'Why not, Uncle?' he asked.

But Hugh shook his head. 'I am not prepared to say; not yet, anyway. They tell me I am old, and getting very woolly in my mind, and it may well be true.' He frowned. 'My thoughts ramble, and odd fancies occur to me which, I suppose, may have no basis in reality.' He put up a hand to massage his forehead. 'It is hard at times, I admit, to determine truth from imagination, and I do dream a lot.' He glanced at Josse. 'It is my rants, I suspect, that have prompted the family to send for you, young Josse.'

He had hit upon the truth, and Helewise, amused, watched as Josse cast around for a diplomatic way of admitting it. 'Well, er—'

Hugh laughed again. 'Don't trouble yourself, my lad!' he said. 'I know my daughters, and I know, too, that what they do is out of love for me.' He paused. 'I am very lucky, to be cared for so devotedly.'

There was a brief silence. Then Hugh went on, 'Harold de Crowburgh was my friend. He was probably my best friend, and that is saying a lot.'

Josse looked at Helewise, eyebrows raised. She, momentarily confused, recovered more swiftly, instantly working it out. 'Harold must surely have been the father of William Crowburgh, Cyrille's first husband?'

'Yes, yes, of course he was,' Hugh said, waving an impatient hand. 'As boys, Harold and I were closer than brothers, and our friendship persisted as we grew up, married and had families of our own. My Herbert and Harold's William were boyhood friends too, just as their fathers had been, although circumstances later separated them, and for many years they saw little, if anything, of each other. Enough of the old affection remained, however, for Herbert to wish to pay his respects when his friend William died.' He gave a great, gusty sigh. 'And so Cyrille came into our lives.'

'She brings with her a fine son,' Helewise said. She wondered if she should have spoken. Was it correct to offer her opinion? Hugh had turned to stare at her, and, nervously, she pressed on. 'Is it not some consolation for her presence, that you have the grandson of your old friend under your roof?'

Hugh sighed again, but he was nodding. 'I suppose so, yes, and it's no fault of the lad who his mother is.' Isabelle, Helewise recalled, had said something very similar. 'He has a look of his forefathers, and I do indeed see dear old Harold in him,' he conceded. 'But – but . . .'

Quite suddenly, Uncle Hugh changed. From being alert, interested and lucid, he turned in the blink of an eye to a puzzled, frail old man, mouth mumbling incomprehensible words, a drool of saliva trailing from his lower lip. Helewise, filled with the urge to help, leaned forward, her hand briefly on the old man's, and, reaching for a piece of cloth, she gently wiped his mouth. 'Uncle Hugh?' She kept her voice low. 'Are you all right?'

He stared up at her, his eyes wild. He tried to say something: 'Mar—', it sounded like. 'Not that one!' he spluttered. '*Mar!*' His voice rose to a shout, surprisingly loud, and he freed his hand from Helewise's, clenching it into a fist and pounding it hard on the bed, still repeating that strange word and shaking his head in impotent, furious frustration. Then, as if he had exhausted himself, his eyes closed and he sank back into his pillows.

Josse was already at the door. 'I'll fetch Editha – I can't think where she's got to,' he said, his voice tense with anxiety.

Helewise heard his footsteps hurrying away along the passage. She stayed where she was, once again gently holding the old man's hand. After some time, she heard footsteps again, but they were walking, not running.

Isabelle appeared in the doorway, carrying a tray, and Editha was beside her. Josse followed them into the room.

Isabelle went to the far side of the bed and Helewise moved out of the way so that Editha could take her place. Editha smiled at her, obviously understanding the gesture. 'Don't worry, he often does that,' she said kindly. 'Josse told us what happened. We think that Father's mind somehow slips at times, and then for a while he is lost to us.' She looked at Hugh, her face full of love. 'He always comes back, though.'

So far, Helewise thought sadly. Catching Isabelle's eye, she read the same, unspoken comment.

She and Josse quietly crept away, leaving Isabelle and Editha with their father. She thought Josse looked distressed. 'He is old, dear Josse,' she said, taking hold of his hand. 'Take comfort from what he said: he is not afraid of death, and he is lucky to have such tender care.'

'Aye, I know,' Josse said gruffly. 'It's just that—' He stopped, and shrugged helplessly.

Just that he's dying, she silently finished for him. There really wasn't any more to say.

They went through into the new extension and made their way to the solar. A wintry sun was trying to shine in a sky so pale that it was scarcely blue at all. A light snowfall had turned the land to patchy white. A fire burned in the hearth, and the little girls were playing beside it. A big chest of cast-off remnants of clothing stood open on the floor; clearly, the dressing-up box.

Josse and Helewise smiled to the family members who were present. Philomena and Henry sat watching the children, and Emma was sitting on a low stool sewing a length of grubby white silk into a headdress of some sort for Cecily, who stood right at her shoulder directing her. Josse led the way to a bench set against the far wall, and he and Helewise sat down.

Presently, Jenna came to join them, and they moved up to make room for her.

'Your daughter is very patient with her little sister,' Helewise said, nodding towards where Emma, her head bent over her sewing, was unpicking a seam and reworking it precisely as Cecily commanded.

Jenna smiled fondly. 'She is.' Turning to Helewise, she said, 'You know she wants to be a nun?'

Was there anything significant in that question? Did she know of Helewise's own past? 'Yes, Isabelle mentioned it,' she replied cautiously. She hoped Josse would not say anything. She was planning to reveal herself to this welcoming, open-hearted family one day, but she was not quite ready to do so yet.

'She'll go to Hawkenlye,' Jenna was saying. She gave a harsh laugh. 'If they'll have her, once—' She broke off. Then, in a very obvious change of direction, she said, 'Do you know it? It has a fine reputation, and we hear well of it even here in Lewes. You live much closer, I believe?'

Helewise met Jenna's clear eyes and found she could not dissimulate. 'I do know Hawkenlye Abbey, very well,' she said quietly. 'I would very much like to tell you about it, and how I come to know so much, but not yet.'

Jenna was watching her, obviously intrigued. She started to say something, then, bowing her head, said politely, 'As you wish, my lady.'

Josse was looking puzzled. 'You said, Jenna, *if they'll have her.*' Jenna turned to him. 'Why should they not?' he asked in a whisper.

Jenna's strong face contracted in a scowl. 'Because my dear brother's wife has taken it upon herself to say to Emma – and to everyone else who will listen, including, in time no doubt, the good sisters of Hawkenlye – that she doesn't think Emma is *suitable.*' The last word, cruelly emphasized, came out as a furious hiss.

'But surely that isn't for her to say?' Helewise protested. 'The call to the religious life comes from God, and if he has deemed a man or a woman suitable, that is all that matters.'

'So you'd think,' Jenna agreed. 'Cyrille, however, has her own ideas, and, since she expresses them with a considerable amount of conviction, Emma has let these ideas influence her. She's so worried!' For a moment, Jenna's eyes filled with tears. With an angry gesture, she brushed them away.

'What is the basis for Cyrille's objection?' Helewise asked.

'I cannot say, although I have my suspicions,' Jenna replied. 'I've asked her to explain, but either she cannot or will not. She maintains that as a truly God-fearing woman, she is uniquely qualified to judge Emma's suitability for the religious life, and furthermore she tells me – and I'm Emma's *mother*! – that she observes aspects of my daughter's nature that I and everyone else miss.' Her face working, she added in a sort of growl, 'She has managed to maintain, or so she informs me, the unique viewpoint of the outsider, who is best placed to appreciate the full picture.'

'But *what* does she observe?' Josse persisted. 'Can there be any basis for her concerns? You just said you had your suspicions,' he reminded her.

'Oh, she drops allusions to "inappropriate behaviour" which, she informs me, is not at all seemly in one who wishes to give her life to God. "Emma will have to do without a good many of the pleasures life has to offer," she told me self-importantly' – Jenna's imitation of Cyrille's careful, precise tones was uncannily accurate – '"and I am not at all sure that will be possible for her."' Slowly Jenna shook her head. 'You almost have to laugh, it's so absurd.'

Helewise was thinking hard. Guessing that Jenna didn't want to say anything to disparage her daughter, she said cautiously, 'It sometimes happens that, before a woman is quite sure that she hears God's call, she experiences the normal feelings and emotions of all the young. Perhaps Emma felt drawn to some handsome young man of your acquaintance?' Jenna had flushed, and Helewise realized she had guessed right. 'Perhaps, even, the young man might have stolen a kiss or a caress. It is what happens when we are young and the blood is hot,' she went on, not allowing either Jenna or Josse to interrupt, 'and, although we are quite rightly instructed that our passions must at all times be under our control, nevertheless I have always felt that a loving God – even more so his beloved Son – would understand, and not condemn a young woman or a young man for allowing themselves to be carried away by youthful affections.'

She paused. Steadily, she stared into Jenna's eyes. After a long moment, Jenna said, 'And would an indiscretion of this nature – if, indeed, it had happened – be sufficient to make a great abbey such as Hawkenlye refuse to take a young woman as a novice?'

Helewise took both her hands. 'Of course not,' she said firmly. 'No woman is born a nun, and all have had a varying number of years in the world before they answer their call. Since not one of us can say we are free of sin, I would judge that every single nun on earth has had to reconcile their past with their future. Why, Hawkenlye has widows and former harlots among its congregation,' she went on bluntly, 'all of whom would have had a great deal more to tell their confessor than some minor misdemeanour committed by a young, unmarried woman.' She smiled encouragingly. 'Nobody will expect her to be perfect.'

'And –' Jenna hesitated – 'and what if a girl, a young woman, believed she had heard God's call, and yet discovered, after a time, that the – er, that the aspects of life she had thought to have given up were too strong, and summoned her back into the world?'

'Nobody is asked to make vows before they are ready, in both their superiors' and their own eyes,' Helewise replied. 'And, before anybody even begins to think of perpetual vows, there is the postulancy and, after a minimum of six months, the novitiate. Both are designed to ensure that both a woman and her community have made the right decision.' She paused. 'Hawkenlye is unique, and run on lines different from other foundations,' she went on softly. 'The man whose vision was behind both it and one or two other abbeys, here and in France, believed passionately in Our Lord's message of compassion and tolerance, and consequently Hawkenlye has a flexibility not known elsewhere.'

Jenna was looking at her, her expression fascinated. 'You seem to know a great deal—' she began. Then – and Helewise actually saw the realization dawn – Jenna gasped.

'Please,' Helewise said softly.

There was no need for more. Jenna nodded, then, tears once more in her eyes, she leaned forward and put a soft kiss on Helewise's cheek. 'Thank you, my lady,' she whispered. 'Your past is your own business, and I will only say that, whatever path brought you to Josse, and so to us, I am *very* glad that you took it.'

Then she was on her feet, and, without a backward glance, hurrying away across the solar and out through the door.

* * *

During the afternoon and early evening, the snow came back. As if the first flurries had just been an experiment, now it came down with its full might. The sky was grey and heavy, with a solid look about it, as if it carried a huge weight and was finally, with relief, beginning to set it down.

The temperature dropped. The family deserted the solar, for, with the icy chill outside, the heavy wooden shutters had been fastened securely over its windows. The room that was made for light and sunshine turned into a gloomy, dark space, where footsteps echoed and nobody was inclined to linger.

The fire in the Old Hall's great hearth was kept well stoked, and, as the short daylight quickly faded beneath the dark grey clouds, more and more lamps and candles were lit. The family closed in around the warmth and the light, snug with blankets, wraps and cushions. Outside, the snow went on falling.

Late in the day, Helewise turned worriedly to Josse. 'Olivar still has not been permitted to join us,' she whispered. Cyrille sat quite close, on a footstool beside Editha, and Helewise did not want her to overhear. 'Do you think he is allowed light and a fire in his room?'

'I hope so,' Josse said fervently. 'It begins to be inhumane, this punishment.' He shifted in his seat, levering himself up.

'What are you going to do?' Helewise hissed.

'Speak to Isabelle.' He looked down at her. 'While Uncle Hugh is unwell, Isabelle is head of the household.'

He strode off across the hall to where Isabelle sat beneath the light of a torch set in a wall sconce, working at a piece of tapestry. Helewise, hurrying after him, watched as he bent down to speak to his cousin. She too got up and, with Helewise a few paces behind, the three walked out into the passage.

'What is it?' Isabelle looked from one to the other. 'Is there something you need?'

'No, Isabelle – your hospitality leaves no wish unmet,' Josse said. Then, as if his unease could brook no delay, he said, 'Helewise and I are concerned for Cyrille's lad. We understand he is being punished by being confined in his room, but surely he has been there long enough? And, given the conditions, will he not be cold and frightened? Unless that is part of the punishment?'

His voice had risen with his anger. Isabelle, with a narrowing of her eyes, said quite sharply, 'Don't get cross with me, Josse, it's not my fault!'

'I apologize,' Josse said instantly. 'I know it's not.'

'Accepted.' Isabelle managed a brief smile. 'I quite agree with you. This treatment is far too harsh for the boy, especially as his crime wasn't all that severe in the first place.'

'What did he do?' Josse asked.

'He went into his mother's room when she was having her afternoon sleep, and, although she repeatedly tells him not to, he amused himself till she awoke by playing with a rather pretty rosary she has, the beads of which are pearls and coloured glass. The inevitable happened, the rosary broke, and some of the beads couldn't be found.'

'It was wrong to have played with something he'd been told not to touch,' Helewise said tentatively. 'But I would have thought a short, sharp punishment would have better driven the lesson home.'

'So would I,' Isabelle said tersely. She met Helewise's eyes. 'You have children, Helewise?'

'Two sons, yes, and now they too have children.' She smiled. 'I was married before.'

Isabelle nodded. 'I thought you probably had been.' Then, returning to the matter in hand: 'If you're going to ask me to speak to Cyrille, and suggest it would be kind to fetch Olivar to join us, then I must tell you I've already done so, more than once, and each time she informs me that it is up to her, not me, to order her child's days.'

'Couldn't Herbert ask her?' Helewise suggested. 'He is making Olivar his ward, isn't he?'

Isabelle frowned. 'Yes, he is.' The frown deepened. 'It's odd,' she went on, lowering her voice still further, 'but Cyrille's attitude seems to have changed. To begin with, she was constantly harping on about it – Herbert's adoption of Olivar as his heir – and she never gave my son any peace. "What if something happened to you before the formalities are complete?" she said once. "What would then become of me and my poor little boy?"' Isabelle's eyes flashed with indignation. 'What did she think would happen?' she added in a sort of suppressed shout. 'Did

she imagine we'd kick her out on her fat little backside and
Olivar with her?' She paused, taking some deep breaths. 'No,
oh, no,' she said softly after a moment. 'Cyrille, I very much
fear, is here to stay.'

'You said her attitude changed?' Josse prompted her.

'Hm? Oh, yes. I first noticed a couple of weeks ago, or maybe
three. She – Cyrille – went quite quickly from wanting Olivar
with her every moment, and sort of pushing him at the rest of
us, as if she was determined to keep him right under our noses
and remind us constantly of who and what he is, to virtually
ignoring him.' She turned puzzled eyes to Helewise and then
back to Josse. 'He, poor little lad, didn't know what to make of
it, which is hardly surprising. One minute she's on at him all the
time, telling him he must behave like a little lordling and keep
his elbows in at mealtimes, not chatter with the servants, sit up
straight and all the rest of it, and the next, she's ignoring him as
if he'd suddenly become invisible.'

'The poor boy must be utterly confused!' Helewise exclaimed.
'How very cruel.'

'I suspect that's why he went searching for her on the occasion
he broke the rosary,' Isabelle said. 'Until she changed in her
attitude towards him, she liked him to be clinging to her skirts.
Pretty much literally,' she added with a grim smile, 'since she's
taken to wearing skirts that trail on the ground at the back, and
gets Olivar to hold up the hem as she walks.'

Stunned into silence, it was a moment before either Josse or
Helewise spoke. Eventually, Josse said, 'What would happen if
one of us quietly slipped away and took the boy some hot food
and something to drink, a candle or two and the means of making
a fire to comfort him?'

Isabelle turned to him. 'I've already done it,' she whispered.
'It may be going too far to dictate to Cyrille how she treats her
own child, but this isn't her house. Yet,' she added in a savage
mutter. Raising her chin – and, Helewise observed with a quiet
smile, looking absurdly like Josse – Isabelle said, 'Tomorrow,
Olivar will be allowed to rejoin us. Cyrille has decreed it.' Then,
with a bow to both of them, she spun round and went back to
her sewing.

*   *   *

It was late. It was cold. It was very, very dark.

The little boy lay huddled deep beneath the bedclothes. He had been alone for a long time now. He had eaten the food that the stern-faced but nice lady had brought – gulped it down so fast that it had made him burp, in fact, in case *She* came and got furious because he'd been eating when she'd said he mustn't – but that was ages ago. He was hungry again now, and there was nothing left.

The nice lady had made a little fire, too, and brought a candle. Both had burned out.

I mustn't cry, he told himself firmly. *I must be as good as gold and I must take my punishment without complaint.* Those were Her phrases. She said lots of things like that. Or she used to, before she suddenly stopped talking to him very much. He didn't know what he'd done wrong. Oh, he knew he'd broken her rosary, and that was why he'd been sent to his room for two days. But she had started not talking to him and not wanting him to be with her – *attend* her, that was what she used to say – quite a long time before the rosary got broken.

He didn't understand.

He didn't mind not having to be with her all the time. He didn't mind that at all. But he did mind – very much – having to be here all by himself.

Especially when it was so cold.

So dark.

So scary.

He thought he heard a noise, and his whole body stiffened with terror.

It came from the corridor.

It was the monster, slithering back to its lair beneath the bed. He could hear a sort of clicking sound. That was its long, curved talons, tapping against the flagstones.

He could hear its breath. It came in quick pants, as if the monster had been hurrying.

His eyes wide, he stared in horror at the door.

It began to open.

Something long and sharp and glittery came through the gap between the door and the frame. The door opened a bit more. Something huge and pale was there just for an instant, then a huge black cloud seemed to burst out into the room.

The little boy's heart was drumming so hard that he could feel it, up high in his throat. He could barely breathe. He thought he was going to be sick.

Deeper black against the darkness, the shape flowed on into the room.

The monster was almost upon him.

Desperate with terror, the little boy dug deep inside himself for courage he didn't think he had. Wild with panic, he drew air into his lungs. Then he opened his mouth and screamed and screamed and screamed until he thought his throat would burst.

He didn't know what happened next. He must have thrown himself right under the blankets and the pelts on his bed, for everything went black. Then, some time later – he didn't know how long – arms were round him, big, strong arms, and a deep voice was speaking quiet words of kindness and comfort.

He dared not open his eyes to look, but instead just pushed himself into the broad chest. A cup was held to his lips, and the deep voice said, 'Drink up.'

He drank. The drink was quite hot and sweet, but with a bitter aftertaste. The powerful arms held him close. 'I saw a big black shape,' he whispered, his voice shaking. 'It came flowing into the room, and I saw its glittery claws and they were *huge*.' Another deep, bone-shaking tremor ran through him.

'Hush,' soothed the deep voice. Held so close, he could hear the sound reverberating in the broad chest, above the slow, steady heartbeat. Boom, boom.

Then the big, strong arms laid him in his bed and tucked him in. 'I am here,' the deep voice said. 'I will watch over you.'

The boy smiled as he snuggled down.

The monster might well come back – it probably would, in fact, because monsters were like that – but it didn't matter now.

He had hoped and hoped and even prayed that the big, strong man who had come out of the shadows and defended him would come again.

And now he had.

Still smiling, relaxing now, secure and snug, the little boy fell asleep.

SIX

J osse half expected that someone – either his cousin Isabelle or Cyrille – would challenge him the next morning for having taken it upon himself to rush to Olivar's aid during the night.

'It may well be true that it wasn't my place to help him,' he said to Helewise as they prepared to join the household, 'but I just couldn't hold back once I heard those screams.'

'Of course not,' she said soothingly. 'But you must have been concerned about the boy already, Josse, to have been within earshot? I didn't hear him.'

'Aye, I was in the Old Hall,' Josse admitted. 'I couldn't sleep. I kept imagining how he must be feeling, all alone on such a bitter, savagely cold night.' He paused. 'It was almost as if I was waiting for something to happen,' he added in a low voice.

'Did he say what had scared him?'

'No. Just something about a huge black shape with long, glittery claws. He was almost beyond words to begin with, and then whatever sedative Isabelle prepared for me to give him quickly sent him to sleep. I stayed with him till it was light, and then Isabelle came back and relieved me.'

'Was there no sign of his mother?' Helewise asked incredulously.

'Not when I was there. Her chamber is over on the other side of the family's quarters, so perhaps she didn't hear him.'

'Did Isabelle comment on her absence?'

Josse sighed. 'Apparently Cyrille believes that the best way to cure a child of night fears is to ignore his terror and force him to overcome it.'

'A little harsh,' Helewise said, tight-lipped.

Josse was frowning. 'The thing is,' he said slowly, 'this really isn't a house where children suffer night fears. Do you know, Helewise, the lad sleeps in the same place I did, when I was a little older than him and the first extension had been completed. I used to wake up sometimes and be frightened, but I always sensed that something in the very fabric of the house was watching over me, and the fear went away.'

'Perhaps things have changed since then,' she suggested. 'The house, after all, has been further extended, and maybe the ancient protective spirit has been disturbed.'

But instantly Josse shook his head. 'Oh, no, it's still just the same,' he said, although he had no idea why he was so certain. He smiled ruefully at her. 'Come on. If you're ready, I'd better go and face the retribution.'

But to his surprise, nothing was said about the events of the night. Cyrille was not present; once again, Herbert said she was resting and would join the family later. The others greeted Josse and Helewise with the usual friendly courtesy. Henry remarked that there had been a lot more snow in the night, and that if it continued, and there was no rise in the temperature, the roads would very soon become impassable.

'I hope, Cousin Josse, that you have no pressing business back at home?' Editha asked him, concern in her pale face. 'It would not be at all wise to risk the journey under the present conditions.'

'No, and anyway I want to stay here to be with Uncle Hugh until – to be with Uncle Hugh,' he replied. Editha nodded her understanding. 'My family won't worry,' he went on. 'Conditions are no doubt much the same back at the House in the Woods, and they'll understand if Helewise and I stay away longer than planned.'

As if his kinsmen had been waiting for the opportunity, now they asked a flurry of questions about Josse's children, his house, what his life was like over there on the fringes of the Great Forest. He answered as best he could, telling them of Meggie and Geoffroi, his own children, and Ninian, his adopted son; how Meggie was hoping to set up home with her Breton blacksmith Jehan le Ferronier and how she had become a skilled healer; how Ninian was now a father; how Geoffroi's world centred around the animals, both domesticated and wild, with which he had such skill. Although Josse had made it clear that Helewise was not his children's mother, his kinswomen were too tactful to ask what had become of her. Josse had a swift, bitter-sweet image of

Joanna: *I do not forget you, my love, and neither do your children*, he said silently to her.

After breakfast, Helewise murmured to him that she would like to visit the chapel, and he showed her the way. He did not go in with her, for he had other things than prayer on his mind. He went on into the solar, hoping that, not having been in the Old Hall, the person he sought must surely be there.

He was: Olivar was kneeling up on the padded stone seat that ran along beneath the solar's small north-facing window. He had pushed aside the heavy wooden shutter that covered the opening, and was peering out at the snowy landscape far beneath.

Not wanting to take the lad by surprise and perhaps risk an accident – it was unlikely he'd fall, but not impossible – Josse deliberately made his footfalls heavy and loud. Olivar spun round, jumped down as if he'd been poked with a stick and said hurriedly, 'I didn't get my shoes on the cushions! I was very careful not to.'

'Then you did well,' Josse said, forcing a grin even while his heart went out to the boy's obvious anxiety. Was the lad habitually punished even for something as minor as that? 'I bet I couldn't kneel up there without dirtying at least a bit of cushion.'

The boy risked a small smile. Then, perhaps recognizing something in Josse's voice, suddenly the smile vanished and his mouth dropped open in astonishment. 'You – you're the big strong man!' he whispered. 'The man who comes in the night to protect me!'

Josse nodded. 'Well, I came last night,' he agreed. 'I knew something had scared you, and I thought I ought to make sure you were all right.'

'Yes, yes, I know,' Olivar said, 'but you've been to rescue me before.' He spoke with utter certainty. 'You always know when I really need you, like that time when she was so cross about – er, well, you just seem to come at the right time to save me or make me feel better.' He risked a quick look up at Josse. 'Andtosavemefromthemonster,' he added in a tiny whisper, running the words together in his fear and his haste as if he hardly dared utter them.

Josse wanted to pick him up and hug him, but he didn't think the gesture would have helped the boy in his very obvious effort to be brave. To take his mind off his pity – it was so strong it hurt – he wondered just what it was that the lad had stopped himself from saying. *She*, surely, must mean Olivar's mother. What had she been cross about, and what did her son fear she would do, to make him so desperate for protection and comfort?

But there was something even more disturbing, and Josse felt he must mention it. 'I couldn't have rescued you before, much as I'd have liked to,' he said gently, 'because I've only been here for a few days, and last night was the first time you needed me.'

But Olivar shook his head, laughing. 'But you did come before,' he insisted happily. 'We can pretend you didn't if you like, and keep it a secret just between us.' He hesitated, and, for a moment, fear came back into his wide blue eyes. 'Just as long as you keep coming,' he added in a whisper.

Touched, and not a little worried, Josse said, in as reassuring tone as he could manage, 'I will. You have my word.'

Helewise stood just inside the heavy wooden door of the chapel, looking around in wonder. It was small but perfectly proportioned, and it was clear that the best craftsmen had been employed in its construction. Graceful pillars lined the north and south walls, rising to fan out at their summits into a tracery of lines like the spread fingers of an open hand. The rood screen, of pale oak, was beautifully carved with images of trees, flowers and leaves, and the altar, again of oak, bore a crisp white cloth edged with a deep border of lace and on which stood a simple but heavy silver cross. Along the southern wall, open to the outside world, were two small stained-glass windows. There was another little aperture over on the northern wall, where the chapel backed on to the solar, and Helewise guessed it was for the use of family members who did not wish to join the congregation but chose to hear mass privately. In a church used by the community at large rather than a family's private chapel, she mused, it would have been called the leper squint . . .

Leper.

A soft chime of – memory? Warning? – sounded in her head. She wondered why.

Helewise walked on silent feet up the aisle towards the altar. She had believed herself to be alone. Now, spotting the short, veiled figure kneeling in the shadow of a pillar over to the left of the altar, she realized she was mistaken.

She stopped, not wanting to disturb the woman's private devotions. She began to edge backwards, towards the door, but she must have made some small sound because the veiled woman suddenly started, spinning round to stare at her.

It was Cyrille.

Embarrassed, Helewise said, 'I am sorry, I didn't mean to disturb you.'

Cyrille, appearing flustered, muttered something, and Helewise noticed she was fiddling with some small object she had been holding: something suspended on a long piece of thread. Although Helewise quickly averted her eyes – it would be embarrassing, she thought, if Cyrille caught her looking – nevertheless, Cyrille's hands disappeared beneath the folds of her veil, fumbling there for a few moments as if she was putting the object away in some secret pocket.

Then she turned bird-bright, pale eyes in a flushed face to Helewise and said, 'You do not disturb me, Lady Helewise, for I sense you are a godly woman, and thus welcomed by Our Lord into this His house.'

It was on the tip of Helewise's tongue to remark that the Lord, in the wisdom of his love and his infinite capacity for forgiveness, would surely welcome the ungodly just as much, if not more, if and when they came. But something in Cyrille's rock-steady, penetrating stare deterred her. She had the feeling that, once an opening for discussing the matter had been given, the two of them would still be talking at bedtime.

I am a coward, Helewise reprimanded herself, *but I do not wish to be shut away in here all day with such a woman.*

She answered Cyrille with no more than a courteous inclination of the head.

Apparently taking this as an invitation to closer intimacy, Cyrille came right up to her, the protuberant blue eyes searching her face intently. 'I expect you have come to pray by yourself,' she said with an understanding nod. 'That's what I'm doing, too. I find I need to spend much of the day in solitude, and this is one of my preferred places.' She nodded again, swiftly, repeatedly, as if to verify her own words. Then, her mouth right up to Helewise's ear, she whispered, 'You would not credit what a very strange and unsettling house this is, my lady.' Again, the nodding.

'I try every day to impose my will upon it, for, in truth, there is so much to be addressed that at times I scarcely know where to begin.' She sighed. 'They do not listen, the people who dwell here. They are stubborn, and too firmly set in their ways, and the voice of sense and reason falls upon deaf ears.'

I do not have to listen to this, Helewise thought. Although she tried hard not to jump to conclusions, she sensed strongly that Cyrille was trying to make her an ally; two women who were not of the family's blood uniting against them.

She wasn't going to be a party to it.

'I am a guest in this house,' she said firmly, 'invited here simply for the purpose of meeting Josse's kin, and not to judge them.' In case Cyrille had missed the point, she added, 'The private affairs of these kindly people, who have welcomed me so hospitably, are nothing to do with me.'

Cyrille had withdrawn slightly, but that appeared to be her only reaction to Helewise's snub. 'You are a godly woman,' she repeated softly. 'I see it in you, my lady. You are close to God, and once were even closer.'

Could she possibly know? Helewise wondered. Had she somehow learned that her position in life had once been very different? What if . . .

Enough, Helewise told herself. 'Throughout my life, I have always tried to be a godly woman,' she said quietly.

Cyrille had resumed her nodding. It was, Helewise thought, quite infuriating; as if Cyrille was implying that she knew exactly what you were thinking, and what words would come out of your mouth even before you spoke them.

'Herbert's mother resents me,' Cyrille said suddenly. Even as Helewise tried to adjust her thoughts to the abrupt change of subject, Cyrille went on, 'She is, of course, Hugh's eldest daughter, and she sees this as imparting the right to the position of senior woman in the household, whereas of course I, as wife to Hugh's heir and grandson, should in fact have that honour.' She shook out a fold of her beautiful gown, as if displaying its quality and costliness for Helewise's admiration. 'Isabelle is a widow, and, in a household where tradition and correct behaviour are given their due, she would by now have moved out into some dower house, leaving Southfire Hall to her son and his wife.'

'Surely, while Hugh yet lives, to discuss any such arrangement, let alone propose its implementation, is premature,' Helewise said. She tried to keep her emotions out of her voice, but without success. Even to her own ears, her tone had sounded crushing; almost rude.

Cyrille, however, either didn't notice or chose to ignore the implied reproof. 'And as for that Emma,' she said, 'well, words fail me.' Unfortunately, however, they didn't. Leaning close to Helewise once more, Cyrille said in a spiteful whisper, 'She says she wants to be a nun, but she's going to find the vows far too much of a challenge, that one, especially the vow of chastity.' She gave Helewise a knowing look. 'She was caught with a young man, you know, and he had his arms around her and was kissing her, and his hands were on her hips and buttocks, and on her breasts that she had thrust upwards by tightening her bodice so severely that she could hardly breathe, and—'

'Did you observe this yourself, Cyrille?' Helewise interrupted. What was the *matter* with the woman? Was it just that she enjoyed passing on salacious gossip, or was there something more?

Cyrille shot her an angry glance. 'No, I did not, but I am perfectly certain it happened. These things are made known to me, my lady!'

The obvious question was to ask, *How?* But, rapidly coming to the conclusion that conversing alone with Cyrille was something to avoid, Helewise refrained. Instead, she allowed the short silence to extend a little and then said, 'I am looking forward to getting to know your little boy today. I do hope he has recovered from his night fright.'

Cyrille didn't answer. Once again, she was toying with the folds of her gown. For a moment, Helewise wondered if she had heard. But then, with a faint sigh, she said, 'Olivar. Oh, yes, Olivar.' Then, raising her head, she looked Helewise straight in the eye and said, 'He must learn not to make such a fuss.' Her eyes seemed to slide out of focus, and Helewise had the impression that her thoughts had suddenly turned elsewhere. She muttered something – perhaps, 'It does not really matter, now' – and then, with the barest of nods in Helewise's direction, she turned and walked away, the flap-flap of her soft slippers on the stone floor fading away.

Helewise sank down on to the low steps before the altar, her skirts billowing around her. Aloud she said, '*Well!*'

Then – for the encounter with Cyrille had deeply unnerved her – she turned round to face the simple cross, knelt, folded her hands and closed her eyes. Something bad had intruded here, she thought. Despite dear Josse's bracing words about the house, some evil element seemed to have evaded its benign, protective spirit and slithered inside, and, whatever it was, it had begun to affect poor Cyrille. Either that, or . . .

No. There was no *or*, she told herself firmly.

'I do not know why, dear Lord,' Helewise whispered, 'but I am uneasy. No, it is worse than that –' she forced herself to be honest – 'I am afraid.'

Bowing her head over her clasped hands, she tried to find the words to ask for help with an undefined problem she hadn't even begun to understand.

The long hours of the day slowly passed. The snow went on falling. Late in the afternoon, a messenger fought his way up from the town, bringing word – by some complicated, involved route – from Jenna's husband, Gilbert. As had been expected, he would not be home before the snow melted; he had dispatched his message while the roads and tracks were just passable, but he had not then been able to leave the coast himself because his business there was not yet complete. Anticipating being stranded, he had had the foresight to warn his family that his return would be delayed indefinitely.

Jenna took the news badly. Watching her from her seat by the fire, Helewise had the sudden thought that Jenna, too, felt the presence of something sinister within the beleaguered walls of Southfire House.

Isabelle came into the Old Hall, spotted her daughter and went over to her. 'Peter Southey needs tending,' she said brusquely. 'Everyone else, including me, has their hands full, so will you see to him, please?'

Helewise, sitting nearby, overheard. 'Jenna has only just sat down,' she said. 'I will go.' Mother and daughter both turned to her. Isabelle's expression was harassed, Jenna's grateful. 'I should be glad of something to do,' Helewise added, getting to her feet.

Josse had been with his uncle for much of the afternoon, and she had found that time dragged, although it wouldn't have been polite to say so.

'Very well,' Isabelle agreed. 'Thank you, Helewise.'

'How is he?' Helewise asked as she and Isabelle walked out of the hall.

Isabelle frowned. 'His injuries appear to be mending, and he says he is not in much pain, yet, when I asked if he didn't find the days very long, alone in his room, and suggested he might like to come and join the household, he said it was out of the question.' Slowly she shook her head, smiling ruefully. 'It did cross my mind that perhaps he wishes to remain isolated until the swelling and bruising of his face improves. He is, I am sure, normally rather a handsome young man, and such men are often vain.'

'I will see if I can persuade him,' Helewise said. 'I agree that he would surely be happier amid other people, and that might hasten his convalescence.'

Isabelle gave a dismissive snort. 'Even if he were fully well, he wouldn't be going anywhere for a while. It's still snowing, and very soon we shall be totally cut off.'

A faint tremor of alarm ran through Helewise, although she could not have said why. Wealthy, substantial houses such as Southfire could tolerate many days, if not weeks, of isolation, for the household would have filled the storerooms and cellars back in the autumn, when nature had produced her bounty and there were meats, vegetables, fruits and cereals in plenty for those to buy who had the means. No doubt the buttery was full of fine wine, mead and ale, and, failing all else, there would undoubtedly be a well somewhere at hand for a family of this size living in a place that had been occupied for generations.

Helewise's moment of apprehension had nothing to do with fears of running out of food and drink . . .

Peter Southey looked considerably better. His face was still swollen and discoloured, but the hot flush of fever had left his skin, and his expression was alert. Having seen to his needs – food, drink, a cold compress on his nose and a fresh chemise – Helewise pulled a stool up beside the bed and sat down.

'Why not come and join us in the hall this evening?' she said without preamble. 'The company is jolly enough, and, after the wine has been passed around, there are often songs and sometimes a story or two.'

Peter eyed her solemnly for a few moments. 'Thank you,' he said. 'I know you mean it kindly, but I will stay here.'

'You will soon have regained your good looks,' Helewise said, with a smile to take any sting out of her words. 'Besides, everyone knows how you got yourself in such a state, and are far more likely to sympathize than to jeer.'

'That is not why—' Peter began. Then, lowering his eyes, he muttered, 'I would rather not.'

'Why?' Helewise persisted. 'It would do you good, I believe.'

'You have all been more than kind enough to me already,' Peter replied, still staring down at his hands, twisting together in his lap. 'Far more than I deserve,' he whispered.

Or that was what Helewise thought she heard; surely not? 'The household have only done what it is to be hoped all good Christian people would do,' she said gently. 'We are taught, are we not, to help our fellow man?'

'Yes, we are, but not when that man has come to—' Again, he stopped; this time, as abruptly as if he had bitten his own tongue. Then, with a change of subject that clearly cost him quite an effort, he looked up at Helewise and said, 'Tell me about the family, my lady. You can be my entertainment, if it would not tire you.'

'Very well.' There was much here, Helewise reflected, to puzzle her, but she did not think Peter was going to offer any explanations just because she asked for them. She gathered her thoughts, then began to describe the various members of the Southfire family and how they related to each other, giving brief description of each one, finishing with Cyrille's young son.

'And I can't tell you much about him,' she concluded, 'because I've barely spoken to him.'

Peter was watching her. 'I heard a child screaming in the night,' he said softly. 'Was it him?'

Helewise wondered fleetingly why Peter should assume it had been Olivar rather than one of the little girls. 'It was.'

'He sounded terrified.'

'He'd had a bad dream.'

Peter was still watching her, eyes narrowed. 'Indeed?'

'Yes.'

'Was it not,' Peter murmured, 'that he saw a dark shape, which seemed to flow into his room, reaching out with sharp, silvery claws?'

Helewise looked at him in amazement. 'How did you – has someone been talking to you about it?'

Slowly Peter shook his head. 'Nobody has mentioned anything.'

She didn't know what to do. Should she tell him that he'd just described virtually word for word what Josse reported little Olivar said he saw? Oh, but what if Peter's fever was rising again, and, by confirming the accuracy of his guess, she contrived to make him worse?

For it *had* to have been a guess. There was no other explanation.

'I—' she began.

But he put out a hand, taking hold of hers. His flesh felt quite cool; there was no fever in his blood. 'I am sorry,' he said. 'I meant neither to upset nor embarrass you.'

She shook her head. She had no idea how to respond.

'The lad is this Cyrille's son, you told me?' Peter said after a pause.

'Yes, that's right.' Helewise, glad of the invitation to talk about something else, hurried on. 'She was the widow of Young Herbert's childhood friend, William Crowburgh. She bore him a son, Olivar, six years ago. Now the boy is being adopted as Herbert's ward and his heir.'

'And you said, I believe, that all the other children in the family are female.'

'Yes, that's right – there's Herbert, of course, Isabelle's son, but no male child has been born since.'

Peter did not reply. The room was growing dark and, wondering if he had fallen asleep, Helewise quietly got up and lit a couple of lamps.

Peter wasn't asleep. He had drawn out the little leather bag he wore around his neck, and he was turning it over between his fingers, running his thumb around the outline of whatever was within. His expression had turned inwards, and Helewise realized his thoughts were far away from the small, cosy room.

She reached out and laid a hand on his arm. 'You are missing your home and your loved ones, I dare say,' she said kindly. 'Since you were heading away from home, on your way to Lewes, nobody will be anxious about you yet, but, if you like, as soon as the snow begins to clear, word can be sent to reassure them.' He did not respond. 'Why,' she added brightly, trying to cheer him, 'news that you are safe might well reach them before they have even begun to be concerned!'

He turned to her, his eyes full of sadness in his battered face. 'You have a kind heart, my lady,' he said, his voice not quite steady, 'and I thank you for your concern. You need not trouble yourself to send any message, however. I am quite alone in the world.'

With that, he turned on to his side, away from her, and, still clutching the little leather bag, closed his eyes.

'He looked so very sad,' Helewise said to Josse as they prepared for bed. 'He said he was quite alone in the world, and, to judge by his grief-stricken expression, I'd guess he has lost someone he loved very much.'

Josse went to sit beside her, taking her hand. 'I am sorry for him, but I confess that, just at the moment, I am more concerned with the fact that, from what you've just told me, he seems to have seen the same apparition that so terrified poor little Olivar.'

Helewise rested her head on his shoulder. 'What's going on, Josse?' He could hear the edge of fear in her voice. 'You keep telling me this is a good place, and that the house has a strong protective spirit, yet two people beneath its roof have now seen something quite dreadful.'

Josse held her close. 'Aye, there's no denying that a – a darkness has crept in,' he agreed. 'But the house will fight back. I know it will.'

She looked up at him, and he read the scepticism in her eyes. 'It's a house, Josse,' she said gently. 'Just stone, wood and mortar.'

There was no arguing with that, and he didn't try.

Presently he got up. 'I'll go and speak to Peter Southey,' he announced. 'I would like to hear more of this dark shape that flows from room to room.'

She must have heard some different tone in his voice, for she gave him a quick look. 'You suspect someone may be playing a trick?'

'I hope very much that they're not,' he replied shortly, 'since it's a particularly heartless trick to reduce a small boy to abject terror. But the alternative—' He had been going to say the alternative, that some evil had entered the beloved ancient home of his maternal kin, was even worse. But he found he couldn't utter the words.

Helewise seemed to understand. 'Be careful,' she said.

Peter lay on his back, his head sunk in the pillows. His eyes were closed, and he was breathing heavily through his open mouth. Josse called out very softly, 'Peter? Are you awake?'

There was no reply.

Josse was about to tiptoe away – even his rudimentary knowledge of nursing told him you didn't wake up a convalescent without good reason – when a log collapsed in the small hearth, sending up a tongue of bright flame which briefly illuminated the room. Turning back to make sure Peter slept on undisturbed, Josse noticed the man's hands.

They were clutched over his chest – over his heart – and they held a small object, which was all but concealed within the clasped fingers. The little leather bag lay empty, tucked just inside the open chemise.

Josse leaned forward.

Memories were firing off inside his head, for, although he had no idea why, the object was familiar. Without pausing to think how, why or where, he knew he had seen it before.

It was carved out of ivory, or perhaps some sort of bone, and it was in the form of a seated woman, crowned and dressed in flowing robes. She supported her right elbow with her left hand, and the fingers of her right hand were pressed to her cheek.

Pity her, poor woman! She's got toothache for all eternity! said the laughing, irrepressible voice in Josse's memory.

It was the queen out of a chess set.

SEVEN

J osse made his way back to the Old Hall. The fire had burned very low, but the glowing embers still gave out heat. He went to sit on one of the settles drawn up beside the great hearth. The past had come vividly into focus, and his mind was filled with its echoes. He dropped his face in his hands, giving himself up to it.

After some time – he wasn't sure how long – he became aware that he was no longer alone. Someone had quietly approached, and sat down beside him.

'I didn't realize that you, too, are a night owl,' said his cousin Isabelle.

'I'm not, usually,' he replied. 'These are, however, unusual circumstances.'

'You feel it too, then?'

He met her anxious eyes. 'Aye, I do.' And how much more, he thought, must she, who had lived here all her life. 'Something has changed,' he added in a whisper.

Isabelle nodded. Then, fiercely, she hissed, 'The house will go on protecting us. This – whatever it is – will pass. It *will*!' She thumped a fist against her thigh for emphasis.

There was a moment's silence. Then she said, in a very different tone, 'I'm glad you're here, dear Josse. You are so much a part of Southfire and its past, and it's right that you are with us at this time.'

The past . . . It just kept cropping up this evening.

He said, 'Isabelle, tell me about Aeleis.'

She sighed. 'I was wondering when you were going to ask.'

'Just because I haven't mentioned her before doesn't mean I haven't been thinking about her,' he said quickly.

Isabelle smiled. 'I know, Josse. You were always such friends, when we were all young. Of course she would be in your thoughts.' She paused. 'I'll tell you what I know, but, I warn you, you may not like it.'

'I'll hear it anyway.'

She laughed softly. 'Never one to hide from the truth, were you?' She took a deep breath, then said, 'Aeleis didn't much like being married to old Godric, and I dare say you remember how she didn't bother to hide her relief when he died, and her joy at being free from his fussing and his everlasting attempts to clip her wings and shut her in her cage.'

'She always resented being told what to do,' he remarked.

'Very true. Well, she stayed on here with the family for a while, but Father and Mother made it plain that they thought she should marry again. They thought they were doing the right thing, and they truly believed Aeleis would only be happy once she had another husband and a few children.' She sounded as if she were defending them, Josse thought, but he hadn't been going to criticize their actions. It was always the way of it, he recalled sadly. Neither Hugh nor Ysabel had understood their strong-minded, independent youngest daughter, and although he had no doubt they loved her, they had tried to turn her into somebody else.

'They actually chose a second husband for her,' Isabelle went on. 'He, too, was many years older than her, and probably wouldn't have long survived being married to her.' She shot Josse a sidelong glance. 'I don't doubt that he'd have died a very happy man,' she said with a grin. 'But, anyway, Aeleis refused him. Father told her she was a fool, for Lothar – that was his name – was a wealthy man with no heirs, but she said she had enough money and certainly wasn't prepared to marry another old man just to acquire more.'

'Did she?' Josse asked. 'Have money, I mean?'

'Oh, yes,' Isabelle replied with a wry face. 'Godric had plenty, and left all he had to her.'

'She would have been an attractive prospect for many a man,' Josse observed.

'And many a man agreed with you, and wore a path to her door,' Isabelle said tartly. 'Mother and Father were deeply distressed. There was a great deal of gossip, and people said Aeleis was acting very immorally, entertaining people – *men* – when she wasn't married to them, or, indeed, to anybody.' She shot a quick glance at Josse. 'Single women and widows are meant to be purer than pure, and they certainly aren't supposed to enjoy male company, but Aeleis simply refused to obey the rules.' She sighed deeply. 'Oh, you could understand her point of view,' she conceded. 'She'd already endured marriage to a tremulous old man, more because other people wanted and expected it than through any desire of her own. Do you know, Josse –' she turned to look at him – 'I don't believe she'd have taken a husband at all had she not wanted to please our parents.'

Remembering vividly the child and the girl Aeleis had been, Josse thought she was probably right. 'What happened next?'

Isabelle looked away, and Josse thought he saw a faint flush stain her face. 'Aeleis got more and more tired of the arguments and the pressure, and the constant parade of men deemed suitable for the role of her second husband. Then one day poor Father *really* made her angry. He meant well, bless him, and he said what he said because he genuinely believes a woman hasn't the brains or the sense to manage her own affairs. He told her she must marry again, and soon, so that "some decent, sensible man" – honestly, Josse, those were his exact words! – could start controlling her wealth and making her decisions for her.'

'Oh, dear,' Josse said with a quiet smile.

'Oh, dear, indeed!' But Isabelle wasn't smiling. 'Aeleis was incandescent with rage, Josse. She yelled at poor dear Father, telling him he had never understood her, that he had no idea that women could manage their own lives without being told what to do and kept under control by men, and she swore at him and said she wasn't going to spend another moment under his roof. Then she packed up her bags, stormed off back to the modest manor she'd inherited from Godric, where, with swift efficiency and a certain amount of ruthlessness, she made the arrangements for it to be managed and the land tenanted, with the incomes accruing to her. Then she disappeared.'

For some moments, Josse simply sat there, silently digesting all that Isabelle had just said. It came as no surprise to hear that Aeleis had run off in a blaze of anger, proclaiming she didn't need any *man* to control her life and her wealth. The bones of that self-reliance, independence and resentment of other, lesser mortals telling her what and what not to do had been there in her childhood, when she had been the mischievous, funny, pugnacious, frowning, dirty little girl whom Josse remembered with such affection. No: what had surprised him was that, having fled Southfire Hall and, presumably, set up her own establishment elsewhere, Aeleis had never contacted her family to say where she was. Whether she was all right. Whether she was happy.

'Have you any idea where she is?' he asked after a while.

'No.' Isabelle's single word seemed to echo in the quiet hall.

'There has been no message at all? No news?'

Isabelle sighed. 'We believe she went to London,' she said. 'A friend of Father's heard some talk, and the woman involved sounded a lot like Aeleis.'

'What sort of talk?' Josse could see this conversation was distressing his cousin, but he did not let that stop him.

'Oh, use your imagination!' Isabelle flashed. 'A wealthy lord, close to the King's circle, takes a new mistress to the Christmas festivities at Windsor. Lovely women always get talked about, and it had already become clear that Aeleis would only grow more beautiful as she grew older. Then there was the whisper of a story that she'd married again, but we didn't know whether or not it was true.'

'Were you able to trace her by investigating these possible leads?'

'We could have done, perhaps, but Father forbade anyone to try.'

Josse dropped his head. So Hugh, distressed and embarrassed by his youngest daughter's wild and unconventional behaviour, had done what any upright, moral, God-fearing man should do, and cut that child out of the family. Josse sighed, feeling suddenly as sad as if he bore the weight of the world's sorrows. An upright, God-fearing man might act like that, aye, and be proud of himself for his courage. But how did a father feel? A father, moreover, who had always given every indication that he loved his three girls, and that the youngest in particular had only to twinkle a smile at him to lift his spirits and brighten his day.

Losing Aeleis, and being held back by his own sense of right and wrong from doing anything to find her or bring her back, must have come close to breaking poor old Hugh's heart.

And now this . . .

He turned to Isabelle, about to tell her what he had just remembered, and why it was suddenly so very relevant.

But she was getting to her feet, a hand up to her forehead as if to soothe a headache. 'I am going to bed,' she announced. 'I'm tired and my head's splitting. Good night, Josse.'

'Good night.'

He watched her stride away across the hall. As the sound of her footsteps faded, he too got up and went in search of his bed.

As he relaxed towards sleep, the present gently faded away and Josse's mind took him back to the past. Eyes closed, he smiled, for it was the past of this house, and the memories were happy ones . . .

'You have to get yourself tidied up now! They'll be sending for us any moment, and you haven't even washed your face!'

Josse's young voice is tight with anxiety. She'll be punished again if she's not neat and clean for supper, and he hates having to witness it. Not because the punishments are harsh – they're not, for Aeleis's father loves her far too dearly to do her physical harm. But being reprimanded at all damages her pride, and when Josse sees her face tighten with distress and reined-in anger, he aches for her.

Also, and more to the point, if Aeleis isn't in a fit state for the evening meal, Josse is very likely to get the blame.

Aeleis abandons whatever it is she's been doing with such single-minded attention. She rubs wet hands down her gown – she appears to have been washing something in a ewer of water, but unfortunately it's not herself – and now, a smile splitting her grubby face, she holds the object out to Josse.

'Look! Isn't she wonderful?'

Josse takes the little figure in his hands. It is a woman, regally dressed and seated on a block. One hand is up to her face.

'It's a chess piece,' Josse says.

'I *know*!' Aeleis is scathing. 'But she's not like the set that Father has. She's made of something different. What d'you reckon it is?'

Josse stares down into the tiny face. The woman – she's wearing a crown, so she must be the queen – has strong features, and there is something powerful about her expression. Josse has seen faces like hers before, on a big brass bowl his family uses back home which, so tradition has it, was acquired from the Norsemen. 'She comes from far away,' Josse says. 'She's made from the tusk of a walrus, and she was crafted up in Viking lands.'

Aeleis laughs scornfully. 'You don't know that!'

He grins. 'No, I don't. I'm just guessing.'

Aeleis has taken back her treasure, and is stroking it with a gentle forefinger. 'She's a brave, strong woman like Queen Eleanor,' she croons. 'She doesn't let anybody boss her around. She makes her own rules and nobody ever *dares* get angry if she gets her clothes dirty.' She puckers up her lips and places a kiss on the figure's forehead. 'She's going to be my lucky charm,' she says decisively. 'I'm going to keep her with me always and for ever.'

Josse has the guilty feeling that the figure, which is clearly very old, may well be valuable. 'Er – where did you find it?'

'*Her*,' corrects Aeleis. Her eyes flash to meet Josse's. 'You're not to tell!' she hisses furiously. 'If you do, I'll tell them you pushed me down the steps and that's how I tore my gown and got that huge bruise on my knee.'

'I didn't!' Josse protests.

Aeleis gives him a very sweet and totally unconvincing smile. 'I know.'

'All right, then.' He surrenders with a grin. 'I promise I won't tell. So, where did you unearth her?'

'In the old cellar. The place we crawled through to.'

Josse remembers noticing Aeleis digging in a corner. 'She was just lying there?'

'No, stupid, she was under the earth. I was just scratching around, looking for treasure, and I found her.' Her eyes light up. 'Do you think there are any more pieces?'

Her excitement is infectious. 'I don't know,' he says, 'but I think we ought to check.'

They wait until the evening meal is over and people are relaxing in the Old Hall, talking, drinking. Nobody notices when the two children creep away. It is dark underground, but then it's always dark there, and Josse has had the foresight to bring two cresset lamps. They dig for what seems hours, but find nothing.

Aeleis is upset. 'I wanted you to have one too,' she says crossly. Then, in the companionable mood of their joint adventure, she adds, 'You can share Queen Eleanor a bit, if you like. Just when you're staying here, and not all the time, but you can hold her sometimes.'

Seeing the fervour of possession in the small face, Josse understands just what a very generous offer this is. He grins at his cousin. 'Thank you,' he says with grave courtesy, 'but she's yours. You are her liegeman,' he improvises, 'and queens don't like it when their loyal servants make free with them.'

Relief floods Aeleis's face. 'All right, then,' she says. She fakes a deeply unconvincing sigh of resignation. 'I'd better do as you say.'

With a smile of pure joy, she gives her queen a final buffing with the hem of her skirt, then hides her away up her sleeve.

And Josse, half-awake in his uncle's house many, many years later, turned over, thumped his pillow and, with a sigh, fell deeply into a profound sleep.

'Peter Southey *must* know Aeleis!' Josse said to Helewise. They had been talking for some time, for he had woken at first light and, restless with the swirl of thoughts and conjectures filling his mind, had disturbed her. Once awake, she had demanded to know what he was fretting about, and he had told her. 'She must be someone important to him,' he continued, 'or, rather, *he* must be important to *her*, for she wouldn't have parted with her queen for anyone she didn't care about very deeply.' Swept along by his own enthusiasm, he added eagerly, 'Do you think he—'

But Helewise interrupted. 'Just a moment, Josse,' she said calmly. 'Before you get carried away making connections where none may exist, let's look at the evidence. Peter has a chess piece, which normally he carries in a little leather sack around his neck, and from just one brief sighting of it, you've convinced yourself that it once belonged to your cousin Aeleis.'

'It was her most treasured possession!' he protested. 'She loved it, and it became her talisman.'

'She loved it when she was a child,' Helewise pointed out. 'She is a grown woman now, and, from what you've been telling me, rather a wealthy one. I'm quite sure she has jewels and golden bracelets and entire chess sets, beside which an old ivory piece she unearthed when she was five years old pales into insignificance.'

'It was her lucky charm,' Josse insisted. 'It's hard to understand for someone who didn't know her when she was little, but she always knew her own mind, even then.'

'Very well,' Helewise conceded. 'But the next point is, how can you be so sure that Peter Southey's piece is the same one? I have seen those carved chess sets, and they are not exactly rare. Peter's piece could have come from anywhere.'

'And yet it has turned up here, in the very place where it was once lost and Aeleis found it.'

Helewise did not immediately reply. Then, with a sigh, she said, 'I grant you, it does seem quite a coincidence.'

Josse's mind ran on. 'He said he was bound for Lewes,' he said slowly. 'He was going to put up at an inn, but he never said what his business in the town was.' He paused, for the direction of his thoughts suddenly seemed incredible.

'Perhaps he wasn't really making for the town,' Helewise whispered. 'Perhaps he was coming here all along.' She looked at Josse, her face flushing with excitement. 'He knew all about Southfire Hall, because Aeleis told him. He was about to come and announce himself when he had his accident. His horse slipped and took a bad fall, and Peter was brought here, and . . . Oh.'

He nodded, grinning. 'And just forgot to say, *Fancy me getting hurt so close to the very place I was heading for! I'm a very good friend of Aeleis's, and she sent me to find you all!*'

'Could he have lost his memory when he hit his head?' Helewise's voice held a note of desperation.

'I don't think so. He remembers other things. You were telling me only yesterday that he said he was alone in the world, with nobody to worry if he went missing.'

Something occurred to him. The same thought must have simultaneously struck Helewise, for, meeting her eyes, he could see her dismay. 'If he's alone,' he said slowly, 'then does that mean Aeleis is dead?' He was surprised at the surge of grief that swept through him.

Helewise took hold of his hand. 'Steady, my love,' she said

gently. 'We race ahead of ourselves, I think. Perhaps they are just friends, and he doesn't presume to imagine she will concern herself if he fails to return. Let us not even consider that Aeleis might be—' She stopped. 'We won't think about it until and unless we must.'

He nodded. She was right, although the sense of dread – lying somewhere near his heart, like a cold, hard stone – did not dissipate.

'I must talk to them,' he announced. 'To Isabelle, anyway, for surely she must suspect what happened to Aeleis, even if she doesn't know, and also to Uncle Hugh.'

'You will distress him,' Helewise said warningly. 'He may well feel much guilt at having acted in such a way that she felt there was no alternative but to leave.'

Josse got to his feet and, squaring his shoulders, headed towards the door. 'If he does, then perhaps it is no more than he deserves.'

He heard Helewise give a gasp, and he knew she thought he was being too harsh. He didn't care.

Left alone, Helewise took a deep breath, composed herself and then went over again in her mind everything Josse had told her, adding her own impressions and recollections of all that had occurred since Peter Southey had been brought into Southfire Hall.

She thought about what happened when they asked him his name. She thought about how he asked not once but twice where he was. She recalled how he had resisted the invitation to go and join the household in the Old Hall. And, most of all, she thought about a young man who seemed to have something on his conscience.

Who, just perhaps, felt very guilty because people for whom he intended to make a specific sort of mischief had treated him with kindness . . . *far more than I deserve*, he said.

A small spark of certainty lit up her contemplation. *Wait*, she told herself firmly. Frowning in concentration, she tried to recall everything Josse had told her. Aeleis had been at Southfire Hall twenty years ago, a young widow perhaps in her early twenties. Then, as Isabelle had informed Josse, her parents had tried to make her marry again, but she had refused, after which she had left the family home and not been seen or heard of since.

Twenty years ago . . . Helewise's shoulders slumped. Only twenty years. No. She was wrong – what she had believed for a moment was the answer to the riddle couldn't be true.

Or could it?

The man's face was badly damaged, after all, and the pain of such a battering, not to mention the dislocated shoulder, would make him look drawn; older than his true age.

She knew she was allowing her imagination to run away with her, making connections and drawing conclusions on the slimmest of evidence. She ought to—

But then something else struck her. It was horrible, and surely so very unlikely that it couldn't possibly be true. She needed someone with whom to discuss it; another, cooler, mind. She would just have to keep calm till Josse came back, and see what he thought.

Shaken, she tried to compose herself for the wait.

Josse strode away up the passage, his mind full of unthinking anger. He really wasn't sure who he was so cross with: Isabelle, for having allowed her little sister to disappear without protest, or Uncle Hugh, for his intransigent attitude that forced Aeleis away. Both, probably.

Editha was seated on a settle by the hearth in the Old Hall. The little girls were running in and out, but otherwise the big room was deserted. Belatedly, Josse realized it was still very early.

Editha beckoned to him, a smile of welcome on her face. He didn't want to stop and talk politely, for he was wound tight with indignation and something else – something that hurt – and needed to hurry on to seek out Isabelle and Hugh. But Editha called out again: 'Josse? Are you all right?' and her tone was so anxious that he had no choice but to go and join her.

She stared at him as he came to stand before her. 'What on earth is the matter?' she asked, her face falling into lines of concern. 'Has something happened?'

'Aye, it has!' he began. His voice was far too loud, so that Editha shrank back. All at once he was contrite. She had no way of knowing what he suspected, and it really wasn't fair to take out his anger on her.

He sank down beside her. 'I apologize,' he said gruffly. 'I shouldn't have shouted at you.'

'Just tell me what's happened!' she pleaded. Then, her pale face losing what little colour it had, she said in a whisper, 'Is it Father?'

'No, no,' he reassured her. She had half-risen, and, taking hold of her hand, gently he pulled her down again. Looking into her wide eyes, he could think of nothing to say other than the truth. 'Peter Southey knows Aeleis.'

She shrank away from him. '*No*,' she said in a tiny voice. 'It cannot be!'

'I believe it to be so,' he replied.

Editha was shaking her head, holding up her hands as if to fend him off. 'I can't believe it,' she muttered, 'I – I—'

He caught her as she slumped into his arms in a faint. She was heavy against him, and, very carefully, he got up, laid her head down on the cushions and swung her feet up. Then, looking frantically around, he spotted a serving woman who had come to tend the fire.

'Go and fetch your mistress!' he cried. 'The lady Editha is unwell!'

The woman dropped her basket of logs and ran back the way she had come. Very soon, Isabelle appeared, swooping down to kneel beside her sister, patting her hands and calling out her name.

Editha opened her eyes. 'Oh, Isabelle,' she whispered, 'Josse says – oh, no!'

Isabelle turned furious eyes up to Josse. 'What have you done?' she demanded. 'You've upset her, that's plain enough, but how? What did you say?'

The serving woman was still hovering, face agog with lively interest. With an impatient gesture, Isabelle shooed her away.

Josse crouched down beside her. 'I only said that Peter Southey must be acquainted with Aeleis, and Editha—'

Editha groaned. 'Hush!' Isabelle said. 'Really, Editha, you ought to be able to hear her name by now without going into a swoon. Now, Josse, what grounds have you for this extraordinary claim?'

'He has Queen Eleanor.'

Isabelle gasped, a hand flying to her face. For a few moments she didn't speak. She merely knelt there, staring at him, her eyes wide with an expression he couldn't read. Eventually she said, 'You're sure?'

He shrugged. 'It looks exactly the same. And what are the chances of a stranger turning up here and coincidentally treasuring a copy of just the chess piece your sister adopted as her lucky charm?'

Isabelle nodded. 'Slim, I agree.' She was looking worriedly at him. In a whisper, she said, 'What does this mean?'

'I don't know.' He rubbed his hands over his face. 'Helewise and I tried to work it out, but—'

'Come along.' Isabelle rose to her feet. 'Editha, you stay here – don't try to get up yet.' She beckoned to the serving woman, lurking in the doorway. 'Don't just stand there, Tildy! Fetch her some water. Josse, you and I will speak to Helewise.'

His mouth opened to protest, but Isabelle was already striding across the hall.

'This is surely a family matter,' Helewise said a few moments later, shooting a furious glance at Josse. 'I am sorry, Isabelle – it was wrong of Josse to discuss it with me first.'

Isabelle brushed the objection aside. Josse, watching Helewise's expression and perceiving her angry mood, was quite grateful for the reprieve. 'It doesn't matter, Helewise. I would like to hear what you think.'

'Really?' Helewise sounded uncertain, and, his eyes still on her, Josse realized she had thought of a possible solution but was reluctant to reveal it.

'Yes. Please.'

Helewise drew a breath. 'I may be wrong – in fact, I'm sure I must be – but I wondered if Peter Southey could be Aeleis's son.'

Isabelle sank down on the bed. 'Her *son*.'

Josse looked at his cousin. She looked shocked, as well she might; he was feeling more than a little surprised himself.

'It could be possible, couldn't it?' Helewise said into the stunned silence. 'Josse, you told me that Aeleis was a widow during the Yuletide you spent here twenty years ago, but that she left—'

'She left this house for good the following year.' Isabelle's tone was distant. Then, eyes coming sharply into focus, she said, 'Could Peter Southey be as young as nineteen?'

'But it would mean Aeleis must have conceived him very soon after that Yule!' Josse protested. 'Yet I recall no mention of any forthcoming marriage. Why, you told me only last night, Isabelle, that she didn't want to marry again! You said she stormed out after a row with Uncle Hugh and that was the last time you saw her.'

'Yes, all that is true,' Isabelle said slowly. 'But—' She glanced at Helewise.

'It is possible, I'm sure, for two people to meet, marry and start a child within quite a short time,' Helewise said carefully.

Isabelle smiled grimly. 'And, of course, babies can be conceived outside wedlock.'

'But you told me there was a rumour that Aeleis *had* married again?' Josse found he didn't want to accept that suggestion. 'We have no grounds for concluding she bore an illegitimate child.'

'All right, Josse,' Isabelle said. She looked at him with affectionate impatience. 'We all know you thought she could do no wrong.'

Helewise said, 'We still haven't decided how old Peter Southey is. His facial injuries make it difficult to ascertain what he usually looks like.'

Isabella nodded impatiently. As soon as Helewise stopped speaking, she said, 'Yes, yes, quite so. If you're right, then Peter's reason for coming here is only too clear.' She paused, looking first at Helewise and then, lingeringly, at Josse.

Helewise appeared puzzled. 'Perhaps Aeleis *sent* him,' she suggested. 'It seems logical, to me.' Watching her closely, Josse could tell she was thinking hard. 'Maybe,' she went on, her expression softening, 'she has instructed him to find out how the family feel about her now, and whether they would welcome her back into the fold.'

But there was another possibility. Turning to Isabelle, trying to keep any hint of accusation out of his voice, Josse asked, 'Does Aeleis know her father is ill?'

'It is difficult, if not impossible,' Isabelle replied stiffly, 'to send word to someone whose whereabouts they have elected not to disclose.'

Helewise, evidently detecting the tension between the cousins and diplomatically changing the subject, said, 'Could we not just ask Peter how old he is?'

'And give what reason?' Josse countered. 'It's hardly common practice, I would have said, to demand that a guest reveals his age.'

'He's not exactly a guest,' Isabelle said, 'since he's only here because ours was the nearest dwelling to where he had his fall, and anyway—'

There was a sudden small noise in the passage. Isabelle stopped in mid-sentence, and Josse hurried across to the door, opening it and peering out. In one direction, the passage came to a dead end where it met the north wall of the solar block. There were a couple of shallow recesses in the stonework, but, going swiftly to check, he quickly saw that neither held a lurking eavesdropper. He ran back past the doorway, going first down the corridor leading past more guest accommodation and ending at the chapel. Nobody was in sight, and surely whoever had been outside – if, indeed, anyone really had been – wouldn't have had time to let him or herself into one of the other rooms and soundlessly close the door. He raced back and took the passage that led to the solar. There was nobody there.

Slowly he went back to Helewise and Isabelle. 'No sign of anybody,' he said. 'Maybe we were mistaken.'

Isabelle frowned. 'I'd like to believe that, but I'm quite sure I heard a footfall,' she replied. Her frown deepened. 'We should not have been discussing such a sensitive matter without first checking that we couldn't be overheard. It was foolish.' With a curt nod to each of them, she hurried away.

Helewise looked at Josse. 'Sensitive? Does she mean because, if Peter really is Aeleis's son, it implies she rushed too quickly into remarriage and pregnancy?'

'No, my love.' He sighed, and, reaching for her hand, sat down on the bed. 'It means that in this family where daughters predominate, the unexpected arrival of a legitimate male child of Aeleis's would force everyone to rethink their expectations.' He recognized he was being blunt but did not regret it. 'Young Herbert has married a widow with a little boy in order to adopt the lad, so as to be sure of a male heir in the next generation. But if Peter Southey is Aeleis's legitimate son, then all that will change.'

Helewise stared at him, her eyes wide with wonder. 'Won't they welcome him?' she whispered, but already she was shaking her head, as if answering her own question. 'If he really is Aeleis's son, then his presence here must surely mean she wants a reconciliation, and has perhaps sent Peter as an emissary to see how they would all feel about her coming home, and . . .'

Her hopeful voice and optimistic words trailed off. Watching her, pitying her, Josse guessed she had just realized exactly what he had: Peter had Aeleis's chess piece, he was grieving, and had admitted he was alone in the world. If indeed Aeleis was his mother, then only one conclusion could be drawn.

The dreadful thought that had occurred to Josse the previous night must be true. Aeleis was dead.

Disentangling his fingers from Helewise's, he dropped his face in his hands.

EIGHT

Helewise had nothing to do. It was early afternoon, of a day that already seemed to have dragged on for an eternity. Nobody was inclined to venture outside, although the sun was trying to shine and, in Helewise's opinion, it would do most of the household good to get into the fresh air and out of the claustrophobic tension that affected them all.

The family had dispersed after the meal, leaving Helewise alone in the Old Hall. Josse had gone to sit with Uncle Hugh. He had been preoccupied all morning, and, when Helewise had remarked that it was a kindly gesture to go and spend time with the sick old man, had muttered something about it not being kind at all since he intended to ask some unwelcome questions. He had looked so distressed. She had tried to cheer him up, tried to convince him that they could not even be sure that Peter Southey *was* Aeleis's son, and so it was surely premature to conclude that, because the young man was grieving and alone, it meant Aeleis was dead.

Josse didn't seem to be amenable to reason. Didn't even, if she was honest, appear to have been listening to her.

Helewise tapped her foot. She couldn't get used to being unoccupied: as long as she could remember, right back to earliest childhood, every minute of the day had had its allotted task or duty. Since leaving Hawkenlye Abbey, the relentless pace of life had continued, for, apart from the busy community at the House in the Woods, there was also her beloved sanctuary to tend. People's need never seemed to decrease.

She did not, she reflected ruefully, make a very good guest. Here she was, for the first time in memory with time on her hands and nothing demanding her attention, so why couldn't she simply go on sitting here in this comfortable seat, a cushion at her back and her toes warmed by the fire, and enjoy it? *I am not accustomed to leisure*, she thought, *and it is probably too late to acquire the habit.*

She wondered how Josse was getting on. She guessed he was going to try to force Uncle Hugh to talk about Aeleis. It was perfectly clear to her, now, that Josse as a boy had had strong feelings for his youngest cousin; knowing Josse as she did, she suspected he had probably loved her. *He loves so many*, she thought with a smile. *He has such a big heart, and is ever ready to be hoodwinked into believing people are better than they really are.*

She pulled herself up short. It was not right to criticize Josse, even in the privacy of her own thoughts.

She got up, pacing round the hall and listening at the various doorways to see if she could detect activity. Where *was* everyone? Stopping by the entrance to the passage leading to the family's quarters, in the original extension, she heard voices. Without stopping to think, she strode off to see who it was, what they were doing and whether she could join in.

Following the sound of the voices, she hurried down the passage as it twisted this way and that and came upon a partly open door. In the small, cosy room beyond, warmed by a little fire and illuminated by several candles and lamps, a circle of women sat sewing, heads bent over their work, talking quietly as they stitched. As Helewise paused in the doorway, Editha and Philomena both gave her a smile and Jenna half-rose from her seat. The three little girls looked up eagerly.

'I am sorry if I intrude,' Helewise began, 'but I wondered if—'

I wondered if I might help, and join in whatever you're doing, she had been about to say.

She didn't get the chance. Cyrille, who had placed herself in the centre of the group and appeared to be organizing the work, stood up and moved over to the doorway, positioning herself right in front of Helewise as if barring her entry.

'Oh, no, my lady,' she said, craning her head on its stocky neck towards Helewise. 'I am working on my needlepoint, but the other ladies are busy with the household mending, and do not expect our *guests* to involve themselves with such work!'

She managed to make *guests* sound almost like an insult. As plainly as if she'd actually spoken the words, her meaning shouted out: *You're an outsider and not welcome in this intimate little circle.*

'I'm sorry,' Helewise said again, flustered and very embarrassed. 'I will leave you to get on.'

Not knowing where she was going, only wanting to get away, she hurried off along the passage. She thought she heard voices, swift movements – as if someone had leapt up, and was perhaps protesting, castigating Cyrille for her behaviour – but she did not wait to find out.

She meant well, and was trying to be kind and considerate, she told herself. *The fact that I am burning with humiliation and furiously angry is entirely my own fault, and indicative of the fact that I am far too proud, and enjoy my normal position of authority and supposed indispensability a great deal too much.*

She strode on, barely aware of her surroundings, all her attention absorbed in the battle not to dislike Cyrille de Picus so much that she yearned to run back and punch her.

After what seemed quite a long time, she came out of her fit of temper. Looking around in some surprise, she found that she had paced right through the house and had emerged in the kitchen quarters at the rear. To her right a storeroom, or larder, opened up, and she could see great hams and joints of smoked meat hanging from stout beams, and barrels of various staples neatly ranged along the walls. To her left was a still room, and from somewhere ahead the sounds of splashing water and chattering voices suggested the servants were still busy clearing up after the meal.

Not wanting to interrupt them, or have one of them ask her solicitously if they could do anything for her, she crept on.

She came to a big, heavy door, standing ajar. Peering out, she saw a covered way leading to the bakehouse, with the dairy some way beyond it. Once again, she could hear voices; the servants were all hard at work. She was about to turn round and creep back the way she had come when a movement caught her eye.

The kitchen quarters were bordered by a high fence made of wooden palings, and in the fence there was a narrow opening filled with a stout gate, which was slowly being pushed open. Intrigued, Helewise watched.

Presently a swaddled figure appeared. Slowly, moving at a shuffle, it came up the well-trodden path to the doorway in which Helewise stood. The path was slushy with melted snow, and the underlying earth had been churned up by the passage of many feet into a slippery squelch of mud.

Afraid that the stumbling figure would fall, she went out to meet it.

'Are you in need?' she asked, stopping a few paces short.

The figure stopped, raising a hooded head. In the hood's dark recesses, Helewise made out a gaunt face with long, shaggy, unkempt grey hair and bright eyes under thick, bristling eyebrows. A scarf covered the nose and mouth, a filthy beard emerging from its lower edge. The hand holding it in place was missing the ring and little fingers. The garments were scarcely more than rags, held together with clumsily sewn string stitches. The deformed feet, half-buried in the mud, were bare.

The beggar stared at Helewise. 'May I please have a cup of water?' he asked in a low, cultured voice that crackled with disuse.

'Of course! Come with me.' She turned and trotted back up the path, her mind already working on how best to help this poor supplicant. A bowl of soup would be best, for if he was starving – and most people who came begging were starving – then solid food would be rejected by the shrunken belly. She looked behind her to make sure the beggar was following her. Perhaps some small pieces of bread, well soaked in the soup, and—

'What do you think you're doing?'

The words, spoken in a tone of horror, cut across her busy thoughts. Spinning round, she saw Cyrille standing on the doorstep, bulging pale blue eyes wide with horror, a fold of her veil held up over her nose and mouth.

'Someone is here who needs our help,' Helewise said, keeping her voice low so that the beggar would not hear. 'He is far gone, I fear, and will walk no further without sustenance.'

Cyrille had not moved. She was staring at the beggar, her eyes unblinking, a few beads of sweat on her forehead. She raised her veil a little higher, peering over the top. Then she turned to Helewise. She did not speak.

'Will you summon one of the kitchen servants?' Helewise asked politely, struggling to conceal her impatience. Cyrille had already put her in her place once, and she didn't want to invite a further snub. 'He has asked only for water, but we should encourage him to take more than that, if he will, and perhaps find him a warm shawl or cloak and some shoes, if that is possible, for—'

To her amazement, suddenly Cyrille leaned forward, grabbed hold of her sleeve and dragged her inside the house, closing the door with a violent bang.

'*He must not come in!*' she hissed. Then, putting her face right up to Helewise's, she added in a ferocious whisper, 'He's a leper!'

'Yes, I know,' Helewise said calmly. Hoping Cyrille wouldn't notice, she drew back, away from the angry eyes and the fast-panting mouth.

'There are women and children in this house!' Cyrille said, her voice rising and her arms folding protectively across her shaking body. 'They must not be put at risk. It is *forbidden.*'

By whom? Helewise wondered. Not, surely, by the level-headed, sensible Isabelle, who would undoubtedly know as well as Helewise that the risk of catching the terrible disease from a quick encounter was so small as to be non-existent. Even among the Hawkenlye nuns who heroically chose to be shut away with their patients, it was rare for leprosy to spread, and, in all her years at the abbey, Helewise had only known of two sisters who had succumbed.

When she was quite sure she had control of herself, she said, 'I understand that you do not wish to admit the man into the house. However, I am prepared to take water and food out to him, and to wait with him while he consumes it. If some warm garment *could* be found, I'll give it to him.'

Cyrille had stopped the frantic panting, and now regarded Helewise critically. Whatever terror had held her in its grip seemed to have relented.

Then, unbelievably, she shook her head. A patronizing smile spreading over the pale face, she said, 'No, my lady. What you ask cannot be done.' Edging closer again, her expression intent, she was nodding as if in confirmation of her own utterance. 'I know about such people – they play on our finer sentiments, yet if we give them the assistance for which they crave, it only serves to undermine their efforts at self-improvement.' Fixing Helewise with a hard stare, she said, 'He must leave immediately, and I suggest you go out and tell him so.'

Barely able to believe she was actually hearing the words, Helewise said, 'But, Cyrille, where is he to go? Apart from the fact that he is so weak he can scarcely walk, half his toes are gone, and the snow is deep.'

Cyrille's face drew into a scowl of distaste, and she sniffed. 'He must go down to the monks in the priory.' She went on staring at Helewise, who had been shocked into immobility. 'Now,' she added firmly.

Then she spun round and strode away.

Flinging open the door, Helewise hurried out to the beggar, who stood slumped against one of the pillars supporting the roof over the covered way. 'I am very sorry, but I cannot help you,' she said. She could feel the hot blood flooding her face. 'This is not my house, and the woman who came to the door has forbidden the giving of food or drink.'

The leper watched her from steady light-grey eyes. He had lowered his scarf, and she saw that he was missing several teeth. 'She is afraid,' he said simply.

'Needlessly,' Helewise said with a frown.

'You know about the sickness?' he asked, a sudden note of interest in his harsh voice.

'A little,' she replied. *Enough*, she thought, *that I am mortified by Cyrille's ignorance and her brutal refusal to act as she should.* 'You should go down to the priory in the valley,' she said briskly. 'The monks there will help you.'

'Yes, I know.' Then, to her surprise, he gave a rueful laugh. 'Nevertheless, I had hoped to avoid approaching them for a little while yet.' He looked straight into her eyes. 'They will help me, yes, but once I am under their care, I will never leave.' He looked up, his face open to the wide sky, his expression anguished. 'And, in truth, my lady, I am not quite ready to bid farewell to this harsh but beautiful world.'

Her heart was wrung with pity. 'What would you have me do?' she whispered.

He smiled. 'What you must, and, despite what I just said, you have my gratitude.' She did not move. His smile broadened. 'I'm asking if you'll help me down the road to the priory,' he prompted.

'Oh! Yes, of course.' Flustered, she tried to think. He was thin, wasting away, but a man just the same, and clearly beyond the end of his strength. She doubted that she could support him alone. 'Wait just a moment, and I'll be back. I will try to find you some boots if I can, for the snow lies thick and you are barefoot.'

He gave her a resigned smile. 'My lady, do not trouble. I cannot feel my feet.'

She ran back down the passage, skidding round its many corners, hoping the house was as deserted as it had been a short while ago. Where was he? She had to find him, quickly. She tried to recall the way to Hugh's room – down there, was it? No, that was the wrong direction, surely . . .

'Helewise? Whatever's the matter?'

Josse stood in front of her, his face creased with concern. Grabbing his hand, she dragged him on with her to the big old chest just inside the entrance, where outdoor clothing was dumped, not pausing for any explanation other than, 'Come with me. We'll need our heavy cloaks and our boots. Oh, *hurry up!*'

Supporting the leper between them, and steadily bearing more and more of his weight as the last of his reserves finally ran out, Josse and Helewise got him down the long hill, along the valley path and up to the gates of the priory.

A big, broad-shouldered man, warmly wrapped in a thick woollen cloak, had been watching their approach from the shelter of a little booth that stood beside the gates. As they covered the final few yards, all three staggering now, he came out to meet them. Josse could have cheered with relief.

'I guessed you were coming here,' the big man said. With gentle hands, he detached the beggar's grip on Josse and Helewise's arms, taking over his full weight and supporting him, apparently as easily as if he had been a child. 'One for us, is it?' He looked down into the beggar's face with a smile.

The beggar made no reply. He stood slumped in the big man's arms, his head fallen on his chest and his face concealed by his hood. He was, it seemed, beyond speech.

'He came to the house but we – er, it wasn't possible to help him, so we have brought him here to you,' Josse said. Helewise had managed to explain the bare facts of what had happened, and, although he was as revolted by Cyrille's lack of charity as

Helewise clearly was, he found himself reluctant to condemn his kinsmen's household by going into detail.

The big man was staring at him. 'Couldn't even spare a pair of worn-out old boots?' he asked softly, jerking his head in the direction of the beggar's feet.

'We are guests in the house,' Josse said curtly. 'It was not for us to criticize the ways of the household.' The big man nodded, but made no comment. 'Will you help him, Brother?'

'He's not a monk,' Helewise whispered. 'The Cluniac order spend their days in prayer and contemplation, and laymen perform all the work of the priory.'

The big man, overhearing, gave her a grin. 'You are well informed, my lady. I am called Gregory, and I am gatekeeper, porter, puller of the plough on occasions and bearer of anything and everything too heavy for other men.' He flung out his chest with a certain amount of pride. 'In answer to your question, yes, we will help him.' With the same gentleness, he handed the beggar back to Josse. 'Hold him up while I open the gates, and then, if you have recovered a little strength, come with me, for I must leave you while I find the prior and the infirmarian.'

A short time later, Josse, Helewise, Gregory and the beggar approached the big limestone building where the sick of Lewes Priory were cared for. It stood to the south of the vast church, and beyond it were a series of stew ponds, now frozen over except for one or two places where the ice had been smashed, presumably for fishing holes. Gregory led the way under a low, arched doorway, and they found themselves in a long, wide room lined on either side with cots, most of them occupied. Gregory, now carrying the beggar in his thickly muscled arms, turned immediately to his left, and they followed him into a section of the infirmary that was segregated from the main ward. It seemed to be a place reserved for initial assessment, and was sparsely furnished with a pair of narrow beds and a table, on which there were several rush lamps. Gregory laid the beggar down on one of the beds. Josse heard him say reassuringly, 'The infirmarian will be here directly. He's a good man; have no fear.'

He stood back. They waited. Presently, a black-clad monk

hurried into the room, two men dressed in plain brown robes at his heels. He muttered a cursory greeting to Josse and Helewise, murmured, 'Leprosy, you say?' to Gregory, who nodded, and then knelt down by the bed.

It seemed intrusive to watch the examination. Josse turned away, walking a few paces back along the corridor to the main ward, and Helewise followed. But the monk's quiet voice still reached them. 'Damage to your hands and feet,' they heard him say, 'and thickening of the skin. Can you feel that?'

'No,' came the soft reply.

'Or that?'

'No.'

There was a long silence. Then, a note of perplexity in his voice, the monk began, 'It's strange, but I don't—'

'I know what's wrong with me,' the beggar interrupted with surprising force. 'There is no need to talk of it, and certainly not right now, for I am exhausted and only wish to sleep.'

'Of course,' the infirmarian said smoothly. 'I will leave you in the capable hands of Luke and Philip here.'

He came bustling out into the passage, glanced at Helewise and Josse, then went on past them. They heard his footsteps steadily fading as he crossed the main ward and left the infirmary.

'Brother Anselm's off back to his devotions, then,' Gregory said, emerging from the little room and staring after the departing infirmarian. 'Still, those two laymen in there know pretty well as much as he does, and they'll look after our new patient.'

He stood looking at them, and Josse realized he was waiting for them to leave. 'Thank you,' he said courteously, 'I am happy to hear it. Come, Helewise – we should return to Southfire Hall before darkness falls.'

Gregory walked with them back to the gates. His attitude towards them had softened, Josse thought. Perhaps, having had the time for reflection, Gregory had concluded that it really wasn't a man's fault if one of the senior women in the house where he was a guest had commanded – in very relentless terms, according to Helewise – that the sick and the impoverished were not on any account to be helped.

As if Gregory's thoughts had been running along the same lines, he said, 'Southfire, you said? The place you're staying?'

'Aye,' Josse agreed. 'My Uncle Hugh's manor. We've come to visit because he's not very well.'

'So I've heard,' Gregory murmured. 'The monks are keeping him in their prayers.'

'I'm grateful.'

Josse had the impression that Gregory had more to say, and after a few moments, he spoke again. 'I'm surprised, I must admit, at a lack of charity from that house. The family has always been generous when it comes to alms-giving.'

Josse hesitated. Should he explain? He glanced at Helewise, and she shrugged as if to say, *Why not?*

So he did. 'My cousin Isabelle's son married last year,' he said. 'His wife has rather firm ideas about how things should be done, and she was quite vehement, apparently, on the subject of donations to the needy.' He glanced at Helewise.

'Indeed she was,' Helewise agreed. 'She is of the opinion that a beggar will be encouraged in his indolence if he is provided with sustenance, and that generosity undermines his efforts towards independence.'

Gregory's eyebrows went up. 'Indeed?' Slowly he shook his head. 'Well, it's a point of view, I suppose. And what of the rest of the family?'

'Nobody else was present when the beggar came to the door,' Helewise said swiftly. 'Had they been, I don't believe he would have been turned away.'

Feeling the need to defend his kin, Josse said, 'It seems to me that disagreeing with the lady leads to more trouble than it's worth. The various members of the family have, I believe, fallen into the unfortunate habit of letting her have her way.'

Gregory nodded his understanding. 'It happens in a place like this, too,' he said, 'even among the holy brethren, their servants and workers, who, you might say, ought to know better.' He sighed, his pleasant face clouded; clearly he spoke from personal experience. 'The kindly give way again and again in the face of the strong will of the conscienceless, and then one day you wake up and find you've backed yourself into a corner, and the one person's rules have become the law that everyone else has to live by.'

'Aye, that describes Cyrille exactly,' Josse said.

Gregory looked up. 'Cyrille?' he queried.

'Aye. She was Cyrille de Picus before she wed my cousin's son Herbert.'

'Herbert of Lewes was his great-grandfather?'

'Aye, and my grandfather.'

Gregory smiled. 'A great man. He died, of course, long before I was born, but his name is still honoured hereabouts. He lost his life on crusade, you know.'

Josse grinned. 'Aye, indeed I do, since he died fighting beside my father.'

Gregory clapped a hand to his forehead. 'I should have worked it out when you said you were Hugh's nephew,' he said. 'You're Josse d'Acquin.'

Josse bowed. 'At your service.'

Gregory didn't speak for a moment. Again, Josse sensed there was something on his mind. Then: 'I probably wouldn't have said this if I hadn't just realized who you are, but, since I have, I feel obliged to.' His eyes met Josse's. 'Not that I can be specific, mind, but something's niggling me about the name Cyrille de Picus. There was some unpleasantness, although for the life of me I can't recall exactly what it was.'

'She was married before,' Helewise supplied. 'To a man named William Crowburgh, by whom she had a son. When he died – last year, or perhaps the year before – Herbert went to offer his condolences, having been a good friend of William Crowburgh's in their youth, and he and Cyrille fell for each other.'

Gregory shook his head. 'No, it wasn't that – it's all news to me, and not as if there was anything amiss in the tale.' His brow creased in a deep frown. 'It was, however, something to do with a marriage; or perhaps a betrothal, and I have the feeling that something very bad happened . . .' They waited. Gregory shook his head. 'It's no good. I can't bring it to mind.'

Josse met Helewise's eyes. He knew, just from that quick look, that she was thinking what he was thinking. 'May we visit you again, Gregory?' she said. 'We would like to check on the health of the beggar, and, if possible, we will try to bring some warm garments for him.'

'And you'd very much like it if I could scratch my head till I've remembered what it was about Cyrille de Picus that rang a bell when I heard her name,' he added with a grin. 'Of course, my lady. Come whenever you like, and I hope I'll have news for you.'

They had reached the gates. Gregory glanced up into the sky. 'Best get on up to Southfire Hall without delay,' he advised. 'Temperature's dropping, and the clouds are building; it'll fall dark early, tonight. You—'

Suddenly, as Helewise and Josse watched, a change came over Gregory. He stopped speaking, and all expression seemed to be smoothed off his face, leaving it bland and vacant. His eyes seemed to be focused on something far away.

'Gregory?' Josse asked anxiously. 'Are you all right?'

Slowly the big head on the massive shoulders turned to Josse. 'You must take care,' said a chilly, distant voice that was barely recognizable as Gregory's. 'There is evil there, and the threat is perilous and imminent.'

'What do you mean?' Helewise asked, her voice shrill with fear. 'Who is threatened?'

Gregory did not respond; it appeared he hadn't heard her.

Then, as suddenly as it had arrived, the brief fugue was gone. Turning back to his contemplation of the skies, Gregory said, in his normal tone, 'There's going to be more snow before moonrise, I'll warrant, so best be quick and get safely within doors. Good evening to you!'

With a cheery wave, he stepped back inside the priory grounds and closed the gates.

NINE

It was a long, hard slog back up the hill. The temperature was falling fast, and the snow and the sloppy mud were steadily freezing into hard ruts and ridges that could turn an unwary ankle. At times they seemed to slip back one pace for every three they took forward. Josse had hold of Helewise's arm, trying to help her, and both were tired and sore by the time they finally reached the house. Although they didn't speak of it, Josse guessed that the events of the afternoon troubled her as much as they did him. For the hundredth time, he found himself wondering why his kinsmen were acting so feebly; why one of them – all of them – didn't stand up to Cyrille and put her firmly in her place.

He looked at Helewise, struggling along beside him, her face red with effort and her breath coming in gasps. *You didn't either, my love*, he thought. *You allowed her to overrule your loving heart and your instinct to act with compassion, and you let that poor, sick, starving man leave Southfire Hall without so much as a sip of water or a heel of bread.*

As, he added honestly, *did I . . .*

He thought again about Southfire and its protective spirit. He thought about the sinister, shadowy darkness that seemed to be stretching out its malicious fingers into every room and every corner. He thought about a happy, cheerful family who were tense with anxiety and at odds with one another. And he thought of a woman who seemed to have put them under an evil spell, so that they allowed her to order their days and impose her own poor judgement and bad decisions when surely every last one of them knew full well that she was utterly wrong and they should not allow it.

It was as if a dim mist was before his eyes, swirling darkly like a black veil being tossed and billowed by a soundless wind. Through the mist he seemed to see the short, sturdy figure of a woman, but then, even as he strained to see better, she changed. In the spot where she had stood he saw a looming shape, a long snout and thick forelegs that ended in sharp claws sensing the air before it, the great bulk of its body curled up as if poised to strike. He blinked several times, and the vision went away.

He saw in an instant what was wrong at Southfire Hall.

For a moment, out there in the deepening grip of the cold and under the lowering sky of approaching night, Josse's thoughts were so terrible that they almost drove him to his knees.

Then he came back to himself. There he was, his Helewise beside him and leaning heavily against him, and they were out in the cold and almost at the summit of their long climb. In his mind there was the echo of something so disturbing that it frightened him, but, try as he might, he could not recall what it was.

He tightened his hold on Helewise, putting his arm round her waist to help her along. 'Not far now,' he said bracingly as the snowflakes began once more to fall.

The family sat round the dying fire in the Old Hall, huddling close around the last of the warmth. The children had been sent to bed; again, there had been no sign of Olivar, who seemed once more to have been banished from the company. Or perhaps, Helewise reflected, glancing surreptitiously at Cyrille, he prefers to keep out of his mother's way. How odd it was, for a mother of an only son to treat him so. Wasn't the normal human instinct to want to be with one's children? That surely applied to boy children in particular, for whom the years during which they were permitted to live at home with their parents were all too few.

As if sensing Helewise's eyes on her, Cyrille turned to her. 'The leper was accepted at the priory, I assume?' she asked.

'Yes,' Helewise said shortly.

Cyrille nodded. 'Yes, yes, just as I said, for I knew that was the right place for one such as he.'

Her smug self-righteousness stung Helewise like a hot brand. Before she could stop herself, she said, 'He would have made the journey down to the priory a great deal more easily had he had a mug of hot soup in his belly and a pair of boots to walk in.'

Herbert looked up, a worried expression on his face. Isabelle did too; she shot an enquiring glance at Josse, as if to say, *What's all this?*

'Cyrille, dear,' Herbert began.

She ignored him. The pale blue eyes fixed on Helewise, the plump cheeks quivering slightly, she said, 'As I told you earlier, I understand people like our poor beggar, and I pride myself on knowing the way they must be handled. Had I allowed you to overrule my own good judgement, word would have got around, and before we knew it we would find ourselves being troubled incessantly by the sick, the poor, the destitute and the plain idle, for it is always easier, is it not, to beg one's bread than to earn it honestly for oneself?'

There were so many points with which to take issue in that little speech that Helewise didn't know where to start. She opened her mouth, but then Jenna spoke up.

'You really shouldn't patronize Helewise in that way, Cyrille,' she said, 'for she is a great deal more experienced than you in these matters.'

Cyrille turned to her, a sugary smile of stunning insincerity on her round face. 'I wouldn't dream of patronizing anyone, Jenna dear, especially a woman so very much older than I,' she said with a smug little shake of her head.

Helewise heard someone gasp – Isabelle, she thought – but, before anyone could comment, Cyrille got up and began pacing to and fro.

'We must be vigilant, at all times,' she declared, 'and, just now, even more so than usual, for much is at stake.' She turned, her eyes roaming in turn over each of those present. 'Charity is all very well, but we would be guilty of *grave* irresponsibility were we to admit a leper into our household.' She nodded quickly several times, as if agreeing with herself.

Helewise watched her closely. Something was affecting the woman deeply, she thought, and, thinking back over the evening just passed, she realized that Cyrille's behaviour had been odd; even more odd than usual. She had seemed restless and agitated, once or twice getting up to pace to and fro. Her eyes had shone and her normally pallid face was flushed. It was almost as if she was hugging to herself a very precious secret, one that she was not ready to share. Since supper, she had been starting conversations, interrupting others relentlessly when they tried to respond, demanding that people pay her attention even if it was clear their thoughts were elsewhere and they needed a little time to themselves.

She had been very rude to poor Herbert, too, giving him a harsh telling-off when he proffered a dish of jugged hare and pushing it away from her as violently as if it had contained something foul and rotten.

It was all very strange.

Breaking quite a long silence, Josse went to sit beside Isabelle and asked her quietly how Peter Southey's convalescence was progressing. Looking across at the two of them, Helewise noticed that everyone else was doing the same. She bent her head, smiling. Dear old Josse! No doubt he had meant the conversation to be private, between him and his cousin, but his idea of speaking softly was normally perfectly audible to everyone else, provided there was no distracting noise.

Isabelle said, 'He is not so good tonight. I persuaded him to get out of bed today and sit on the settle, and Editha and I helped him to walk round the room and up and down the passage. I fear it may have been too much for him, for this evening he has been complaining of a worsening headache.'

'The effect of his fall?' Josse said.

'Undoubtedly,' Isabelle agreed. 'I've prepared a specific for him containing both willow bark for the pain and various herbs to make him sleep. He's already had a dose, and I shall check in the night and see if he requires more.'

'I could do that, if you like,' Helewise offered. 'Peter's room is, after all, much closer to ours than to your quarters.'

Isabelle gave her a grateful smile. 'Thank you,' she said. 'I must admit, I should welcome a chance to sleep the night through with no disturbance.'

Cyrille had edged closer. 'I do hope you know what you're doing, Isabelle,' she said primly. 'Myself, I have always considered it a little perilous to mix treatments for the alleviation of pain with sleeping draughts.'

'In my experience, it is common practice, providing the

herbalist is well versed in her craft,' Helewise said with polite reasonableness, 'as I am quite sure Isabelle is.'

Isabelle muttered something, which, fortunately, was inaudible.

'I'm sure I didn't mean to imply otherwise, but we should not take any chances with our poor invalid,' Cyrille persisted.

Isabelle said shortly, 'I don't intend to.'

Cyrille made a face like a small child who has just suffered a telling-off. 'Oh, dear,' she said. 'Somebody's getting overtired.'

Isabelle shot to her feet, her face scarlet, and with a brief 'Goodnight', strode out of the hall.

Cyrille had subsided again, a smug little smile on her face, and was back in her seat, her sewing on her lap. Nobody spoke; the Old Hall fell silent. Once again, Helewise reflected, the entire family – herself and Josse included – had meekly sat back and allowed Cyrille to vent her opinions, insulting and unwelcome as they were, with barely a word of protest.

Dear Lord, Helewise prayed in silent desperation, *what on earth is wrong with us all?*

Before joining Josse in their room at the end of the passage, Helewise went to look in on Peter. She found Isabelle standing beside the bed, a small earthenware bottle in her hands. Hearing Helewise behind her, quickly she put it down on the little table, next to the ewer and the wash cloth.

'I was going to administer another dose of the draught,' she said softly, 'but he is sleeping soundly at present and I see no need.'

'No, it would be a pity to wake him,' Helewise agreed. 'I will return later, and give him more if he is restless and in pain.'

'Good. This much –' Isabelle indicated with forefinger and thumb on the side of the bottle – 'in warm water.' She pointed towards the fire in the small hearth. 'I've left a pot of water there. It ought to suffice.' She went on staring at Helewise. 'Sure you don't mind?'

'Quite sure.'

'And – er, you won't sleep right on till morning?'

'Oh, no. I'm used to waking in the night.'

Isabelle nodded. 'I see,' she muttered. Then, with a nod, she left the room.

*   *   *

Peter Southey opened his eyes. Something had disturbed him, and, in the weak light of the gently smouldering fire, he peered round the room, trying to make out what it could have been.

He thought he saw movement: a deeper darkness in the shadows, over there in the doorway.

'Is anybody there?' he hissed.

I should not feel so afraid, he told himself. *I am a grown man, not a child like that poor little boy who screamed and screamed.*

He tried to raise himself up on one elbow, but the effort caused a shooting pain through his injured shoulder, and an even worse pain – like a knife stabbing his skull – in his head. He lay back, a groan escaping him.

He closed his eyes. Perhaps, if he could sleep again, the pain would go away.

Something – some change in the light – penetrated his pain. He opened his eyes. The room looked different . . . oh, yes; the fire had died right down, so that now the room was almost in total darkness. *I must have slept*, he mused, *for the embers were still glowing when last I was aware.*

The pain was still there, relentless, and steadily worsening. His hand felt across his chest and he grabbed at his lucky charm, fumbling at the strings of the little leather bag and pulling out the chess piece. He put it to his lips, kissing it. *Help me! Help me!* He gave a soft cry of agony, trying to form the words to pray. *Dear, merciful Lord, please send someone to me! I cannot bear this!*

Then, *Oh, thank you, Lord*, somebody was there. The fire had been tended. An arm was insinuated behind his head, raising him on his pillows, and he felt the hard edge of the medicine cup touch against his lips. He struggled to sit up. 'Do not disturb yourself,' a soft, gentle voice whispered right in his ear. 'There is no need, for I will support you. Drink this, now.' Obediently he parted his lips, and the hot liquid was carefully poured into his mouth. By a hand well used to the action, he thought vaguely, for whoever it was tipped the liquid at exactly the right rate, allowing him time to swallow before the next mouthful came. 'It is a draught prepared by Isabelle,' the quiet voice continued, 'and you must drink it down straight away, while the full potency is in it!' He obeyed, greedily sucking in the liquid. It was heavily laced with honey, but the bitterness of whatever gave it its power broke through the intense sweetness, almost making him gag. 'Steady, steady,' soothed the calm voice. 'Not so fast!'

But Peter went on gulping it down. He would have drunk anything, just then, if it promised to relieve his agony.

Presently he noticed that the mug had been taken away from his lips. He made a small sound of protest – it was surprisingly hard to speak, for already sleep was fast overcoming him – and the quiet voice said reassuringly, 'No more now – you've drunk it to the dregs.'

He murmured his thanks, although the words were no more than a vague mumble. He was aware of movements; one or two quiet sounds; footsteps, soft, as if someone walked on tiptoe so as not to disturb him.

He smiled, already half in dreams. *No need to step quietly on my account*, he thought to himself. He could feel the chess piece, safe in his right hand, and, as always, it gave him comfort. *A horse galloping down the passage would not keep me awake now . . .*

Some time before dawn, when the first light had not yet shown in the eastern sky, Helewise woke, quietly got out of bed, took a warm shawl and, wrapping herself snugly, hurried along the passage to attend to Peter.

The fire in his room still glowed red, and she glanced at him quickly as she went in. He was asleep, and she wondered whether it would be best to leave him. She decided to wake him; he had already slept long, and might soon be stirring. Another dose of the draught administered now would provide many more hours' sleep, and that was the best thing for a man recovering from a serious head injury.

She bent down beside the hearth, picking up the jug of water. It was still warm; hot enough, she thought, to dilute the thick potion and make it drinkable. She went over to the bed, picking up the earthenware bottle and measuring out the right amount into the small cup set beside it. She poured on the water.

'Peter,' she said softly. 'Peter, wake up, for it is time for another dose of medicine.'

There was no response.

'Peter?'

She stood utterly still, holding her breath, listening.

Then, dropping the bottle on the floor, she bent down over Peter's sleeping form. She put her hand to his throat. She pressed her ear to his chest. She put her cheek against his slightly parted lips. She took his hands in hers, first the right, then the left.

Shaking, she straightened up. The words came readily to her – how many times she had said them! – and she took her time. Then she turned away from the bed, left the room and, at first walking steadily, then breaking into a run, flew down the passage to find Josse.

TEN

J osse, Helewise and Isabelle stood over the dead body. After a swift dash back to Peter's room to verify Helewise's dreadful news, Josse had hastened away to the family's quarters and quietly roused his cousin. Now, watching her as she stood white-faced, repeatedly shaking her head as if to deny what lay before her, Josse wished he could have left her peacefully sleeping.

Helewise took hold of Isabelle's hand. 'It is what quite often happens after a bad blow to the head,' she said, her voice soft and soothing. 'I have seen it several times. The patient seems to be improving, and is encouraged to resume a normal, active life, and then it is as if some grave injury hidden within the hard bones of the skull asserts itself, the patient falls unconscious and, sad to say, there is nothing anyone can do to save him.'

Watching Isabelle, Josse wasn't at all sure she'd taken in Helewise's kind words. She did, however, seem to appreciate the gentle tone and the hand holding hers.

'I gave him only a modest amount of the preparation,' she said, not for the first time. 'Enough dried willow to ease the pain, so that he would sleep, and enough of the soporific to ensure he stayed asleep.' She gave an anguished cry, stifling it swiftly with her free hand. 'I have given far more powerful doses in the past with no ill effect!'

'Helewise is right,' Josse proclaimed, 'and I, too, have observed deaths that occur several days after a fall and a blow to the head. You cared for him devotedly, cousin, and there is nothing to feel guilty about.'

'He's dead, Josse!'

'Aye, I know, but through no fault of yours,' he insisted. Realizing that standing there helpless beside the body was not helping Isabelle to cope with the shock, he said briskly, 'Now, there is much we must do. The body must be laid out, arrange-ments must be made to remove it to some private spot within the house, and we must consider how and where he is to be buried.' He thought swiftly. 'Fortunately we know who he is, and we must set about discovering where he comes from so that we can inform his family.'

'He is all alone in the world,' Helewise whispered. 'Remember, Josse?'

Isabelle said softly, 'Do you think he really is Aeleis's son? Because if he is, we'll have to seek her out and tell her he's dead.'

Josse felt they had enough to deal with without the added distress of planning how they would break the news to Aeleis. Ignoring the sudden surge of love for her that rose up in him, he said firmly, 'The idea that Peter was her son was no more than speculation. It cannot be permitted to affect our efforts to locate his kin, if, indeed, he has any. All we have to go on is his name, and the fact that he was on his way to Lewes, and—'

'He wasn't really going to Lewes at all,' Isabelle said impatiently. 'He was coming *here*, to us, and he had Aeleis's Queen Eleanor with him to prove he was her son.'

Josse sighed; this was getting him nowhere. Forcing a smile, he said, 'Isabelle, will you attend to the laying-out and the temporary care of the body?'

Isabelle seemed to make an effort. Disengaging her hand from Helewise's, she squared her shoulders and nodded. 'I will. I'd better go and wake Editha so she can help me.'

'I'll help, if you like,' Helewise offered. 'It is still very early, and it's a pity to disturb Editha when I am already awake.'

Isabelle turned to her. 'Thank you. Let us do it together.'

'What will you do, Josse?' Helewise asked.

Josse had been staring round the room, noting what few possessions had arrived with the dead man. 'I shall go through his belongings,' he said, 'and see if they reveal any clue as to where he came from.'

Peter Southey had travelled light. Apart from his garments – chemise, padded tunic, hose, cloak and boots, all of good quality but showing signs of hard use – he had a leather purse, attached to his belt. It contained money; a substantial sum. Nothing else. He also had a pack, containing a change of personal linen and a spare pair of hose, as well as a soft, sweet-smelling woollen blanket. Josse, a seasoned traveller himself, understood why a man would carry such an item. Blankets supplied by wayside inns – if, indeed, they did supply them – were usually filthy, verminous and hard as a board from too much use and too little washing.

He found Queen Eleanor on the floor beside Peter's bed. Reverently he picked her up, brushed off a piece of fluff and returned her to the little leather bag on its thong around Peter's neck. 'She's back with you now, safe and sound,' he whispered, bending down low over the dead man. 'She'll go with you to your grave.'

Then, sensing that his presence in the small room was impeding the women in their sad work, he left.

He was in no mood for company and, to his relief, he found the Old Hall deserted apart from two or three servants coming in and out, seeing to the fire and preparing the board for the first meal of the day. He stood for a moment, undecided. Then suddenly he knew what he must do. Hurrying on across the hall, he went through the arch into the family's quarters and strode through the maze of passages, open spaces and interconnecting rooms until he reached Uncle Hugh's chamber.

He had gone to seek him out yesterday, angry and upset because nobody seemed to be able or willing to tell him what had become of Aeleis. But, yesterday, he had been frustrated because first Hugh was sound asleep and then, once he woke, his mind was wandering and he thought Josse was his father.

I shall do better today, Josse vowed, pausing in the doorway. *It is very early still, and he will be fresh from his night's sleep.*

I will *have some answers.*

He straightened his tunic, drew a deep breath and went on into the room.

To his relief, Uncle Hugh was sitting up in bed, eyes bright and alert, looking expectantly towards the door as if the very thing he wanted was someone to come in and entertain him with a good, long conversation. One of the household had already been in to tend him: his sparse hair lay smooth on his scalp, and his cheeks were still slightly damp from shaving. The room was adequately warm, and a tray beside the bed held an empty mug and a wooden platter bare but for some crumbs and a hard rind of cheese.

'Good morning, Uncle!' Josse greeted him. 'You're looking well.'

'Yes, my boy, and I feel well, too.' Hugh smiled cheerfully. 'Today is going to be a good day, for the sun is out and presently we shall all go outside and enjoy the fresh air.' *Ah*, thought Josse. Should he break it to the old man that snow lay on the ground, and nobody would be venturing out unless they had no choice?

But Hugh was still speaking. 'You're up early – something on your mind, is there? A question you want to ask?'

There seemed no point in denying it. 'Aye.'

'Ask away!' Uncle Hugh hummed a few notes of an old folk melody.

'I want to talk to you about Aeleis.'

The humming stopped in mid-tune. Hugh's happy smile vanished and his fingers began to play with the sheet. 'Aeleis,' he echoed in a whisper.

'I'm sorry if it pains you to think of her,' Josse hurried on, 'but it's important that we find out where she is, and what's become of her.'

Hugh's eyes shot to meet his. 'Why?' he demanded. There was a definite touch of ice in his voice.

'Something's happened.' It sounded inadequate, but Josse wasn't ready yet to explain about Peter Southey and the chess piece. 'You heard a rumour concerning her, didn't you? One of your friends told you about the exploits of a beautiful woman at court, and you thought it was Aeleis. You—'

'*She wouldn't listen!*' Hugh burst out, so loudly that the words seemed to bounce off the stone walls. 'I told her, over and over again, that she should marry again, and Lothar Wellstone would have been a good match, for he was steady and wise and would have curtailed all her nonsense! He'd have reined her in, all right, and that was what she needed, a hard, firm hand. She needed a husband, and children, and she made it perfectly obvious she wanted a man in her bed, and that's precisely why God gave us marriage, to satisfy those urges that otherwise turn us into animals, although, in heaven's name, I never expected to find a *woman* who would demonstrate such base needs, and my own daughter at that.'

Embarrassed, for in his right mind Hugh would never have

given vent to such a furious, frank tirade, Josse stared down at the floor.

'I tried and I tried,' Hugh was mumbling, a tear hanging on the lashes of his right eye. 'But she wouldn't listen.' He looked at Josse, but it was as if he saw right through him, and Josse knew the remarks were not intended for his ears. 'I know my daughter, you see,' Hugh said softly. 'She's always been far too fond of sex and as an unmarried woman – yes, even as a widow – she'd just go on giving rise to the most vicious gossip, carrying on like she did!' He stopped, panting, his lips wet with spittle.

'Didn't the rumour mention one particular name?' Josse asked. He was disgusted with himself for preying on the old man's confusion. But he had no choice. Aeleis must be found, and Uncle Hugh held the only key. 'An important man – a nobleman, perhaps – with whom she attended a court Christmas at Windsor?'

Hugh looked at him vaguely. 'Eh?'

'The rumour you heard, Uncle; the tale about Aeleis that upset you so much.' He forced himself to speak calmly and patiently. 'What was the man's name?'

'What? His name? No, No, I don't know any name. If I once did, it's gone now.'

'Was it Southey?'

'Southey.' Uncle Hugh frowned. His lips moved, as if he was repeating the name silently. 'No. It wasn't Southey. It was some foreign-sounding name – Norman, like as not.' Josse waited, not daring to prompt or interrupt. 'De Chanticleer?' Hugh ventured. 'De Chamois?' He shook his head. 'De something, anyway.' He smiled, like a child who believes he has successfully repeated his lesson and can now relax.

'And what did you hear about this man and Aeleis?' Josse asked softly.

'Rumours, how I hate rumours!' Hugh burst out suddenly. 'Even when people deserve to be talked about because they refuse to behave with the decency they should, still the world is too quick to judge and too harsh in its condemnation.' He fixed Josse with a hard stare. 'De Chamois wasn't a bad lad, although if you'd listened to all the stories about him after it happened, you'd have taken him for the devil incarnate,' he said.

De Chamois. Josse memorized the name. 'What happened, Uncle Hugh?' Josse prompted.

Hugh waved a hand. 'Oh, he refused to obey, like so many of the young these days. Like my Aeleis, you know.' He seemed to have forgotten they'd just been talking about her. 'She wouldn't marry where she was told to, either. Mind you,' he leaned forward confidingly, 'we all had a bit of sympathy for him, and he was a very handsome fellow, everyone agreed.'

'Why did you sympathize?' Josse asked.

'Because of what they were all *saying*!' Hugh exclaimed peevishly, as if Josse should have realized. 'Everyone was gossiping because it was scandalous, the way they were carrying on, and *he* wouldn't listen, either, another one who thought he knew better than those older and wiser, and he went his own way, and then *she* got her heart broken, that poor young girl, although she wasn't as young as she made out, not by a long chalk, and then William . . . William . . .' Abruptly the old man's face crumpled into confusion, and he stared at Josse in helpless appeal. 'William Crowburgh, do you mean?' he asked.

'No, Uncle,' Josse said gently. 'We were speaking of Aeleis, and you were trying to remember the name of the man who took her to the court Christmas.'

'William Crowburgh was never at court.' Hugh shook his head decisively. 'His father Harold was my friend, you know, and his boy William had a son, and he – he—' Once again, the puzzled frown creased his brows.

Josse sighed in frustration. Was it worth one more try to bring his uncle's rambling thoughts back to Aeleis? 'We urgently need to find out whether Aeleis remarried,' he began, 'and it would be extremely helpful if you could—'

But Hugh's wandering mind was now far away. 'Young Herbert went over to pay his respects, you know,' he said, once again lowering his voice as if he feared people were listening. 'They'd been boys together, he and William, and, for all that they'd seen very little of each other for many years, nevertheless Herbert felt it right to go over there and express his condolences. Now the little lad's here, and Herbert has a wife, and . . .' His words trailed to a stop. 'He's married her, you know.'

'Cyrille, yes, I know,' Josse agreed. 'Olivar's mother, and William Crowburgh's widow.'

Hugh looked at him uncomprehendingly. 'I don't trust her,' he muttered, just as he had done before. 'She—' Then, sharply, 'She's *here*?' A sudden light of hope flared in the tired old eyes.

'Aye, she's here,' Josse said, forcing a smile. He couldn't think why his uncle seemed so excited by the news of Cyrille's presence, especially when the old man had just reiterated his mistrust of her. 'I'm sure she'll come and sit with you, if you'd like that.' He wasn't sure at all.

But Hugh's thoughts had fractured again. Now, his face working with distress, he was muttering incoherently to himself. 'We should go outside, while the sun's out,' he said suddenly, glaring at Josse. 'Get them to saddle my horse, Herbert, for I have to see to this and try to sort it out, for it's all a muddle and I don't understand.' He threw off the covers and struggled to get out of bed, skinny old legs waving around as if he was feeling for his slippers.

Gently but firmly, Josse pushed him back, rearranging the sheet and the blankets and tucking the old man in. 'Don't go out now, Uncle Hugh,' he said calmly. 'It's very cold. The sunshine is misleading.'

Hugh looked trustingly up at him. 'Shall I go later?'

His heart wrung with pity, Josse took the old man's hands in his. 'Aye, Uncle, if you think you should.'

'I have to put it right,' Hugh said, but with less conviction now. 'I have to – have to—' He yawned. Then, briefly alert once more, he said angrily, 'They don't *know*, you see! Only I know, and I can't seem to sort it all out in my mind.' He shook his head in frustration.

Josse stroked the frail old hand. 'Have a sleep,' he advised. 'I'll leave you for now, and come back later when you've rested.'

'Will you?' Hugh looked up anxiously at him. 'Will you help me? It has to be sorted out, you see, because it's not right, and nobody realizes.'

'Of course I'll help you.' Josse watched as the eyes slowly closed. Hugh's breathing slowed and calmed, and presently his mouth dropped open and he began to snore softly.

Josse got up and tiptoed across to the door. Just as he was about to close it behind him, he heard his uncle say quite clearly, 'Martyr.'

Deep in thought, Josse wandered back through the family quarters. There were one or two indications that people were stirring, but he hurried on past outside, not being ready yet to talk to anybody, and especially not to break the news of poor Peter's death and deal with the inevitable questions that would follow. Approaching the archway through to the Old Hall, he noticed that the door out to the courtyard stood ajar.

The sun was rising, and the first of its rays shining through a gap in the clouds made long shadows across the open space. Suddenly desperate for fresh air, he went outside and down the steps.

Ah, but it was good to be out of doors!

He walked over to the main gates, but nobody had yet drawn back the heavy oak bars that fastened them, and he was loath to disturb the regular routine of the household by doing so himself. Hearing sounds from the stables over to the right of the gates – somebody was whistling – he went to investigate.

The stables, like everything else at Southfire Hall, clearly demonstrated that this was a well-run establishment. There was a row of stalls over to the right, where a pair of stable lads were just finishing the morning mucking-out. There were sounds of quiet munching as perhaps half a dozen horses tore at their hay. One of the lads looked up and wished Josse a cheery good day.

The whistler turned out to be Garth; Josse found his uncle's head groom in the end stall, grooming a chestnut gelding with big eyes set beneath a broad forehead. Down its face ran a narrow, pale stripe, which, merging with the star on its brow, gave the impression of a roughly-formed cross.

'Good day, Garth,' Josse greeted him.

Both man and horse turned interested faces towards him. 'Morning, sir,' Garth responded. 'I've already seen to your horse, and your lady's, if you were requiring them?'

'Thank you, but not for now,' Josse replied. He was staring at the chestnut gelding which, he noticed, had two white feet, the left fore and the right hind. 'That's a fine animal.'

'He is that,' Garth agreed, running a hand the length of the horse's gracefully-arched neck, beneath the long pale ginger mane. 'He'll be ready directly, too, and pretty much recovered from his hurts, if his master's ready to ride him again. Though they'll have to take it nice and easy, the pair of them, to begin with.'

'This is Peter Southey's horse? The man who had the fall?'

'Yes, sir.'

Josse looked into the horse's deep, dark eye, and the horse looked right back. It gave a quiet whicker. *You know, don't you?* Josse said silently, then wondered why on earth he'd had such a fanciful thought.

'I'm sorry to have to tell you, but Peter Southey is dead,' he said to Garth.

'Is he? Ah, now, that's a pity,' Garth said. He sighed, once more stroking the gelding's neck. 'Not that it's any great surprise, since that was a nasty fall.' He reached inside his tunic, pulling out a small, wrinkled apple which he fed to the horse. Over the loud sounds of crunching, he murmured to it, 'We'll have to get you back where you came from, won't we, my beauty?'

Back where you came from . . .

'Do you recognize the horse, Garth?' Josse demanded.

'Well, not this chestnut specifically,' Garth admitted, 'but I reckon I know right enough who sired him.'

'Go on.'

'There's a fine old knight lives over northwards a step. Well, he's probably dead long since, so it'll be his son now, or maybe even his grandson. Anyway, they've got a place up on the downs, where it's good horse country. The old knight went on crusade, and, like many another, took a fancy to those strong little horses the Saracens ride, or so they tell me. Brought a stallion home with him, he did – way back in my grandsire's day, this was – and bred from it, putting it to one of his brood mares. Started a line of strong, neat, clever, handsome horses exactly like this one.' He pushed back the gelding's bright forelock, and the horse's ears pricked with interest. He turned his nose towards Garth, snuffling inside his jerkin in search of more titbits.

'You're sure?' Josse said.

'Certain,' Garth replied. 'This horse came from Sir Godfrey Hellingsham's stables, or I'm a Saracen myself.'

'And is it far to this place?'

Garth considered. 'It's the other side of Henshaw, over on the north side of the downs and along a little valley. Normally I'd say it's a morning's ride. Given the present conditions, however, you'd have to allow a deal longer.'

'Thank you, Garth.' He slapped the old man's shoulder. 'I may be needing my horse after all.'

Helewise and Isabelle had shut the door of Peter's room for privacy. Now, with quiet and respectful efficiency, they set about their task.

'His wounds had begun to heal,' Helewise said softly, as carefully she wiped the dead man's face and tidied his hair. 'You nursed him well, Isabelle, for there is no sign of infection on his body.'

Isabelle carried on with her sponging of the long legs, now stripped bare. 'He was a good patient,' she replied. 'Did as he was told, which is more than most men do.'

Helewise smiled.

They carried on with their work, neither speaking, and a peaceful, thoughtful calm spread through the little room. It was quite unusual, Helewise reflected, to feel such a sense of peace in the presence of the very recently dead. She remembered Josse's phrase, *the spirit of the house*. Was that what this was, then? The house's cherishing, protective spirit, doing its work?

If so, then this was, just as Josse maintained, a rare house indeed . . .

Bathing the dead man's mouth and chin, she noticed something. 'He was eager for the medicine you prepared for him,' she said with a sad smile, glancing up at Isabelle. 'Look, there's a little cut on his lower lip, where he must have banged the cup against it in his haste to drink the contents.'

Isabelle came over to stand beside her, peering at the body. She leaned closer. 'And a tiny bruise on his chin, look, just below the cut.' She straightened up. 'I was careless,' she said, her expression distressed.

Helewise watched her. 'You did your best,' she said. 'You did not spare yourself in your care of him.'

'I had help,' Isabelle muttered.

'Yes, perhaps, but you took the main burden, even though you do more work in this house than all the other women put together.'

'Jenna does her share,' Isabelle protested. 'Editha does what she can, and Philomena has her hands full with those energetic daughters of hers, and Emma quietly helps wherever she's most needed.'

'Yes, I know.' Helewise hesitated. 'I wasn't really referring to them.'

'Oh.' Isabelle raised her eyebrows. 'I see.'

Then, with a faint smile, she resumed her work.

Josse found Helewise in their room, where she was taking a little time to collect herself before going to join the family in the Old Hall.

He took her in his arms. 'Was it bad?' he asked gently.

She nodded. 'He was just a young man, Josse, with the most fulfilling and rewarding years of his life before him, and we all thought he was getting better.' Her voice broke on a sob.

He wiped the tears from her face. 'Aye, I know,' he said. 'It's hard, and I have no comforting words to offer you.'

They stood for some moments, standing close. Then he said, 'I'm going to ride over to see Sir Godfrey Hellingsham.'

Her head shot up. 'Who?'

'According to Garth, Peter Southey's horse came from his stables, and it's more than likely he can direct me to Peter's home and his kin.'

'So we have decided not to believe Peter when he said he is all alone in the world?' she responded, raising an ironic eyebrow. 'I don't want you to go riding off, Josse! The weather is bad and the road conditions will be frightful!'

'It is milder this morning,' he replied. 'I have already been outside, and there has been no more snow. The clouds will clear and the sun will break through soon,' he added optimistically.

'But what do you hope to achieve, even given that this Sir Godfrey recognizes the horse and reveals the identity of the man who bought it from him?' Helewise said anxiously. 'He'll just say "Peter Southey", and we already know that.'

'He will be able to tell me where Peter came from,' Josse said, fighting his impatience. 'Then I'll go there, and, even if what we guess is right and Aeleis is—'

'We *know* she's dead!' Helewise cried. 'Peter had no-one to love and miss him!'

'Perhaps he was lying!' Josse exclaimed angrily. 'Perhaps there was some reason he wanted to conceal his relationship to her, and deny her very existence!' He made a sound of exasperation. 'But even if it's true and Aeleis *is* dead, she and Peter must have lived somewhere,' he went on more calmly. 'There will be servants, neighbours, distant acquaintances, some cleric of the parish – oh, *I* don't know, but I refuse to believe there isn't one single person on earth who can tell us why he sought us out.'

All at once, the fierce angry protest left her. She slumped against him, pressing her face to his chest. 'Let's not fight, Josse,' she muttered. 'I know you're only doing what you feel you must, but I worry about you.'

He smiled, knowing she wouldn't see. 'Aye, I know.'

Her face still muffled, she said, 'If you insist on going, then I'll come with you.'

'No, you won't,' he said firmly.

She raised her head. She had, he noticed with dismay, her determined expression. 'Neither you nor anyone else should ride out alone in this weather,' she said. 'It is foolhardy.'

She had a point, he had to concede. 'Then I'll ask Young Herbert to accompany me.'

She gave a snort. 'And you think Cyrille will allow that?'

'Well, I suppose I could ask Henry . . .'

'No, you can't. Isabelle just told me he's heading down to the coast this morning, now that the weather's warmed up a little, to arrange the delivery of some more supplies.'

Josse held her at arm's length, staring into her eyes. 'Somebody else evidently believes it's safe to travel today,' he observed. Before she could think of a suitably repressive response, he went on, 'I'm going to ask Herbert, anyway. I'll tell Isabelle where I'm going and why, and that I'd welcome Herbert's company so the two of us can get to know each other better.' He grinned. 'That ought to do it.'

There was something else. Knowing she would understand,

he added quietly, 'Look after Olivar. I hope we'll be back by tonight, but if not . . .'

She did understand. She whispered, 'Of course I will.'

A short time later, Josse and Isabelle went to seek out Herbert, eating by himself at one end of the board in the Old Hall. 'Josse needs you to ride out with him today,' Isabelle told her son. She explained about Garth having recognized Peter Southey's horse, and the hope that they would in this way be able to trace where Peter had come from.

'I'm sorry to hear he's dead, Mother,' Herbert said. 'You didn't spare yourself in your care of him, and it's sad it should end like this.'

'Sad for Peter, in particular,' Isabelle said tartly, although Josse noticed that Henry's words – and the kindness with which he had spoken them – had softened her tense expression.

'Of course I'll go with you, Josse,' Herbert said, getting to his feet and brushing crumbs off his tunic. 'I'll fetch my heavy cloak, and I'll be ready to leave as soon as you want to go.'

Josse and Isabelle watched him hurry off. Josse wondered if the alacrity with which he'd agreed to the outing suggested he welcomed an excuse to get out of the claustrophobic atmosphere in the house. *If so*, Josse admitted honestly to himself, *then I'm the first to agree with him.*

Very soon, Herbert was back. He carried a thick, fur-lined cloak interlined with padded wool, and he had put on a stout pair of boots. But he no longer looked as cheerful as he had a little while ago: Cyrille was trotting along behind him, and it was clear she wasn't happy.

'Good morning, Cyrille,' Isabelle greeted her. 'It is unusual to see you at this hour. I hope all the activity didn't disturb you?'

'I was told of that poor young man's unfortunate demise,' Cyrille said, 'and, naturally, I found it impossible to sleep after that.'

'Naturally,' Isabelle echoed faintly.

'And now my husband tells me that he has to go out on some ill-conceived expedition to try to trace where our late guest came from,' she went on, glancing at Josse with narrowed eyes and an icy expression, as if she knew full well who to blame for this idiotic enterprise. 'And all because you failed to take my advice,' she finished, turning back to Isabelle, a note of triumph in her voice.

Josse, watching intently, hoped Cyrille wasn't going to say, *I told you so . . .*

She very nearly did: 'I warned you, Isabelle, did I not,' she went on, 'that the mixing of pain-relieving herbs with those that promote sleep is a delicate matter, and one perhaps best left to the hands of a skilled practitioner.' She gave a smug little nod, which said, as clearly as words, *I would not have made such an error.*

Isabelle said nothing. She simply stood there, facing Cyrille, her unblinking eyes fixed on her until eventually Cyrille was forced to look away. 'Oh, well, you must all do as you see fit,' she said, with an attempt at nonchalance. 'If anybody needs me, I shall be in my chamber.'

Isabelle shot a furious look at the plump little figure hurrying off down the hall. Watching her, Josse was quite surprised she overcame the temptation to give her daughter-in-law a good kick to hasten her on her way.

Josse and Herbert were setting off. Herbert had brightened up again as soon as they were out of doors, and now looked decidedly cheerful. He knew the way to Henshaw, and was confident that they would find Sir Godfrey's stables without difficulty; his was, it appeared, a well-known name in the vicinity.

As the two of them rode out through the gates, Helewise stood at the top of the steps watching. Josse turned round once, and she gave him a wave and an encouraging smile. She went on standing there until they were out of sight.

She prayed for them. Putting her whole heart in the quietly muttered words, she begged that they would uncover the information they sought and return, swiftly and safely, to Southfire.

For she had a premonition: although she did not know where or how, or to whom, she was utterly certain that something awful was going to happen.

ELEVEN

Josse and Herbert kept up a good pace. Their horses were full of energy after too many days shut up in the stables, and eager to go. For some time, the ride was too exhilarating and too energetic to allow speech but as the horses slowed to an easy trot and the two men positioned themselves side by side, Herbert looked across at Josse and said, 'She's not as bad as she seems, you know.'

There was no point in saying innocently, *Who isn't?*

'Er—' Josse began.

'Oh, I know how it looks,' Herbert hurried on. 'She's a good wife to me, though, in her own way, and I was so lonely after Maud died that I—' He stopped. 'But you don't want to hear about that,' he muttered. 'She likes to be in control at all times, both of herself and others,' he went on after a brief pause, 'and she thinks she knows best how to do things, and she has all these little ideas for making our lives more comfortable that she really wants us to adopt – for our own sake, of course, not hers – because she really cares about us all.' His voice had risen. He waited until he was calm once more, then added quietly, 'Josse, you have to try to see it from her point of view.'

'Aye, I suppose so,' Josse said doubtfully.

'The trouble is,' Herbert said, 'she thought she was going to be mistress of Southfire. When she agreed to marry me, I might have inadvertently given that impression, you see, because she'd always said what a beautiful old house it is, and how much she'd admired it from afar, which you can easily understand because it's so much bigger than anything she'd ever known. I can't say for sure, because it's not the sort of thing a man asks his wife, but I believe she comes from – er, from rather humble stock, and I sense her life has been hard.'

'Did she and Olivar not inherit from William Crowburgh?' Josse asked.

'Good God, no,' Herbert said fervently. 'Poor William suffered a series of disasters, apparently, and when he died he was virtually penniless. It was one of the reasons I first fell for Cyrille,' he hurried on, 'because, after William's death, she was put in such a frightful position and she was being so brave about it.' He added thoughtfully, 'I suppose what she needed most was security, and the prospect of being the mistress of Southfire Hall was—'

'She cannot be mistress until you are master,' Josse interrupted bluntly, 'and you won't be master until your grandfather dies.'

'*I know!*' Herbert cried. 'And, even then, there's my mother. You see, Cyrille doesn't really understand how our family works, how we've always lived quite happily all together, with no need of someone to be *in overall charge.*' His pronunciation of the words suggested to Josse that he was quoting his wife. 'She – Cyrille, I mean – seems to think that the moment Grandfather is dead, I will move my mother out into some dower house that I'll somehow conjure up out of thin air, and that not only will Mother disappear from Southfire, she'll also take Editha, Jenna, Gilbert, Philomena, Henry, Emma, Cecily, Brigida and Philippa with her.'

'Aye,' Josse murmured, 'she makes that plain enough.'

Herbert looked amazed. 'You – you'd noticed?'

'Of course, lad,' Josse said impatiently. Then, more kindly, 'Does she not understand that, even if it would be appropriate to find different accommodation for Isabelle, you cannot abandon your responsibilities to the rest of your kin? Responsibilities,' he went on relentlessly, 'that will only intensify once you are master of Southfire Hall.'

'No,' Herbert said miserably. 'No, Josse. She doesn't even begin to understand that. And, anyway, Southfire is our home!' he cried plaintively. 'Our family's lived there for generations, and we all love it. That's why the first extension was built, back in Grandfather's day, to make room for an expanding family, and why we've now added the new extension, with the solar, the chapel and all that extra living accommodation.' He hesitated. Then he went on, his voice soft and almost dreamy, 'It's the only place any of us really want to live, you know. It's as if we belong to the house, and somehow it's a part of us – it's in our family's blood.'

'Cyrille is also a member of your family,' Josse pointed out.
'You made her so when you wed her.'

'Yes,' Herbert whispered. For a moment, his expression was
utterly bleak. Then, attempting a smile, he said, 'We've let the
horses catch their breath. Come on, let's push them on.'

He kicked his mount to a canter, and Josse, doing the same,
thundered after him.

Back at Southfire, Helewise was in the chapel praying for the soul
of Peter Southey, whose body now lay covered with a heavy cloth
on a trestle before the altar. He had died alone, with no friend to
hold his hand and no priest to hear him make his peace with God.
Helewise felt the urge to speak on his behalf. 'We believe he was
a son of this family, Lord,' she said softly, looking up at the plain
silver cross, 'and, if we are correct, then he had returned to the
place that ought to have been his home.' She hesitated. 'Even if
he planned to declare his position, and demand his rightful place
in the line of inheritance –' she remembered Peter's odd comment
that the family had treated him far better than he deserved – 'nevertheless, we cannot say for certain that he was scheming to do
wrong, or to rob another of what was rightfully his.' She paused.
There was no need, really, to explain all this to the Lord, and she
had the feeling she was doing it more for her own benefit, to try
to set her own scattered thoughts and emotions in order. 'He was
lonely, Lord,' she went on after a while. 'He was sad, and I believe
he was grieving. Comfort him, dear Lord, and let him feel the gift
of your love, so that he may find peace.'

She dropped her face on to her folded hands and stilled her
mind. Soon, a sense of calm flowed over her.

Coming out of her meditation, she went back over the events
of the morning. Peter's death. Cyrille's cruel words to Isabelle.
Josse riding away.

She didn't want to think about Josse, and so she returned to
Cyrille. The flare of intense dislike for the woman seemed even
more wrong than usual, here in this holy place, and she tried to
fight it. *Cyrille is not at ease here in this household, amid this
close and affectionate family*, she told herself. *We – I – should
try to understand her, and in that way perhaps come to appreciate
why she behaves as she does.*

The core of dislike remained.

Helewise recalled how, in her previous life, they had been encouraged to overcome antipathy towards another by trying to perform a kind act for them. She smiled grimly: her instant, powerful reaction against doing any such thing for Cyrille told her just how much she needed to.

She knelt in prayer for a little longer. Then she stood up, turned away from the altar and strode out of the chapel.

Cyrille was not in the Old Hall or the solar. When Helewise finally asked Isabelle if she knew where she was, Isabelle said shortly that she was resting in her quarters. Helewise nodded her thanks and went to find her.

The part of the house that Cyrille and Herbert occupied was comprised of a small, square hall with other, smaller rooms on three sides, reached through low archways. The rooms were sumptuously furnished, to a standard of comfort and luxury not found elsewhere in the house. The rushes on the stone floor were fresh, and in places topped with thick furs. The furniture was of oak, polished to a rich, golden shine; the hall smelt of beeswax and lavender. There were hangings on the walls, the brilliant colours of the wools a clear indication of their high cost. Large candles burned in elaborate silver holders; proper candles, Helewise noted, like the ones usually reserved for church on feast days. A fire burned in the hearth, and a basket of logs sat beside it.

Yet, for all this display of extravagance, the room was empty . . .

Or so she had thought; just then, however, as she stared around and wondered which doorway led to Cyrille's bedroom, she heard a tiny noise from beneath the long table set against one wall. A mouse? She listened, but the sound did not come again.

Bending down, she raised the stiff white cloth that covered the central section of the table and peered underneath. Crouched on the rushes right in the corner was Olivar.

'Hello!' Helewise said softly. 'Are you hiding?'

His blue eyes were huge with fear, the pupils widely distended. He nodded.

'If I know boys,' Helewise went on conversationally, sitting down beside the table, 'and I do, having raised two of my own, I would guess somebody is trying to make you wash your hands, or do your lessons, or go outside and fetch more firewood, or any number of things that adults insist boys do when they'd far rather be playing.'

Olivar tried to speak, but the words didn't come.

'It's all right,' Helewise said quietly. 'I won't tell.'

'I'm not sure I'm meant to be out of my room,' Olivar finally managed, his voice so low she had to strain to hear. 'She said two days, and I think it is two days, but if it isn't and I ought to be there still, she'll send me back for another two days.' He gulped back a sob. 'I don't like it on my own.' He looked at her, misery in every line of his face. 'And,' he added in a tiny whisper, 'I'm afraid the monster will come back.'

Helewise crawled in under the table and took him in her arms. He was trembling, and she guessed from his runny nose that he had recently been crying. He leaned against her with a sigh; a sound that went straight to her heart. Remembering her resolve to be kind to Cyrille, she almost laughed.

But then an idea occurred to her. 'Your mother is resting, I'm told?'

As soon as she said *your mother*, Olivar stiffened. 'Yes,' he said. 'She's lying on her bed with a blanket over her and earlier she said she was sick. I wasn't trying to listen,' he added urgently, defending himself as if he expected accusations to be hurled at him, 'I'd just gone to see if there was anybody who would tell me about leaving my room or not, and I heard her talking to Father.' He leaned closer to Helewise and whispered confidingly, 'He's not actually my father because he's dead, but I have to call him Father. She said so.'

Helewise waited till she was sure her voice would sound normal. 'I know what we'll do,' she said with a cheerfulness she was far from feeling. 'I'll go in and speak to your mother, and ask if there's anything I can do for her. She might need another blanket, or perhaps she feels like a hot drink or something to eat. People quite often do feel hungry, you know, after they stop feeling sick.'

'Yes,' he agreed, 'that's what she says.'

'Well, there you are, then. And after we've done whatever she requests of us – we could do any little tasks together, couldn't we? – I'll say I've got lots of jobs to do today and I could really do with a hand, and would it be all right if you were my helper?'

'What sort of jobs?' Olivar asked warily.

'Oh well, now, let's see,' she improvised quickly, 'I have to go to the stables to see if my mare is all right, and maybe take her out for a ride as I'm sure she's getting fat and lazy, and then I have to go to the kitchens and see if the cat's had her kittens yet, and then I thought I'd offer to take the scraps out to feed the chickens, and after that I thought I'd sit in the solar and see if I can come up with a design for a piece of tapestry, and then—'

'I want to be your helper,' Olivar said eagerly.

Helewise got out from beneath the table and held out her hand to Olivar, who followed her. 'In that case,' she said firmly, 'I shall go and speak to your mother.'

Mutely Olivar indicated which one was Cyrille's room, and, after hesitating briefly on the doorstep, Helewise called out softly, 'Cyrille, may I come in? It's Helewise.'

There was a rustle of bedding, and Cyrille said, 'What do you want?'

Helewise went on into the room. It was small and cosy, with several candles burning to enliven the gloomy daylight penetrating through the one narrow window. Cyrille lay on the high bed, propped up by a bank of pillows, a thick woollen blanket pulled up to her shoulders and a glossy fur pelt over her legs.

'Isabelle told me you were resting and I came to ask if you needed anything,' Helewise said pleasantly.

'I *need* to be left alone,' Cyrille said ungraciously. 'Oh, well, since you're here I suppose you can pour a cup of water for me.' Imperiously she pointed at a jug and a mug, set on a small brass tray beside the bed. Well within her reach, in fact, but Helewise smiled and did as she was bid. She handed it to Cyrille, who took it without a word and drank a few sips.

Go on, Helewise ordered herself. 'I met Olivar outside,' she said. She was surprised at how nervous she felt. 'He seems to have nothing to do, so, if you have no objection, I wondered if I could have your permission to enlist his help with a few tasks I have to do today?'

Cyrille's eyes shot to hers, their expression suspicious. 'What do you want him for?' she demanded. 'He's a clumsy boy. He broke my rosary,' she added, her mouth working, as if the offence had just occurred and she was in the throes of her first, furious reaction.

'I will try to encourage him to be more careful,' Helewise said meekly. She despised herself for her duplicity but, if it was what it took to take Olivar away with her, it was worth it.

Cyrille studied her through narrowed eyes, as if suspecting an ulterior motive but unable to work out what it was. Then suddenly she said, 'Oh, do what you like with him.'

Not giving her any time for second thoughts, Helewise bowed her head, said, 'Thank you, Cyrille,' and backed hastily out of the room.

Olivar, who had quite obviously been listening to every word, sprang away from the doorway as she emerged and pretended to be very interested in the wax pooling at the foot of one of the candles. He looked up at her, blue eyes intent. 'Is it all right?' he whispered.

She grinned. 'Yes. Come on –' she held out her hand and instantly he took it – 'let's go and say good morning to my horse.'

For Helewise, Olivar's company was the perfect antidote to the distress of Peter Southey's death. Although Olivar had been suitably respectful when informed that the injured man had sadly died, he was too young to pretend a grief he didn't feel, and since he hadn't known Peter, it was foolish to expect him to be upset.

They didn't get very far with Helewise's invented list of jobs. Olivar fell in love with Helewise's grey mare and, as far as you could tell with a horse, Daisy reciprocated the sentiment. The mare had been shut in her stall for several days and was as eager to get outside and stretch her legs as Olivar was to take her, and very quickly Helewise had her tacked up and ready. She didn't think she should let Olivar go beyond the gates, but the home enclosure was generously sized and both boy and horse seemed content to go round and round inside the perimeter walls, trotting, cantering and even managing a jump, made of two empty barrels and a long pole, kindly put up by old Garth.

'Sits a horse well, for a young 'un,' Garth observed, standing beside Helewise and watching Olivar with critical eyes.

Helewise nodded. 'He does indeed.' She smiled. 'I think I'm going to have a job getting him to stop.'

'Maybe he'd like to groom her too,' Garth suggested. He chuckled. 'It'd save me the job.'

Olivar leapt at the suggestion. For the remainder of the morning, having been instructed by Garth, he groomed Daisy till her coat shone.

Back inside, Helewise and Olivar went into the Old Hall to thaw out their fingers and toes by the fire. Emma, noticing their arrival, brought hot drinks for them, and some honey cakes studded with a few precious raisins, fresh from the oven. The smell of the cakes attracted the three little girls, and they stood eyeing Olivar suspiciously.

'How come you're allowed out into the hall?' Cecily asked belligerently. 'And are you going to talk to us, or stand there all aloof like you usually do?'

'Cecily!' Emma reproved her. 'Manners!'

Olivar looked at Cecily, appearing quite unembarrassed. 'She – er, Mother's being not very well, and she's lying down, so she said I could be with her.' He jerked his head in Helewise's direction.

'Do you want to play with us?' Cecily demanded.

Olivar hesitated. 'I'm not really meant to, and she wouldn't like it,' he muttered, flushing.

'If your mother's in her room, she won't know, will she?' Cecily pointed out.

'We're not playing with *dolls*,' Brigida piped up, as if such an activity was utterly despicable, and despite the evidence of the collection of dolls lying discarded beside the hearth. She leaned closer to Olivar and said in a very audible whisper, 'We're going to play hide and seek.'

Olivar's eyes widened. 'Hide and seek,' he breathed.

'Come on,' Cecily said, jumping up and cramming the last little cake in her mouth. 'I'll be it, and you lot can count to a hundred and then start looking.'

'Don't go anywhere near Cyrille's room! We mustn't disturb her!' Emma called out after her.

Cecily turned, gave her elder sister a resigned look as if to say, *I'm not likely to, am I?* and then raced away.

The short daylight faded, and evening came on. Josse and Herbert had not returned. Helewise told herself it was silly to worry; any journey endured under present conditions was bound to take a lot longer than usual, and in all likelihood they had arrived at their destination, spoken to the man they had gone to find and, the day by then being advanced, been pressed to stay the night.

Take care, my dear Josse, she thought.

Resigning herself to a night without him, she put on a brave face and went to join the rest of the family as they settled down in the Old Hall for the evening meal. The children had been sent to bed, and Helewise herself had taken Olivar. He had gone to say goodnight to his mother, and, after her cursory acknowledgement, he had scurried back out to Helewise and she had accompanied him on to his own little room, at the end of the passage.

There was something she had to tell him.

'Josse isn't here, Olivar,' she said, kneeling beside the bed and holding his hand, 'and so he won't be able to keep an eye on you as he promised.'

Olivar went sheet-white, and his face filled with dread. 'What if—' he began.

She stopped him. 'I am here,' she said, 'and although I do not believe you are in any danger, I will protect you.' She felt his small hand grip hers. 'You know where I sleep, don't you? Over on the other side of the Old Hall? You came and found me there, on the day I arrived.' He nodded. 'Well, I want you to promise me that if at any time you feel lonely or scared, you will come and find me again, just like you did then.'

'All right,' he whispered.

She bent over to kiss him good night, then walked softly away. *Cyrille won't be very pleased*, she thought, *if he does come to me for comfort and she finds out.*

She realized she didn't really care.

The evening meal was all but over, and they sat on round the long board. Cyrille had emerged from her room to join them, and had tucked into her food with gusto. Conversation had been sporadic; it was as if the household were respecting the presence of Peter's body, lying cold and alone in the chapel. And also, perhaps, Helewise reflected, they were all too aware of the absence of Josse and Young Herbert. Others had expressed the same conclusion that she had drawn – they'd been invited by Sir Godfrey Hellingsham to stay overnight and would reappear the next day – and Helewise was heartened by their confidence and good sense.

All the same, it was hard to look at the two empty places and not worry a little.

Cyrille was helping herself to a honey biscuit, dipping it in her goblet and sucking the liquid from it with evident pleasure. She had demanded the rich white wine, having rejected the customary sweet red with some vehemence.

Helewise studied Cyrille's bent head. An extraordinary idea had just occurred to her. On the face of it, it seemed very unlikely; but, on the other hand, it explained virtually everything.

She thought back over the past few days, considering one by one the quirks of behaviour that Cyrille had displayed. Her exaggerated horror at the presence of the leper and the imagined threat he posed; her refusal to eat hare or drink red wine; the repeated gesture of clasping her hands over her breasts or stomach; even – Helewise's eyes opened wide with shocked realization – that strange moment in the chapel, when she had come across Cyrille fiddling with some small object on a length of thread.

Could it really be true?

But then Helewise's good sense took over from her instincts, and she knew she must be wrong. According to what she had told the family, Cyrille was thirty-two years old; she had a son of six, and thus would have been twenty-six when she gave birth to him.

Helewise did not believe Cyrille was as young as that. She added a good seven or eight years on, and that was being generous; she could not accept Cyrille as being much younger than forty. And, besides, if Helewise's sudden suspicion was right, then without doubt everyone would know by now, since Cyrille would surely be keen to demand every last act of consideration, every small gesture to ensure her comfort and well-being.

Horrified suddenly at her deeply unkind and uncharitable thoughts, Helewise felt herself flush. Instantly penitent, she began a silent prayer of abject apology, vowing even as she prayed that she must take the very first opportunity, and each and every subsequent one, to make amends to Cyrille for her wicked specu-lations. *Yes, she has no idea what I was thinking*, she told herself firmly, *but that is no excuse whatsoever.*

She sat there, head down, burning with shame and horror and trying desperately to come up with something kind to think about Cyrille. Then she thought, *What if my instinct is right?* She tried to convince herself that, in this matter, what she sensed in her heart must give way to what made sense in her head.

But she discovered she couldn't.

TWELVE

Josse and Herbert made better time than anticipated, for once they had completed the long, steady climb up on to the downs, they found that the well-drained higher ground had not been as badly affected by the weather as the lowland. Musing on this, Josse remembered Joanna telling him about the old ways; the greenways and the ridgeways, the dry hill ways and the sweet ways which wound all over the country, and how they were as old as man's occupation of the land and indicated that the earliest ancestors had shared a disinclination to get their feet wet unless there was no choice.

Josse had ridden along the downs with Joanna. He felt her presence acutely this morning.

As they topped the downs and began the descent on the north side, Herbert raised his arm and, pointing ahead, said, 'That's Henshaw, down beyond that patch of woodland. See? You can see the church, over by that big yew.'

'Aye, I see,' Josse said. He glanced at the sky, estimating that noon had not long passed. 'We've done well, lad.'

Herbert grimaced. 'We still have to get down this rather steep incline, and then we'll have to find where Sir Godfrey lives, and it could be quite some way out beyond the village.'

Aye, and there might be a second Flood and a small plague of locusts, too, Josse thought. He hadn't realized his cousin's son was such a pessimist. 'Well, let's just hope for the best,' he replied, grinning, 'and maybe we'll find the place is just past the church and we ride straight to it.'

In fact, both Herbert and Josse were half right. They found Sir Godfrey Hellingsham's manor easily – the first person they asked gave clear, concise directions and, since it was easily the biggest house for miles, it would have been hard to miss – but it was a good five or six miles north-east of Henshaw, bordered by lush,

gently sloping meadowland to the south and, on the valley side
to the north, small fields and orchards.

They rode through wide-open gates into a big cobbled yard,
bound on two sides by walls of small bricks interspersed with
rows of flints, on one side by an elegant house, and on the fourth
by a long row of stables, beyond which were several workshops
and a smithy.

Hearing the sound of their mounts' hooves, a dozen horses
put their heads out over the stable doors, ears pricked with interest.
Several stable lads looked up from their work, a brindled bitch
came up and barked at them and a big man on a grey trotted
over and wished them good day, dark, bushy eyebrows raised
questioningly over round brown eyes.

'Am I addressing Sir Godfrey Hellingsham?' Josse asked,
pulling Arthur up as the man approached.

'Yes. Who are you?'

'I'm Josse d'Acquin, and this is my cousin's son, Herbert of
Southfire Hall.'

Sir Godfrey stared at them both. 'Southfire I believe I know.
Down Lewes way?' He glanced at Herbert, who nodded. 'Acquin,
now, that's not a name I recognize.'

'No, I'm not surprised,' Josse said with a grin. 'It's where I
come from but not where I live, which is the other side of the
Great Forest, although I'm presently a guest at Southfire.'

'Well, now that we all know who we are,' Godfrey said,
returning the smile, 'why don't you tell me what I can do for
you?' He looked over their horses, eyes darting about so that
they seemed to be everywhere at once. 'Nice enough creatures
you have there,' he remarked, 'although many now say that you
haven't ridden till you've ridden a horse with the blood of the
Saracen mounts.'

'It's about one of your horses we've come,' Josse said, 'but
I'm afraid I'm not here to buy one.'

Godfrey's smile widened. 'Fair enough, but don't blame me
if I try to change your mind. *Tib!*' he yelled suddenly, making
them jump.

One of the lads came running over. 'Yes, Sir Godfrey?'

'Take our visitors' horses and look after them,' Godfrey ordered, 'since they've come a fair step today. Oh, and take mine, too.' He dismounted, handing his reins to the lad, and Josse and Herbert did the same. 'Now, follow me into the house,' Godfrey went on, leading the way, 'and we'll have a drop of ale while we talk.'

A short time later, seated on a padded settle before a good fire with a pewter mug of rather fine ale in his hand, Josse began. 'An injured man was recently tended at Southfire Hall,' he said, 'both he and his horse having suffered a bad fall. We believed the man was on the mend, but the blow to his head must have been worse than we thought, and he died during the night.'

'God rest his soul,' Godfrey said reverently, and both Josse and Herbert muttered, 'Amen.'

'We know nothing of the man except his name, and we need to find out where he came from so that his household can be informed of his death,' Josse went on. 'We had no clue, until one of the grooms at Southfire happened to remark that the dead man's horse was one of yours.'

Godfrey was nodding even before Josse finished speaking. 'Yes, I had an idea that's what you were going to say,' he said. 'They're very distinctive, my horses. It was my grandfather who brought the first Saracen stallion to these parts – he was Sir Godfrey, like me and like my father, too – and he had the idea of—' Josse gave a discreet cough and Godfrey, picking up the hint, said, 'Well, you haven't come here to hear me drone on about bloodlines and brood mares, have you?'

'No,' Josse agreed.

'Go on, then,' Godfrey said, smiling. Clearly, he had taken no offence at having his little lecture curtailed, and Josse, who had an idea that this might be something that happened quite a lot, guessed he'd probably had to become used to it. 'Describe this horse to me.' Leaning forward, his expression suddenly serious, he said, 'Is it all right? You said it had a fall?'

'It's fine,' Josse assured him. 'My uncle's groom has taken extremely good care of it. Him, I should say, as he's a gelding. Chestnut, with a ginger mane, and white markings on his face that look like a crudely drawn cross. He has two white feet, the front left—'

'And the back right,' Godfrey finished for him. Then, with utter certainty, he sat back and said, 'That's Mickle.'

'Mickle?' Josse echoed.

'I know,' Godfrey agreed, grinning. 'He was born at Michaelmas, you see, and my little daughter reckoned we should honour the fact in the foal's name, especially when she saw that great cross on his face. "He's blessed, Father," she says to me, "and should have a saint's name." "Well," I says, "by rights the saint's actually an archangel called Michael, so we should call him Michael," and she said that was a daft name for a horse.' His grin widened. 'So the little fellow got stuck with Mickle, although I'm sure that's not what he's called now.'

'I don't know,' Josse admitted. It wasn't one of the things you asked a sick man, he reflected, not really having much importance when compared to concussion, a broken nose and a dislocated shoulder. 'So you recall who you sold the horse to?'

Godfrey was frowning. 'I've been trying to think,' he said. 'It was a good few years ago, and Mickle must be getting on for nine or ten now, so I'm that glad to hear he's still fit enough to survive a bad fall.' He fell silent.

'Could you ask your little daughter?' Herbert asked.

Godfrey looked up with a grin. 'The small girl who named Mickle is now a happily married woman with a young daughter of her own,' he said, 'and she lives a fair few miles away. She'd remember, though; you're right there. She loved Mickle, and it was hard on her, the day the stable lad took him away, for all that she knew very well the horse would go one day because that's what we do here. Breeding and selling horses is what puts bread on the board and clothes on our backs, and—' Abruptly his impressive eyebrows went up and his face brightened. 'Stable lad!' he repeated. 'Yes, it's coming back to me. Although the lad came and collected the animal, he came later. It was a lady who purchased that horse – she came riding by one sunny morning on a pretty little mare and said she wanted the best animal in my yard, and it had to be good-looking because it was going to be a gift for a handsome young man. Oh, yes, I remember her, all right!'

'Tell us about—' Josse began, but Godfrey didn't need any prompting.

'She was a lovely one, and no mistake!' he said, smiling and misty-eyed at the memory. 'She came in here with me, sat just where you're sitting now, and we talked and talked till noon and beyond, and laughed! I've never known a woman make me laugh like that.'

'What was her name? Could it have been Southey?' Josse put in.

'Southey? No, no, it wasn't that. She was a beautiful woman – mature, shapely, bright-eyed and as sharp as a tack,' he went on, 'and I don't mind admitting that morning with her was the best I've spent in many a long year, before or since, and, seeing as how I was a widower by then, I did no harm to anyone by appreciating that woman's company like I did, though I can't speak for her, although that's her own business, and not for me to criticize.' He paused for breath.

'Where did she come from?' Josse asked. If Godfrey either couldn't or wouldn't reveal the woman's name, perhaps he would at least tell them where she lived.

'Eh? Oh – north-eastwards of here, right over towards the forest. Place had a funny name and it stuck in my mind, so whenever someone mentioned it afterwards, I couldn't help but think of her . . .' They waited. 'Pard's Wood!' he exclaimed triumphantly. 'Told you it had stuck in my mind! That's where she came from, my lovely lady.' His eyes were dewy with memory.

'North-east?' Josse said after a while.

'Hm? Yes, yes – like I said, it's right on the fringe of the forest, although nowadays I dare say they've cut back the trees a bit, since that seems to be the way of it, with folk wanting to clear the ground to make space for fields and orchards and houses, still, they've a right to live, same as all of us, and—'

'Could we ride over there by nightfall?' Josse interrupted; you had to interrupt Godfrey, he had realized, otherwise he would talk all day.

'Reckon so, if you got moving sharpish, even in these conditions,' Godfrey said. 'It's not far, six, eight miles, maybe, but—'

Josse stood up, and Herbert did too. 'Then we'll take up no more of your time, and be on our way,' Josse said. 'Thank you for your help. I'm sure it'll enable us to find our man's household and, hopefully, his kin.'

'I pray it will,' Godfrey said, accompanying them out into the yard. The lad brought out their horses and, as they mounted,

Godfrey gave them directions to Pard's Wood: 'Follow the track down into the valley, then go along by the stream and on to the forest road, and if you find yourselves in under the trees, you've gone too far!'

With the sound of his hearty laughter still ringing in their ears, Josse and Herbert rode out through the gates.

The route was quite easy to follow, although down there on the low-lying land, water from the partly melted snow had mingled with the heavy soil to make a gooey, sticky mud that slowed their speed and quickly tired the horses, who at times had to make huge efforts to raise their feet out of the mire. When finally the small outcrop of oak, beech and ash which they had been told to look out for came in sight – a sort of outlier group standing sentinel for the great forest beyond – the daylight was beginning to fade, and the temperature was dropping fast. Josse and Herbert looked at each other with expressions of relief.

They rounded a bend in the track and, in among the trees, saw a small manor house set within its own square courtyard. The front of the yard was bordered by a paling fence in which was set a pair of wooden gates, presently closed. The other sides of the courtyard were formed of thick hedges rising higher than a tall man's height and comprised of mainly yew, hazel and a thick tangle of brambles.

They approached the gates. Above them rose a pediment, and in its apex there was a carved wooden figure . . . No, a face, Josse realized as he studied it; an animal's face, a little like a very big cat but with slitted eyes and a wide-open mouth from which the canine teeth curved outwards and down like two vicious blades. The creature's face was marked with faded paint and seemed to be spotted.

'I do believe that animal's a pard,' Herbert said quietly. 'It suggests we've come to the right place.'

'Aye,' Josse agreed. 'I just hope there's somebody here, because we can't go any further tonight.'

'We'll have to go in and find shelter in some outbuilding if the place is deserted,' Herbert said, sounding alarmed. 'It's going to be fearsomely cold once night falls.'

'Let's see, shall we?' Josse said calmly.

He went up to the gates and, leaning down from the saddle, tried to open them. They were barred. Standing up in the stirrups and looking down into the yard, he yelled, 'Halloa the house! Is anyone within?'

'Can you make out anything?' Herbert called anxiously.

'No. There's no light to be seen, and the stable door's wide open, so I imagine they've—'

He stopped. As if, hearing him, someone within the house had struck a light to come and investigate, a faint yellow glow had appeared inside a tiny, square window. Moments later, there was the creak of hinges as a door opened and a quavery male voice demanded, 'Who's there and what do you want? The mistress and the master aren't here and I don't know when they'll be returning, so it's no use asking.'

'I am Josse d'Acquin and my companion is Herbert of Southfire Hall, by the town of Lewes,' Josse called back. 'We seek the household of Peter Southey, who sought refuge at Southfire following an accident, but—'

'Never heard of him!' the old man replied. 'Young master here isn't called Peter Southey, and, like I said, he's away.'

'He had a chestnut gelding with a cross-shaped face marking and two white feet,' Josse cried desperately, fearing the old man would bang the door and leave him and Herbert out in the cold night.

Silence. Then the old man said, 'Sounds like Mickle, right enough. You've got him, then? The horse?' He was advancing now across the yard towards them. 'What's he doing in Lewes?'

There was the sound of heavy bars being drawn back, and the gates opened. 'You'd better come in,' the old man said grudgingly.

Josse and Herbert rode into the yard and dismounted. Since the old man showed no intention of inviting them inside the house, Josse realized he would have to ask his questions out in the cold. 'The horse is definitely your master's Mickle,' he said. 'We've been to see Sir Godfrey Hellingsham – we've just come from there – and he confirmed that the horse was brought by the mistress of Pard's Wood.'

'Yes, that's right.' The old man nodded. 'Nine, ten years back, that was. Wanted him to have the best, she did, and she knew where to buy it.'

Aeleis was always generous, Josse thought. It was totally unreasonable, for he still had no proof, but he was convinced this was Aeleis's house, and it was she who had purchased the best horse that money could buy for her precious son.

He came out of his brief reverie. Both Herbert and the old man were staring at him expectantly. 'Er – what did your young master look like?' he asked the old man. He was wondering if the dead man had given them a false name, and, as he thought about it, he remembered.

The scene was vivid in his mind. He had asked the young man what his name was, and he'd begun to say something – a single syllable sounding like *Pa* – and stopped. Then he asked where he was, and someone, Isabelle, probably, had said Southfire Hall. Then, some time later, after they'd asked if anyone would be worrying about him, and should they send word, Josse had asked him again what his name was, and he said Peter Southey.

But Peter didn't start with Pa. And Southey . . . Isabelle had just said Southfire Hall, so was Southey the first name that came into the young man's head, having just heard something similar?

You lied to us, Peter, Josse said silently.

'What does he *look* like?' the old man was repeating, scratching his head as if not sure how to respond to such an outlandish question. 'Well, like any other young man, I reckon. Fair hair, long, down to his shoulders. Can't say I approve, but it's not for me to say, and the young make their own fashion.'

Josse thought hard, trying to make up his mind. The evidence was strong, but what if his conclusion was wrong? He glanced at Herbert, but Herbert seemed at a loss. He gave a faint shrug, as if to say, *It's up to you.*

Turning back to the old man, Josse said, 'I believe, from what you've just said and from your confirmation that the chestnut gelding belonged to your young master, that I have bad news. If the man who was tended at Southfire Hall and your master are the same man, then I'm afraid I have to inform you that he's dead.'

The old man shook his head. 'No, no, no, you're wrong,' he said confidently. 'Reckon somebody must have stolen Young Master's horse – this Peter Southey you mentioned – because Master's nowhere near Lewes.' He smiled smugly at them both.

'You're sure?' Josse demanded. 'Absolutely sure?'

'I'm sure all right!' He looked affronted, as if Josse had called him a liar. Then, leaning closer to Josse, he said, 'Mistress took sick, see.'

Sick! Oh, no, no! But she might not be Aeleis, he reminded himself firmly. *And*, said a faint voice in his head, *sick is better than dead* . . . 'Go on,' he ordered.

'Master, he sends for the healer down in the village, and she helped as she could, eased Mistress's discomfort a bit, but then she says she reckons there's no more she can do and Mistress needs better care than she can offer, which was honest of her, if nothing else.' He sniffed. 'Anyway, Young Master says what did she suggest, and she says, only one place as can help Mistress now, and that's the nuns.' He nodded encouragingly, his expression earnest. 'Good, they are, see. Make the sickest of folk well. With God's help,' he added piously.

Josse felt a strange sensation in his chest. It was as if, somewhere deep inside himself, he had been aware all along that this was how it would be.

'Your mistress is at Hawkenlye Abbey,' he said tonelessly.

'But, Josse, that's just near where you—' Herbert began.

'Yes, of course she is!' the old man said over him. 'Rode off there – ooh, more than a week ago now, more like eight, maybe ten days. They had to wait, see, for a morning when it wasn't too cold and Mistress had passed a good night, else the journey would have been too much for her, and even as it was, Master said they should have got a litter or a cart, only Mistress said not to fuss and she'd manage as it wasn't far, and—'

'How far?' Josse barked. Surely the old man must be wrong.

'Well, if you take the road that runs westwards round the forest and then bend north and east, it's maybe fifteen miles,' the old man said. 'Only they didn't go that way, see? Young Master, he says they're taking the track *through* the forest, and that cuts a good seven, eight miles off.'

Josse shook his head, trying to understand. He had been so sure he'd broken through the veil of mist that Peter Southey had woven around himself, and identified him as Aeleis's son. But what if he was wrong? If this old boy was to be believed, then Aeleis was ill and her son had taken her to Hawkenlye, and that was where they both were now. But if that was true, then why did Peter Southey have Aeleis's precious Queen Eleanor chess piece?

Throwing up his hands in exasperation, Josse thought, *He probably stole it, along with the horse, and Herbert and I have come all this way for nothing.*

'What should we do, Josse?' Herbert asked.

Josse, realizing that the silence had gone on rather a long time, turned to him. 'I think I may have seen connections where none exist, lad,' he said heavily. The old man, he noticed, was listening intently, a fascinated expression on his face. 'Maybe the woman and her son who live here at Pard's Wood are two strangers. Maybe Peter stole the chestnut gelding from the Hawkenlye stables, and the chess piece was in the saddle bag. Maybe,' he concluded heavily, 'Peter Southey has no link with Aeleis.'

'Aeleis is Mistress's name,' the old man said. Then, frowning, 'Why didn't you *say?*'

Josse felt a great shiver, running right through his body. Then he seemed to be filled with a warm glow, as if he had moved within the orbit of a blazing fire. *Aeleis*, he thought.

All at once it didn't seem to matter much who Peter Southey was, or why he had the horse and the chess piece. Aeleis was at Hawkenlye, taken there by her son, and Josse was going to see her again, just as soon as he could get there.

He glanced up. Through a gap in the clouds, the western sky was still glowing, although the sun had set some time ago. He would cut through the forest, he thought, just as Aeleis and her son had done. He didn't know the way, at least, not all of it, but if he headed off north-eastwards, sooner or later he was bound to come to a place he recognized, and after that it would be easy. The great forest trees were bare; it was always more straightforward to find your way among them in winter.

Having made his decision, he was desperate now to be off. 'Herbert, you stay here tonight,' he said, turning to the younger man. 'If that's all right?' He looked at the old man, eyebrows raised.

'Suppose so,' the old man grumbled.

'Thank you. Then, first thing tomorrow, I want you to ride back to Southfire and tell them what we've discovered.'

'What *have* we discovered?' Herbert asked plaintively.

'That Peter Southey's horse was purchased by Aeleis, for her son, but that Peter can't be that son because he and Aeleis have gone to Hawkenlye Abbey because she's ill,' he said, all in one breath. 'Tell them I've gone to Hawkenlye to see Aeleis –' even saying the words made his stomach give an odd sort of flip – 'and that I'll find out from her son where and when the horse was stolen, and how he wants to go about getting it back.' He frowned. It was very hard to think about anything other than the prospect of his imminent reunion with Aeleis.

Herbert put a tentative hand on his arm. 'Josse, there are other women called Aeleis,' he said gently. 'Are you sure you're not jumping to the wrong conclusion?'

Josse stared at him, something like fever pounding in his blood. 'I'm not wrong!' he whispered. 'I can't explain, but I *know* it's her.'

Herbert looked very worried. 'Very well, but won't you at least wait till daylight before you go haring off to find her? The forest is perilous, Josse, especially at night.'

Josse was touched by the concern in Herbert's face. 'Don't worry, lad,' he said, smiling. It wasn't the moment to explain about Joanna, and how, the forest having been her natural home, he knew he would never come to harm there. 'I'll be all right.'

'But—'

Josse was already swinging up on to Arthur's back. 'I'll return to Southfire as soon as I can,' he called down. 'Give Helewise my love.' A stab of something that felt quite a lot like guilt went through him, but he ignored it. He put his heels to Arthur's sides, the big horse sprang forward, and Josse clattered out of the yard and off down the track leading into the forest.

THIRTEEN

Night had settled on Southfire Hall. The household had retired, and Helewise sat by herself in her room. She had not made any preparations for bed; she had the strongest sense that the late evening mood was not as restful as it appeared, and she was very concerned about Olivar.

She believed she understood, now, the change in his mother's attitude towards him. To begin with, coming with her little son to Southfire as Herbert's bride, naturally she would have been anxious for Herbert to become the boy's new father, and a true part of the family in the law's eyes as well as those of herself and Herbert. Undoubtedly this would explain why, as Isabelle had described, Cyrille hadn't wasted an opportunity to parade the child before them, extolling his virtues, encouraging him – even bullying him, if Isabelle was to be believed – to behave like a proper little lord, and punishing him when he failed to meet his mother's very high standards.

Then all that had altered. Constant vigilance and hard-handed discipline had changed to indifference. Helewise had witnessed Cyrille's new attitude to her son with her own eyes: only this afternoon, when Helewise asked if she might take Olivar off to assist her, Cyrille had said, *Do what you like with him*. Would a proud, ambitious mother, eager to see her son take his place in the family inheritance, have said those unkind words? Surely not, unless whatever ailed Cyrille physically had also addled her mind.

But now Helewise knew what ailed Cyrille; or, at least, she believed she did. Cyrille was suffering the spells of sickness and the lassitude because she was in the early months of pregnancy. And, proudly and happily carrying her new husband's child – *Is she really?* Helewise thought, for, despite all the evidence, she still found it hard to believe – then the reason for her changed attitude towards Olivar became apparent. It was harsh and it was cruel, but the fact remained that Olivar, son of Cyrille's first husband, had been pushed into second place by the child she now carried in her womb.

What, though, if the baby proved to be a girl? This family, after all, abounded in girls. But then, in a flash of insight, Helewise realized that Cyrille would not even have considered that possibility. Wanting – needing – a boy child, she would have convinced herself that she was bearing one.

And so poor little Olivar was superfluous to requirements.

'*Oh!*' Helewise exclaimed aloud. 'Oh, it's *too* cruel.'

He was a child to be proud of, she reflected, irrespective of his parentage. He was polite, obedient, willing and affectionate, yet he was no timid little weakling. He had entered into the hide-and-seek with Cecily, Brigida and Philippa with great enthusiasm and, judging by the grubby state of all four children when eventually they were rounded up for supper and bed, he'd abandoned all his mother's rules about keeping his hands and his clothes neat and clean, and not venturing anywhere that she'd forbidden, without a backward glance. Moreover, it appeared he had been the leader in some of the wilder ventures, as Helewise overheard Cecily telling her mother in awestruck tones that Olivar had gone on into the 'scary dark bit' where the little girls usually feared to venture. 'He's *really* brave,' Cecily had added, looking at Olivar with wide-eyed awe.

Was he feeling as brave right now? Helewise wondered. Now that it was dark, the household was asleep, his lively companions of this afternoon were no longer with him and the monster that lived under the bed was limbering up for its nocturnal offensive?

She stood up. *I cannot leave him there on his own*, she thought. *I no longer care what his mother thinks or if she is angry with me for interfering, and if she threatens to punish Olivar because he is so frightened, then I shall get angry with her too, even if she* is *pregnant.*

She nodded fiercely, confirming her resolve. Then she stuck a taper in the fire and lit a lamp, carrying it before her like a weapon as she headed off along the passage, across the Old Hall and into the family's quarters. She was not sure where Olivar slept, but Josse had said it was on the opposite side from Cyrille's chambers, and she knew where they were. Accordingly, she set off down the passage to her right, walking soft-footed, ears straining for any soft noise.

She heard it immediately. Somewhere close at hand, a child was crying in terror. The sound was deeply distressing, for it was quite clear that whoever was making it – and it had to be Olivar – longed to howl and scream for help but, not daring to, had stuffed a fist in his mouth to stifle all but the softest whimper.

Along to the right, beneath a low arch, a door stood ajar. Helewise rushed forward, tripped on an uneven flagstone, dropped her lamp and everything went dark. She stumbled on towards where she thought the open door was, fumbling at it, pushing it wide open, and just as she threw herself into the room, something came at her. She raised her hands to ward it off, and felt a cold, slippery, clammy substance . . . *What was it?* Oh, God, oh, dear Lord, was it Olivar's monster, extending a dreadful, terrible, claw-tipped feeler towards her?

She opened her mouth to scream, but then, amid her rising panic, she heard an all too human sound: someone was panting, hard, as if they had just expended a great deal of energy; as if, she suddenly realized, they too were very scared.

She shoved out at the unseen thing with all her might, and her hands encountered flesh, muscle and bone beneath the repellent, slippery fabric. '*Get out!*' she hissed. Beside herself with fury, anger burning through her and destroying reason and moderation, she yelled, 'Get away from here and leave him alone, or I'll pursue you and I'll *kill* you!'

Suddenly the thing wasn't there any more. Feeling around wildly, staring into the darkness, she cried, 'Where are you? Where have you gone? Come back, you coward!'

She paused, gasping, trying to hold her breath long enough to listen.

Nothing.

Then, from inside the room, a very small voice said, '*Help.*'

Olivar was in Helewise's arms when Isabelle burst into the room carrying a lamp, Jenna at her heels with what appeared to be a cudgel in her hands.

'What happened? Is he all right?' Isabelle put down her lamp and crouched beside the bed, eyes on Olivar, hand on his forehead stroking back the thick fair hair.

Olivar buried his face against Helewise. 'Not hurt,' Helewise said softly. 'Frightened, though. Could we have some more light?'

Isabelle gave a *tut* of impatience. 'Of course. I should have thought. Jenna, put down that stick and light some candles, please.'

The soft light spread through the little room, chasing the shadows back into the corners. Olivar, responding, raised his head. 'Has it gone?' he whispered. His blue eyes were huge, and his face was deathly white.

'Yes,' Helewise said.

Jenna – kind Jenna, Helewise thought – made a show of going out into the passage, raising Isabelle's lamp and staring hard in both directions. 'Nothing to be seen out here,' she said with a reassuring smile.

Isabelle looked at Helewise over Olivar's head. 'Did *you* see anything?' she asked.

Helewise nodded, putting a finger to her lips. Then she said robustly, 'Just a shadow, and it's gone now.' Olivar's whole body shuddered. 'However, both Olivar and I have had a bit of a fright,' she went on, 'so, if nobody minds, we're going to stay together for the rest of the night and keep each other company.' She felt Olivar relax in relief.

'What a good idea,' Isabelle said, for Olivar's sake speaking with determined cheerfulness. 'Jenna, fetch some more bedding, and then I think we'd all better go back to bed.' As she got to her feet, she mouthed to Helewise, *Tell me in the morning?* and Helewise nodded.

She held Olivar in her arms until his soft, steady breathing told her he was asleep. Then, still lying beside him, she moved over to give them both more room, snuggled the blankets up over her shoulders and started to think.

It had been no phantom or ghostly presence haunting this ancient house that had so frightened Olivar. Josse was quite right, she reflected; she too had come to sense the house's spirit, and it was indeed benign and protective. If there was a ghost here, then it was a loving one.

But what had come erupting out of Olivar's room just now – this very room, she thought with a shiver – had been made of flesh and blood. It had breathed. Beneath the strange, chilly garment it wore, it had been warm; she had felt it. So who was it? Out of the six adults – the *thing* had been too big to be a child – and the handful of servants in the household, who could have taken it into their head to don some weird costume and frighten a small child out of his wits? And tonight wasn't the first time; two nights ago, it had been Josse who had raced to Olivar's aid, and, from what Olivar had told him, it had happened before.

Who could be doing such a very cruel thing, and, perhaps even more important, *why*?

Resigning herself to several hours' more wakefulness as she set about trying to puzzle it out, Helewise made herself relax and began to think.

Josse soon discovered that riding through the Great Forest in the rapidly deepening darkness wasn't nearly as easy as he had anticipated. Quite soon, he began to regret his impetuosity, reflecting ruefully that Young Herbert had been right about it being wiser to wait till morning.

He managed to follow what seemed like a good, straight track, going in roughly the right direction, for some miles after entering in under the trees as he left Pard's Wood. He was not familiar with this area of the forest, but presently the first stars began to appear, and, with a certain amount of relief, he located the North Star. He grinned, realizing that its position demonstrated he was indeed going north-eastwards.

Then the track gave out. Abruptly, with no warning, a great tangle of bramble and hazel appeared before him like a hedge. It was far too big and high to jump, and, in any case, the track leading up to it was neither level nor straight enough for him to put Arthur at the obstacle with sufficient speed. He would have to go round it.

He managed to find a way, eventually, but by now clouds had gathered, and he could see the stars only intermittently. When finally he made out the North Star again, he had travelled too far east. This, however, proved to be an advantage: although he now had considerably further to go before he emerged above Hawkenlye Abbey, he now knew where he was, and soon found his way to a reasonably well-defined track.

Speaking encouragingly to Arthur, he kicked him into a trot and hurried on his way.

The abbey lay at the foot of a long, gentle incline leading down from the forest. Barely a light showed, and the gates were closed for the night. Riding up to them, Josse dismounted and tapped softly, calling out, 'Is anyone there? It's Josse, Josse d'Acquin.'

To his surprise and relief, a gap appeared between the gates and a veiled head appeared, eyes peering up at him. 'Do we know any other Josses?' Sister Madelin said, smiling. 'I've no idea what you're doing here at this time of night, Sir Josse, and I'm sure you're not going to tell me, but you'd better come in.' She glanced at Arthur as the big horse followed Josse. 'And let me take care of your horse,' she said, a faint note of disapproval in her calm voice. 'You have clearly been riding him hard.'

'Has Abbess Caliste retired yet?' Josse asked as they walked across the forecourt.

'No, I think she's in the church,' Sister Madelin replied. She glanced at Josse. 'Please, sir, don't keep her up,' she added. 'Whatever trouble has brought you here, the abbess needs her sleep.'

Josse was about to protest, but, realizing that Sister Madelin's concern for her superior was utterly reasonable, stopped. 'No, I'll try not to,' he said meekly. 'Thank you for looking after Arthur.'

She nodded in reply, and went on towards the stables.

Abbess Caliste was emerging from the abbey church as Josse approached. She held out her hands to him, for a moment just looking up at him, a smile increasing the serene beauty of her face. Then: 'A late-night visit, Sir Josse, usually presages ill. What can we do for you?'

'I believe my cousin is here, in the infirmary.' *Oh, let her still be alive,* he prayed. 'Her name is Aeleis, and her son brought her to you ten days or so ago.' He looked at Abbess Caliste, who, he knew, was aware of every patient in the infirmary and how well, or otherwise, they were doing. Silently he begged her to smile and say, *Oh, yes, Aeleis! She was quite unwell but she's much better now.*

But Abbess Caliste wasn't smiling. Reaching out to take Josse's hand, she said, 'Oh, Josse, I'm so sorry. We've done what we can for her, and she's not in pain now, but I'm afraid she has not got very long in this world.'

Josse felt himself slump down on to the church steps. He put his elbows on his knees and buried his face in his hands. *Aeleis, my little Aeleis,* he cried silently, *I've found you again, but now I'm going to lose you.*

After a little while, he felt a warm presence beside him as Abbess Caliste sat down and put her arm round him. 'She will not die tonight, and probably not in the next few days,' she said gently. 'You have been given the gift of some precious time with her, Josse. Don't waste it in sorrow that it cannot be longer.'

He raised his head to look at her, only then realizing he had tears on his face. 'Can I see her straight away?' he demanded, wiping his sleeve over his eyes.

'Of course,' Abbess Caliste replied. 'She's in a room by herself, so you can be with her as much as you want and nobody else will be disturbed.' She got up, holding out her hand. 'Come with me.'

Sister Liese came to greet the abbess as she and Josse entered the infirmary. Sister Liese gave Josse a smile of welcome, then turned enquiringly back to Abbess Caliste. 'Sir Josse is cousin to Aeleis,' Caliste murmured, her mouth up close to the infirmarer's ear. Sister Liese, with a compassionate glance at Josse, nodded and, beckoning, led the way down the long ward and into a little corridor leading off to the left. Stopping beside a partially open door, she said, 'She is in here.'

Sensing that he wanted to be alone with their patient, the two nuns quietly walked away.

Josse did not hesitate. He went on into the little room and stared over to the bed, where a woman lay propped up on many pillows. She had an unruly mass of fair hair striped thickly with silver, which had spread out beneath the simple white coif she wore as if the little cap had given up trying to contain it. Her eyes were closed. Her face was very pale, and in it the features

– short nose, wide mouth with even now the hint of a smile, determined chin – were as fine, as clearly defined, as when she was a girl. Under the bedcovers, her body appeared to have retained its strong, athletic build: like many of the women of her family, she was wide at the shoulders, long in the legs, yet full-bosomed.

But Aeleis was no longer the free-striding, fresh-air-loving woman she had once been. As he stood listening to her short, laboured breaths and to the air that bubbled and wheezed in her chest, Josse understood, with a sinking of the heart, the reason for those many pillows. And he knew that Abbess Caliste had told him the truth.

Trying to step quietly, he approached the bed. Her smile widened and, in a husky, croaky voice, she said, her eyes still closed, 'You've never been able to perform any sort of movement without making so much noise that you instantly give yourself away, Josse, so it's no use trying.' She opened her eyes – greenish-blue like Isabelle's but paler, although with the same golden lights – and stared up at him. 'They all seem to know about you here,' she went on, 'and, although personally I can't begin to fathom it, they all sing your praises.' She shook her head in amazement. 'My cousin Josse, the nuns' favourite!'

'Hush!' he hissed. 'They'll hear!'

Aeleis laughed, and it was the same merry, hearty sound he remembered so well. Now, however, the laugh ended in a cough and a struggle for breath.

'Same old Josse,' she said when she had recovered. 'Go on, then, tell me why you're here.'

He met her bright eyes. 'Er – I was passing, and they said there was a patient in the infirmary called Aeleis, and I thought, that's my cousin's name, and—'

She laughed again, but in a more controlled manner. 'Oh, rubbish,' she said firmly. 'You've probably heard somehow that I'm dying, and, like the loving cousin you are, you've come to hold my hand.'

She was still staring at him, a challenging expression on her face, and he knew he couldn't lie. 'Aye,' he said.

She nodded. 'Thank you for being truthful.' She was looking up at him expectantly.

'What?' he said.

'Go on, then.'

'*What?*'

'Hold my hand.'

He pulled up a stool, sat down as close to her as he could and took one of her hands in both of his.

There was a short pause as if, simultaneously, the two of them were acknowledging and accepting what was coming. Then she said, 'How did you hear? Who told you?'

He knew she didn't want him to say, *Your cranky old manservant at Pard's Wood.* Hard though it would be, he must reveal the whole story.

'I was at Southfire Hall,' he began. 'Helewise – she's my wife – and I went to visit. Your father's sick, Aeleis, and wandering in his mind, and the family sent for me.'

The news of Hugh's illness sent a brief spasm of distress across her face. 'I'm sorry to hear it,' she said softly. 'Go on.'

'While I was there, a young man was brought into the house. He'd had a bad fall, and he and his horse were both injured.' He forced himself to continue. 'Aeleis, he said his name was Peter Southey, but I believe that was an invention.' He squeezed her hand tightly. 'He had Queen Eleanor in a little leather bag on a thong round his neck, and I knew then he was somebody you loved very much. He was your son, wasn't he?'

'My son,' she breathed, the words barely audible. Then, instantly: '*Was?*'

'He died, Aeleis. I'm so very sorry. Isabelle and Helewise nursed him day and night, and we all thought he was getting better, but then one morning we discovered he had died in the night.'

Her eyes had closed again, and her face seemed to have fallen in, so that all at once she looked very old. 'Did he suffer?' she whispered.

'No, I'm sure he didn't. Isabelle was treating him with her willow-bark remedy, and he rarely complained of pain.'

Two tears spilled down her cheeks. She raised her free hand to wipe them away. She drew a shallow breath, sighed, then, opening her eyes, looked at Josse. 'I sent him away,' she said. 'He didn't know how sick I was. I told him to stop getting on

my nerves hanging around me, and to go away and *do* something.'
She smiled faintly. 'He was never very good at inactivity. I didn't
want him to watch me die!' she burst out suddenly. 'I meant it
for the best, but oh, Josse, Josse, what have I done?'

She was crying hard now, with the same jerky, painful sobs
she used to emit when she was little and some imagined slight
had touched her fiery temper and made her yell with frustration. Just as he had done all those years ago, Josse took her
in his arms, stroked her hair and simply held her until the
storm was past.

Some time later – she had mopped her face and he had poured
out some thick sweet-smelling medicine into her cup from the
jug beside the bed – she said, 'I'll tell you about him, if you
like.'

'Aye,' Josse said, 'that I would.'

She patted the bed. 'Settle down by me here, then, I can't go
on craning my neck to look up at you. That's better.' She leaned
against him with a soft sigh of contentment. 'He wasn't really
called Peter Southey; his name was Parsifal de Chanteloup.' A
chime of memory rang in Josse's head, and he heard Uncle Hugh's
voice: *It was some foreign-sounding name – De Chanticleer? De
Chamois? De something, anyway.* Hugh had almost got it right.
So Aeleis *had* married the man called de Chanteloup, just as the
rumour had said, and this boy Parsifal – Josse could imagine
Uncle Hugh's face when he heard the whimsical name – was the
result of the union. '. . . and, as you surmised, Josse,' Aeleis was
saying, 'I did indeed love him very much.'

He realized he'd missed a bit of her explanation, but he didn't
ask her to repeat it. 'Your father had heard something about you
being at a Windsor court Christmas,' he said, 'and he thought
you'd been causing scandal by your behaviour, so he'll be pleased
to know you did marry your de Chanteloup, and bore him a son.'

She gave him a strange look. Then she said mildly, 'Yes, such
things were always so important to Father. He placed respecta-
bility far above happiness.'

'You have been happy, Aeleis?' Josse asked. Suddenly it was
very important to know she had.

She smiled. 'Oh, yes, Josse. The years we've spent together
have been happier than anyone has the right to expect. We had

such a time! He was such *fun*, always ready to try anything I suggested, and he didn't care what anybody thought or if people took offence and refused to have anything to do with us. We had each other, and that was more than enough for both of us.'

Did she mean herself and her son? It seemed so. What, then, became of her husband? 'Did your husband—'

'Parsifal made enemies, though,' she was saying, her face sombre. 'One in particular, but, given the qualities of that particular person, one was more than enough. Parsifal believed she had the power to curse, Josse, and, no matter how hard I tried to persuade him there were no such things as curses, and it was all an unfortunate coincidence, he wouldn't believe me.' She sighed again. 'Sometimes, lying here, I wonder if he was right.'

'Who cursed him, and why?' Josse asked in a whisper. Despite himself, and despite Aeleis's robust rejection of the efficacy of cursing, he had just felt a cold shiver down his back.

'He was once betrothed to a woman,' Aeleis said. 'His uncle arranged it, and—'

'Your husband's brother, you mean.' It sounded as if her husband had indeed died, for why else would his brother take it upon himself to arrange the lad's marriage?

She waved away the interruption. 'And both he and the woman's father thought it would be a good match. His uncle – his name was Bertrand – became more and more desperate as Parsifal grew from boyhood into manhood, because he was constantly getting into mischief and causing scandal, and Bertrand, being such a rich and important figure, could bear anything but scandal.' She grinned. 'So, hoping it would make Parsifal settle down and turn into a dutiful young nephew, he – Bertrand – found a decent, obedient, devout young lady from somewhat humble stock, persuaded her family that Parsifal was the ideal husband, and the marriage contract was drawn up.'

Once again, Josse was hearing Uncle Hugh's voice: *She got her heart broken, that poor young girl, although she wasn't as young as she made out, not by a long chalk.*

'But Parsifal wouldn't have it,' Aeleis said with pride. 'He wasn't a man you could push around, and, although he was young then – eighteen, at most – he refused utterly to do as Bertrand commanded. He would have nothing to do with it: he didn't let

Bertrand tell him anything about the bride, and he wouldn't agree to meet her. In the end, one of her kin – her father, I believe – took matters into his own hands and rode over to Bertrand's house with the young woman to demand a confrontation, but Parsifal got word they were on their way, lost his temper, packed his belongings and stormed out of Bertrand's house, never to return.'

Sensing that he was not seeing the full picture, Josse said tentatively, 'Couldn't you have persuaded him to see reason? Could you not have suggested he explain to the girl why he didn't want to marry her? It might have been braver than running away, and it certainly would have been kinder.'

'*I* persuade him?' Aeleis laughed. 'Oh, Josse, dear, dear old Josse.' She laughed again, coughed, and then bent forward, trying to draw breath.

'I'm sorry if I appear judgemental,' he began, 'but—'

She lay back against her pillows, smiling indulgently at him. 'Shall I tell you why Parsifal refused to marry the lady?' she asked, mischief glinting in her eyes.

'Aye, I wish you would,' he said gruffly.

'Because he was already in love with someone else.' She was staring right into his eyes. 'He met her at a deadly dull gathering of important and wealthy lords and ladies, and she winked at him. She was everything he was and more; adventurous, wild, reckless, beautiful, hedonistic, selfish, charismatic. They recognized straight away that they belonged together; that they were halves of the same soul. They fell deeply and passionately in love, and they vowed that they'd never be parted.'

'Not parted except by death,' Josse murmured, staring down at her hand in his.

'Perhaps not even then,' Aeleis whispered, although he barely heard.

'Can you understand, dear, lovely Josse?' she asked after a moment. 'I don't care for the good opinion of most of the people in this world, but, now I'm approaching death, I find I'd quite like to know I have yours. I was so *bored*!' she exclaimed before he could answer. 'I'd married fussy old Godric to please Father, and, when he died, it seemed too good to be true. Then they tried to push another old man at me – someone *steady*, Father said, as if that was any recommendation – and I knew I had to get away. Then, only a matter of weeks afterwards, I knew I'd been absolutely right, and I never once looked back.'

Josse was working it out in his mind. 'Pard's Wood was the house Godric left you, was it?'

She nodded. 'Yes. I'd let it, but then subsequently I realized I needed it after all. As soon as I knew what I wanted, I went back, told my tenants they'd have to leave, and I moved in. Then, once I was no longer on my own there, everything became even better.'

'You bought a horse for him,' Josse said dreamily. 'A good-looking horse for a handsome young man.'

'Mickle.' Aeleis smiled. 'Yes, I did, and I flirted all morning with that saucy old rogue Godfrey Hellingsham, and got a third knocked off the price.'

He looked up into her eyes that shone like aquamarines.

'You know, don't you?' she said quietly.

'Aye.' He smiled. 'Only you, Aeleis, could have kicked over the traces so spectacularly. What was it, sixteen, seventeen years?'

'Seventeen.' She chuckled. 'He was eighteen, I was into my thir-ties, but they all said I looked much younger. Not that I kept it from him, you understand – he had to know what he was taking on, and, much as I adored him, I'd rather have lost him than lied to him.'

He nodded. 'Aye, you always liked openness.'

He went on staring at her, loving her just as he had when they were children, just as, probably, he had always done.

She gave a vast yawn. 'Sorry, Josse, but I'm almost asleep. I get very tired, although heaven knows why since all I do is lie here.'

He got up, carefully laying her hand down on top of the sheet. 'Of course,' he said.

'Will you come back in the morning?' she asked, settling on her pillows, her eyelids drooping. 'I have so much more to tell you.'

'I will.'

She stared at him. 'Thank you for coming. Thank you for telling me about Parsifal. Lots of people – most people, probably – would have kept it from me and let me die thinking he was alive and happy. But I'd far, far rather know.'

He smiled through his tears. 'Aye, that's what I thought.'

Her eyes were closing. She muttered something – it sounded like *He'll be waiting for me, and I can almost see him, now* – but it was probably his imagination.

FOURTEEN

Helewise's sense of foreboding was present right from the moment she woke up, early the next morning. Quietly, so as not to disturb the sleeping child, she got up and went over to peer out of the small window, set high in the wall. Dawn had broken, and the low sun in the east was making long shadows on the land. There was a new sound: that of running water. The temperature had risen overnight – she could tell that from the sweet air blowing in her face – and melted snow must have increased the flow of the stream that ran in the narrow valley to the north of the house, high on its spur of the downs.

Olivar stirred, sat up and rubbed his eyes. He smiled at her. 'Is it time to get up?'

'It's morning, yes, although still early.'

Olivar got out of bed, reaching for his outer tunic and his boots. 'I'm hungry. Cecily says that if you go along to the kitchens and the cook's in a sunny mood, she'll give you a bit of bread when it's just come out of the oven, so is it all right if I go and see? Cecily and the others'll be there, they said so, and I promise I won't get in anyone's way.'

'Of course it's all right.' Helewise returned his smile. 'Off you go.' Before your mother wakes up, she might have added. She was quite sure this was not a venture of which Cyrille would approve. Little lordlings didn't go scrounging in the kitchen.

She listened to the sound of Olivar's feet, running away up the passage. With the resilience of childhood, he appeared to have put the terrors of the night behind him; or, more likely, she reflected, he was eager to proceed with the excitements of the day, in the company of his three new-found friends, in order to help him forget.

She followed him out of the room, making her way past the network of rooms, passages and open halls that made up the family's quarters, out into the Old Hall and along to the chamber she shared with Josse. Josse! Would he be back today? Was he all right? With an effort, she suppressed her anxiety. He would return as soon as he could, for she was well aware he'd know she was worried about him.

And not only about him. She had vaguely imagined that, once away from Olivar's room, where that malicious apparition had materialized, the good spirit of the old house would reassert itself and her mood would improve. This, however, was not proving to be the case, and, judging from the tense expression on others' faces, she was not the only one feeling uneasy. As the family gathered to break the night fast, she saw Isabelle muttering to Jenna and Editha, all three looking anxious. Emma sat alone, a preoccupied frown on her face. Philomena had her arm round Brigida, and Philippa sat on her lap. It was as if she sensed a threat and needed to keep her little daughters close to her.

The children, however, were surreptitiously watching their cousin and ringleader, and Cecily, in turn, was making urgent faces at Olivar, sitting beside Helewise. As soon as Cecily had finished eating and been given permission to leave the table, the two younger girls demanded to go too. With a quick look at Philomena, who shrugged, Isabelle said, 'Very well. But don't go far, and keep out of mischief!'

'That applies to you, too,' Emma said sternly to her sister, her glance including Olivar as well.

Olivar, evidently less adept at subterfuge than his playmates, said brightly, 'We're going to—'

Cecily gave him a hard shove and, before he could finish his remark, she said, 'We're going on with our hide-and-seek game! We've thought of *dozens* more places to hide, but we'll be careful not to get dirty!'

With that, and quite a lot of giggling, the four children sped away.

Jenna sighed. 'They ought to be able to go outside soon, if this thaw continues,' she said. 'It's not good for them to be restricted to the house. They need the good fresh air, and space to run around.'

Helewise met her eyes. 'Olivar will benefit from their company,' she said quietly.

'He seems better this morning. Did he sleep?' Jenna asked. 'Did you?' she added with a smile.

'Yes, we both did.' Helewise leaned closer, lowering her voice. 'Somebody tried to frighten him last night, and not for the first time.'

Jenna nodded grimly. 'I know. Any ideas?'

Helewise hesitated. She did have an idea, but it was a horrible one and she was reluctant to mention it yet. 'I will see what I can discover,' she whispered.

Jenna regarded her, one eyebrow raised. In that moment, Helewise was sure that she understood; that she shared Helewise's suspicion. But all she said was, 'Good luck.'

Saying vaguely that she might go along to the chapel later, and perhaps also go and see if Uncle Hugh felt like some company, Helewise slipped away from the Old Hall. As she had lain waiting for sleep, and again when she woke this morning, she had kept thinking about how that *thing* last night had vanished. Had it been a ghostly presence, such a disappearance was to be expected. But, for one thing, Helewise didn't believe in ghostly presences. For another, she had touched the thing. Beneath that repellent outer skin, she had felt bone and warm flesh. For something that was undoubtedly human to vanish, there had to be some secret doorway, passage or flight of steps which it had utilized.

It was Helewise's firm intention to locate it.

After quite a long time of dead ends and flashes of intuition that proved baseless, she found a tiny, low opening in the north-east corner of the chapel, hidden behind a pillar. With a three-wick cresset lamp in her hand, she descended into the earth down an ancient spiral stair and found herself in a low-ceilinged crypt. No, not a crypt, she decided, raising her lamp to look around; it was just a space, dark, dank, full of bits of rough, unshaped stone and odds and ends of timber. Over to the left, Helewise could make out a rising flight of wide steps, worn and with some of the stones missing. Picturing the Old Hall above, she realized these must once have been the steps leading up to the original main entrance, on the south side of the hall. Crouching low, she went on past the base of the steps. Was she now in Josse's childhood playground? Would she come across the ancient heath that he and Aeleis had uncovered? The place where Aeleis had unearthed her precious chess piece?

It was dark down there, and the shadows beyond the light of her lamp seemed to gather and multiply. *Go on*, she commanded herself sternly. She discovered that there was a solid earth wall to her right, which must be the outer boundary of the house and its extensions. But she found she could squeeze through a rough arch to the left, on the far side of which she could stand up. She looked around. This must be the undercroft beneath the Old Hall. It was well constructed, with a flagged stone floor, stone walls and stout pillars holding up the mass of the hall above.

She stood still for a moment, orientating herself. She was under the hall, and so the foundations of the first extension, where the family had their quarters and where the *thing* had vanished, must be ahead and then a little to the right . . .

Determined now, her fear dissolved by hot anger, Helewise went on.

In the late morning, Helewise heard the sound of hooves, and voices calling a greeting. She was back in her room, brushing off the dust and dirt that soiled her skirts and her sleeves following her explorations underground. She smiled grimly. What a lot she had to tell Josse.

Racing through the Old Hall, out of the main door and on to the steps, she stared down into the courtyard. There was only one rider, now dismounting from his sweaty horse. It was Herbert.

Isabelle stood beside him, and Jenna was behind her. He was speaking urgently to them, and all three looked anxious.

Helewise flew down the steps. 'Where's Josse?' she demanded. 'Is he all right? Why—'

Herbert handed his reins to the stable lad and took her hands. 'He is perfectly all right, Helewise, and he sends you his love.' She let out the breath she'd been holding, smiling now with relief. 'As I was just saying to Mother and Jenna, we found the place where Peter Southey's horse came from, and then we found the house where he lived, but there was nobody there except an old servant. That's as far as I'd got.' He paused. Then, looking at Isabelle, said, 'Mother, it was Aeleis's house, but—'

'Pard's Wood?' Isabelle cried incredulously. 'No, no, it can't have been, she can't possibly have been living there without our knowing!'

Herbert frowned. 'How do you know the name?'

'Because it was Godric's house! He left it to Aeleis when he died, but I thought she'd moved away long ago.' Slowly she shook her head. 'Did you see her? How is she?'

'Mother, I just said there was nobody there except the servant,' Herbert repeated. 'I'm afraid to say she's not well. Her son's taken her to Hawkenlye Abbey, and Josse has gone there too to speak to them.'

'So Peter Southey wasn't Aeleis's son?' Helewise said.

'No. Oh, I don't know,' Herbert said in exasperation. 'Josse had some idea that maybe he – Peter – stole the horse and found the chess piece in a saddle bag, although that would surely have meant that the horse was stolen after Aeleis and her son got to Hawkenlye, and somehow that doesn't seem very likely.'

'The abbey is secured at night,' Helewise said absently, 'and nuns or lay brethren are usually on duty all day, both in the stables and on the gates.' Three pairs of eyes turned to stare at her; one with incredulity, two with understanding.

'You know a lot about it,' Herbert said with a smile, eyebrows raised enquiringly.

'Er – yes.'

Jenna came to her rescue. 'So when will Josse be back?'

'I don't know. He just said he'd come as soon as he could.'

'Come inside,' Isabelle urged. 'It's milder today, but you've had a hard ride and you will become chilled if you stay out here.'

'And I should go and find Cyrille!' Herbert looked very guilty, as if, Helewise thought, he could already hear the scolding voice that asked what he thought he was doing, standing out in the courtyard gossiping with his mother and his sister, when he should have shown his wife the respect that was her right and reported first to her.

Isabelle, she noticed, was staring after him as he hurried away, an expression on her face that suggested she was thinking the same.

The day went on. Helewise, desperate to share her thoughts, her discoveries and her conclusions with Josse, ached for his return.

At times as the long hours dragged by, she considered confiding in Isabelle. *But what if I'm wrong?* she thought. To raise such awful suspicions would, if she was mistaken, only serve to make a bad matter very much worse . . .

I'm not wrong, she told herself.

She was sitting alone in the solar when all at once an image came into her mind of Peter Southey's dead body: once again, she saw with her mind's eye the cut on his lip and the small bruise on his chin. Then swiftly another image imposed itself on that one: a gesture that she and no doubt others had observed many times. She thought about it, and then she knew why those images had appeared.

She got up, walked on soft feet across the solar and along the passage to the chapel. In the soft light of the candles left burning around the trestle table before the altar, she folded back the cloth and stared at Peter's dead face. She reached inside his chemise – her fingers touched the cold flesh and she tried not to shudder – and took out the chess piece in its little leather bag. Extracting it, she placed it against Peter's mouth, just as she had seen him do.

Queen Eleanor's protruding hand fitted exactly the cut in Peter's lip, and her bent knee pushed against the bruise on his chin.

'You used to kiss her, just like this,' Helewise said softly to him, 'because she belongs to your mother, who you loved.' She wiped a tear from her face. 'You were holding Queen Eleanor when they came for you, weren't you? You'd been dosed with Isabelle's soporific, and you'd have been deeply asleep.' There had been, she recalled, a small piece of amber-coloured fluff adhering to the chess piece when Josse picked it up from the floor beside Peter's bed. 'They slipped into your room and held a pillow over your face until you were dead,' she breathed, 'and the pillow drove Queen Eleanor into your flesh and left these marks.'

With gentle hands, she replaced the chess piece in its bag, put it inside his chemise and once more covered his face with the cloth.

Now, the urge to confide in Isabelle was even stronger. *Wait for Josse*, she told herself.

She bided her time and held her peace.

*   *   *

Olivar and the three little girls appeared, breathless, tingling with suppressed excitement and not a little grubby, to eat with the family, then, as soon as they were excused, raced away again. All three were flushed from their exertions, and, to Helewise's eye, had an air of conspiracy, as if they were planning even more thrilling escapades for the rest of the day. Cyrille did not put in an appearance. She sent word with Herbert that she would like to be provided with food and drink in her own quarters, and Isabelle, with no comment but an expression that made words redundant, gave the necessary order.

Helewise lay on her bed. She was exhausted, the broken night, Olivar's terror and today's long explorations, discoveries and musings having combined to wear her out. She closed her eyes, drifting quickly into the sort of half-sleep in which it is almost impossible to distinguish sounds in the real world from fragments of lurking dreams.

She thought she heard whispering; a childish voice hissed a command . . . *whishwhishywhishhisshiss*. There was some giggling, quickly hushed. Helewise dreamed of her sons, small boys again, plotting how to steal a pot from the kitchen so they could go and gather frogspawn. *Don't you let your little brother fall in the pond*, she said to Dominic. *Hold his hand firmly, for the water is high.* There was a soft thud, as if some object had been thrown. Then – was that a faint cry from somewhere near at hand? No, it was Leofgar, in her dream, protesting because his big brother had taken her command to heart and grabbed his wrist in a grip that hurt.

The images faded. Faint sounds seemed to come from a long way away. Helewise, falling into a deep sleep, heard no more.

The body fell a long, long way. Emerging from the little window in the north wall of the solar, it looked for a few seconds as if it would go on flying through the air for ever.

Of course, it didn't.

Southfire was built upon a height, and the north side of the house stood over a long, deep drop. Down, down it went, off the edge of the escarpment and into the valley below where the stream ran, bubbling its way along to add its waters to the River

Ouse in Lewes. From the other, west-facing windows of the solar, the drop wouldn't have been nearly so great. With the vestiges of snow still lying on the ground to soften a fall, tumbling out of one of those windows would have been a survivable accident.

Nobody, though, could long survive that fall from the little north window.

For some time the body did not move. Then the eyes slowly opened. Looked about. Unease came into them, then fear.

'Where am I? What's happened?' a whimpering voice asked.

'I'm lying on the slope beneath the solar,' the voice answered itself. 'I – I *fell*, out through the north window.'

Presently, the thought came to her that she should try to move. The grass beneath her was wet with melting snow, and she knew she must be very, very cold. 'But I don't *feel* cold,' she whispered.

With dawning horror, she realized that she couldn't in fact feel at all. From the chest down, it seemed as if her body just wasn't there. She couldn't feel the cold, wet ground beneath her. She felt no pain, although after such a fall, pain there must surely be.

'I am paralysed,' she said aloud. Screwing up her face with effort, she tried to move her left foot. Her right foot. Her legs. Tried to lift herself off the grass.

Nothing.

She had a little movement in her right arm. Aware, somehow – perhaps from some deep and unconscious survival instinct – she knew she should try to move up the slope.

Away from the rising waters of the stream.

But then suddenly, looking down, a wonderful thought stuck her and she was filled with relief: the water was lapping over her feet and her legs, pushing now against her backside, and it would be – surely it had to be! – very, very cold, for the stream was flooding with snow melt. 'It's not paralysis, it's the numbing effect of the chill!' she cried joyfully. 'I'm all right! I'm going to be all right!'

With new determination, she stretched out her right arm, grasped a clump of grass tightly in her fingers and pulled with all her might. Her body stayed exactly where it was. Some of the grass stems broke off in her hand.

She tried again. And again. And again.

She thought she should try with her left hand, but for some reason, although it wasn't under water yet, that hand did not respond.

She lay back on the cold ground. It didn't feel quite so cold now.

She thought quite a lot of time had passed. It was growing dark. Had she slept? Oh, oh, how could that be? Panicking, she raised her head, looking down the length of her useless body.

The water now reached her waist.

Opening her mouth wide, she let out a scream of fury, frustration and terror.

Time passed.

Someone was standing over her. She managed to move her head a little, but not enough to see who it was. It occurred to her that, whoever he or she was, the person was deliberately keeping out of her sight.

'Help me,' she snapped. 'I can't move my legs, and I need you to pull me clear of the water.' There was no response. 'Hurry up!' she commanded. 'What in God's name are you waiting for?'

'Please,' whispered a very soft, husky voice. Man or woman?

She couldn't believe what she was hearing. '*What?*'

'Say *please*. You're so rude,' the voice murmured conversationally. 'You expect such high standards in others, yet you do not deem it necessary to observe them yourself.'

She spluttered in fury. '*Do as you're told!*' she screeched, craning round, trying again to see who was there.

She heard a quiet movement; the person had stepped further away.

'No,' came the soft whisper.

A shiver of dread ran through her. Frantically she tried once more to move; to wriggle up the steep bank a little and get herself out of the icy water.

Then there came the terrible sound of a quiet laugh. 'So the fall didn't kill you,' the low voice said. 'A pity, really.' A gentle sigh, as if this soft-spoken man or woman were rueing nothing worse than a morning without sunshine. 'We shall just have to see what the flood waters can do.'

The ground echoed to the gentle vibration of light footfalls as the speaker walked away.

The water continued its inexorable rise.

Half an hour later – the longest, most terrible half-hour in all the world – her face was under water.

And she was dead.

Then something quite strange happened. The sky was overcast, and, with the rise in temperature and the melting of the snow, a thick, white blanket of mist flowed over the ground, rolling down the hillside and pooling in the valley. Cloud and mist, it would seem, would have their way with the day, smothering the world in white.

But, at the precise moment of death, as if the very heavens were celebrating, a gap appeared in the enfolding white above and the sun poured through. It radiated the scene with light and warmth and, to anyone with the ears to hear, it seemed as if a brief, beautiful chord of deep joy rang out.

Then the clouds massed together once more and the ray of golden light went out.

FIFTEEN

Josse was roused from profound sleep by a kind-faced little nun gently shaking his shoulder. Sister Liese had found a bed for him in a disused recess in the infirmary; she had said it would be best if he did not go far away.

Remembering, Josse shot up, grabbed the little nun's hand and said hoarsely, 'Is she dead?'

'No, Sir Josse,' the little nun whispered, 'but she is awake and wishes to talk to you.' She was, he noticed, surreptitiously rubbing her hand.

'Sorry,' he said gruffly. 'I didn't mean to hurt you.'

She smiled gamely. 'I'm sure you didn't. Go along to her room, and I will bring you a hot drink.'

He nodded his thanks, then struggled into his boots.

Aeleis looked wide awake, her blue-green eyes watching the doorway as he went into the room. A faint yellowish light could be seen through the small window set high in the wall: morning had come.

He went up to the bed, and she made room for him to sit down. He took her hand. 'So, what have you got to say to me that's so important you have to have me woken up in the middle of a beautiful dream?' he asked with a grin.

She smiled back. 'Food or women?'

'What?'

'The *dream*.' She made an impatient sound. 'Come on, Josse! You used to be quicker than this!'

'Oh, food. There's—' He had been about to say, *There's only one woman for me*, but that wasn't strictly true. There was Helewise, and there always had been, ever since he'd first set eyes on her, but there was also Joanna. And the cousin who now lay on the bed beside him.

She was watching him closely, but made no comment. Nor, he noticed, did she answer his question. Perhaps she felt there was no need.

'What's the matter with you, Aeleis?' he asked gently.

'I can't breathe, Josse,' she replied. 'When I try to take air inside me, it's as if the space where it ought to go is already full, of thick liquid that I swear I can feel moving in my chest.'

He was horrified. It sounded truly awful. He tightened his grip on her hand. 'Can't they do anything?'

'They do. They bring bowls of steaming water with special herbs and distillations in it, and when I inhale the steam, it helps a lot.'

'Can they cure you?' He had to ask, but he already knew what she would say.

'No, dear heart, they can't.'

They sat in silence for a while. Then – perhaps she had waited until she could speak without her voice breaking – she said, 'Parsifal found a moppet, you see.'

'A *what?*'

'A moppet. A wax doll, made to look like me, with dark yellow wool hair, blue-green beads for eyes and, according to Parsifal, a patch pocket on its skirt made out of a scrap from one of my handkerchiefs, although I always thought he added that bit for verisimilitude.' She smiled faintly.

'What was it for?' he whispered.

'Oh, you know that as well as I do, Josse!' she exclaimed. 'You may say firmly that it's all nonsense, and nobody can harm someone else by such methods, but it does feel a little different when it's done to you, and you realize you're the focus of such extreme malice.'

'And Parsifal found this doll?'

'Yes. He found it out in the stables, head-down in a water trough.'

'He—' But then Josse was struck with the awful relevance of that. The doll made in Aeleis's image had been put into water. Now, Aeleis was dying because her lungs were filling up with liquid. A shiver of atavistic dread ran through him, and he shuddered.

'Parsifal believed he knew who had made the moppet, who had put it in the trough, and why,' Aeleis said, her breath wheezing in her chest. She coughed several times, then spat into a piece of rag.

'Don't try to talk!' Josse implored, watching her with deep anxiety. 'You should rest, Aeleis.'

She shook her head violently. 'I have all eternity for resting,' she said shortly. '*Listen*, Josse, and don't interrupt. I must tell you this.'

She started to speak, but the coughing would not let her. Communicating mainly with signs, she got Josse to summon the infirmarer, and Sister Liese, understanding, brought a bowl of hot water. Aeleis was helped into a sitting position, a cloth was draped over both her and the bowl, and for some time she simply breathed in the fragrant steam. The coughing stopped.

For the moment.

Sister Liese took the bowl away. She caught Josse's eye as she left the room. She mouthed, 'Not long, now.'

I have to be brave for Aeleis, Josse told himself. There was something she very much wanted him to know, and so he must put aside his own instinct – to take her in his arms, tell her he loved her and hold her against him until she fell into the final sleep – and somehow help her achieve her desire.

But, whatever she needed to tell him, she wasn't going to be able to confide in him today. Aeleis's attack, far from subsiding, steadily became worse, and soon she was gasping for every tiny breath. Sister Liese asked Josse to step outside while she and her nuns treated their patient, and he waited in the passage, terrified that the infirmarer would emerge with tears on her cheeks to tell him Aeleis was dead.

He waited for what seemed hours. Then, finally, Sister Liese came to find him. 'She is still alive,' she said, her eyes, full of compassion, on his. 'She is asleep, for we have given her a powerful soporific. When she can't breathe, she begins to panic, you see, which of course merely exacerbates the problem.' She sighed, shaking her head.

'Will she—' Josse began, but he couldn't go on.

'She will die quite soon now, Sir Josse,' Sister Liese said calmly. 'She will sleep for the remainder of today, and I shall give her more of the sleeping draught tonight. After such a long rest, she may be sufficiently recovered to talk to you in the morning.' She smiled. 'I shall pray that it is so, for I understand she has something she wishes to tell you.'

'Thank you,' he managed. Then, clearing his throat, he said, 'What should I do? Would it help if I sat beside her?'

'I doubt it,' the infirmarer said, 'although, of course, you would be welcome to do so.'

He stood staring down at her, undecided.

'If I were you,' she said kindly, 'I would take myself off for a walk in the vale, breathe in its healing air, think, pray, perhaps, for the fortitude to help your cousin out of this life when the time comes, and then, when you are restored, return to her bedside.'

It was, he discovered, exactly what he most wanted to do. 'I will,' he said. 'Would you please tell Abbess Caliste where I am, if she should ask? I wouldn't want her to think I'd just walked away.'

Sister Liese smiled. 'She wouldn't think that, Sir Josse, but I will tell her, anyway.'

He didn't go down to the vale. He set off in the opposite direction, up the long slope behind the abbey, past St Edmund's Chapel and into the forest. He didn't think too much about where he was heading, simply letting one foot fall in front of the other, keeping up a good rhythm which, quite soon, soothed his turbulent thoughts and brought him some peace. Presently he came to the little clearing where Joanna had lived, in her little hut. He stood for a long time, staring at the simple wooden structure, its door fastened with the same knot – very likely the same piece of rope – which Joanna had always used.

He allowed his memories of her to fill his mind. They were bitter-sweet. She had loved him, and he knew it, but even more than him she had loved the strange life she had chosen, out in the wild with her herbs, her animals, her magic. Sometimes – and it still hurt to remember – she had not been there when he had needed her badly and gone to find her. She hadn't been physically absent at those times, he now knew. It was just that she wanted to be alone, eschewing even the company of those who loved her.

But at other times she had generously and wholeheartedly given herself to him, and she was the mother of his two beloved children, Meggie and Geoffroi, and also of his adopted son, Ninian.

'For better or worse, lass, you were a part of me, and I of you,' he said softly. He patted the hut's stout wooden wall – he had no wish to go in – and turned away.

Sometimes Meggie stayed in the hut. Probably, he reflected, his feet had led him straight to the hut because unconsciously he had hoped to find her there. Now, thinking about it, he realized she was much more likely to be over in the old charcoal-burners' camp, where, with the Abbess Caliste's permission and encouragement, she and her young man were restoring the old forge and building themselves a modest dwelling. Jehan le Ferronier was a blacksmith, and, as he had pointed out winningly to the abbess, the Hawkenlye area really needed someone on the doorstep to shoe horses, mend ploughshares, make a pair of door hinges, and, in general, provide all the services for which local people normally had to trudge down to the big forge in Tonbridge.

Josse was tempted to seek out Meggie and Jehan. He could remove his tunic, roll up his sleeves and get to work alongside them. But then he wondered if he would be welcome. They were building their future along with the forge and the little house, and maybe Jehan, anyway, would rather do it without Meggie's father butting in. *No*, he decided, *I'll leave them be.*

He walked on, following paths and tracks at random, letting the deep peace of the sleeping winter forest penetrate right into his soul. Much later – and promoted almost entirely by hunger – he looked up into the sky, realized the day was almost over, and set out on the long walk back to the abbey, supper, some time sitting with Aeleis, if it were permitted, and then his bed.

Abbess Caliste, on hearing from Sister Liese that Josse had gone walking, knew where he would be. She knew, too, that before too long he would be facing a great sorrow, and that such things were easier when you had the company and the support of someone you loved.

After nones, she slipped out of the abbey's gates and set off into the forest. She was back in time to finish her day's tasks before vespers and when, after the usual meagre supper and the final office of the day she at last went to bed, it was with the comforting thought that Josse would not be alone in his sorrow.

Her final thought before sleep took her was a prayer, imploring the Lord to make Aeleis's passing as easy as it could be.

Next day, a damp, misty morning broke over Southfire Hall. Warmer air had encountered land still cold from the recent snow, and dense fog lay in the valley on the north side of the house. Peering out through the small window of her room, Helewise thought it looked like clouds.

She had been awake for a long time, watching since daybreak for the first sign of Josse's return. She hadn't slept in her own bed. Instead, she had tucked Olivar up, waited until he was asleep, then lain down across the foot of his bed and covered herself as best she could with blankets and pelts. She knew she couldn't leave him, for he was subdued and plainly distressed, reluctant to talk to her, and she guessed his fear and apprehension were increasing as the night advanced. She had slept only fitfully, quite sure that at any moment the *thing* would come slinking and creeping along the passage and into Olivar's room. She wished she'd had the foresight to arm herself with Jenna's cudgel.

There had been no sign of it, all night long.

There was no sign, now, of Josse, either. She prayed that he was all right. Even more fervently, she prayed he would come back today.

'And how is Cyrille this morning?' Isabelle asked her son as the household assembled in the Old Hall. 'I take it she requires a tray in her room again?'

Herbert flushed. 'Er – I don't know,' he confessed.

Isabelle stared at him. 'Didn't she issue her orders as you left to come for your breakfast?' she demanded.

He looked down. 'She – we – er, she prefers to sleep alone,' he said quietly. 'She says she gets a better night that way, so I've moved into the small room next door.' He raised his head and met his mother's eyes. 'I haven't seen her this morning,' he confessed. 'She shut herself in late yesterday and told me she wanted to get on with her sewing and didn't want to be disturbed.'

'And got one of the servants to take her supper in, I suppose,' Isabelle retorted.

'She does like to be alone sometimes,' Herbert said apologetically. 'And she gets awfully tired.'

'I really can't think why,' Isabelle said tetchily. 'It's not as if she overworks herself.'

There was an awkward silence. Somebody cleared their throat.

Isabelle pushed her chair back and got to her feet, making an exasperated sound. 'I'd better go and ask her if she wants anything,' she muttered crossly.

Helewise watched her stride away. Was she about to confront her daughter-in-law? Was this at last going to be the great, explosive argument they all seemed to be anticipating? She waited. Nobody spoke. The children – the three little girls and Olivar – all seemed very absorbed with what was on their platters, and not one of them spoke or even raised their head.

The sound of Isabelle's returning footsteps reached them. 'She's not in her room,' she said as she entered the hall. 'Where do you imagine she's gone, Herbert?'

He stared at her. 'I – I don't know,' he stammered. 'Out for a walk?'

Isabelle went on glaring at him for a moment. Then she said resignedly, 'She'll no doubt let us know when she wants some food. In the meantime, I suggest we all carry on with our meal, and then proceed with our tasks for the day.'

The sun's gentle heat increased as it rose up in the sky. By mid-morning, the mist had all but cleared. In the solar, Helewise strode up and down, trying to tell herself she was enjoying the warmth coming in through the south-facing window, but in reality only there so that she could keep returning to the little north-facing window to see if Josse was approaching.

Leaning against the wall, staring out over the valley, she noticed how high the water was. The stream had broken its banks, and had turned into a fast-flowing river, full of melted snow and tumbling down the valley towards the Ouse. The water level must have risen even higher during the night, she noted absently, because there was a line of water-borne detritus part of the way up the steep slope in front of the house.

Suddenly she stiffened. There was something else there, lying on the wet grass.

Her heart began to beat very fast.

She raced out of the solar, down the passage and into the Old Hall, calling out as she ran to Jenna, Editha and Emma, busy with some activity at the table, 'Fetch help! There's someone out on the stream bank!'

She flung open the main door and flew down the steps, across the courtyard and out through the gates, turning to her left, running along in front of the wall until she stood at the foot of the high north face of the solar. She paused, not knowing how best to descend, frantically looking for the safest way down. The incline was far too steep to go straight down, so she followed the contours and took a zigzag path, desperately trying to keep her footing and very aware of the rushing waters not far below.

Was he still alive? She ran on. *He'll be so cold*, she thought, *and I didn't think to bring anything to wrap him up in.* She risked a quick glance behind her. Isabelle, Herbert, Jenna and some of the servants were coming out through the gates, two of the servants carrying bundled blankets. *Good*, Helewise thought. The sooner they encouraged a little warmth into him, the greater the chance he would survive.

She skidded to a halt beside the figure lying on the muddy grass. She bent down, staring into the dead face. It *was* a dead face: there could be no doubt. The flesh was marble white, the slightly parted lips were blue, the wide eyes did not blink in the bright sunlight and the body lay utterly still.

Just to be sure, Helewise put her fingers to the throat, feeling under the sodden white linen of the gorget. There was no pulse of life. She put her cheek against the nose and mouth. There was no breath, and the flesh was so cold that it almost hurt.

Helewise stood up and said a prayer for the soul of Cyrille de Picus.

SIXTEEN

It was clear even to Josse's ever-optimistic eyes that Aeleis would not survive the day. He had been at her side since before dawn, sometimes talking to her of their childhood – lying with her eyes closed, it was nevertheless apparent that she enjoyed listening, for she smiled frequently and sometimes even managed a laugh – and sometimes simply holding her hand while she slept.

He recognized the approach of death. Aeleis's face was totally devoid of colour, and her lips had a blue tinge. Her flesh seemed to have shrunk, so that the fine bones of her skull could be traced.

In the mid-morning, she opened her eyes and asked for a drink. Josse leapt up and summoned one of the nuns, who prepared a warm herbal draught sweetened with honey. Aeleis drank it with evident pleasure.

'Now then, Josse,' she said briskly when the nun had gone, 'I've been thinking, and trying to work out why Parsifal went to Southfire Hall. Don't tell me it was to inform my family that I was ill, because I made sure he didn't know I was sick enough to bring the relatives flocking. And don't pretend either that he'd gone on my behalf to see Father, because, as I told you, we didn't know he was failing.'

'We thought—'

'Who's we? You and Isabelle and the family?'

'Well, yes, but mainly Helewise and me.'

'She's your wife, you said?'

'Er – aye.'

'Is she nice, does she really love you and value you as she should, and would I like her? Would she like me?' she added as an afterthought.

He grinned. 'Aye to all four. Helewise and I reckoned Peter – Parsifal – had come because he wanted to see how your kin felt about you. Whether they'd welcome you if you were to come back.'

She watched him through narrowed eyes. 'You all thought he was my son,' she remarked. 'No doubt it occurred to at least one of you that he might have turned up looking for his share of the inheritance. As my legitimate son, he would have been entitled to claim his rightful due.'

'Aye, that was pointed out,' he admitted. 'Isabelle said it would have ruffled a few feathers, since Young Herbert's married a woman with a son by a previous marriage, and is in the process of adopting the boy as his son and heir.'

'Herbert's married? What's she like?'

'She was the widow of his friend William Crowburgh, and he met her when he went to offer his condolences after William died.'

Aeleis sank back on her pillows, closing her eyes. Josse wondered if she had fallen asleep – it would hardly be surprising, since all this talk must surely have tired her – and for some moments he studied her face. He could read nothing in it; it was as if she had deliberately wiped away all expression.

Then she opened her eyes again and said, as if there had been no pause, 'But *would* a son of mine have made any difference to that?' She frowned, clearly thinking hard. 'Herbert is Isabelle's son, and she's older than me, so I'd have thought that the inheritance would have gone down through him.'

Josse stared at her. *Now why didn't any of us think of that?* he wondered.

'It's irrelevant, anyway,' Aeleis said dismissively, 'because Parsifal wouldn't have gone to Southfire either to see if the family were ready to welcome back their disreputable daughter or to claim his inheritance.' Her eyes held Josse's now, the intensity of her gaze almost making him uncomfortable. 'There *is* a reason why he would have gone, but it's nothing any of you could have thought of.'

And she told him what it was.

Afterwards, when they had talked for as long as Aeleis's strength allowed, and she was lying back pale and exhausted, Josse said, 'I'm so sorry he's dead. Not only because you've lost someone you loved so much, but also because he won't have been able to achieve what he set out to do, and have the revenge he sought.'

She looked up at him, a sparkle of the old mischief in her eyes. 'Don't you be too sure about that, my dear old Josse,' she said. Then, giving him an odd look, she murmured, 'Parsifal was a very unusual man, and he once told me that the most powerful magic happens when you reflect someone's curse back upon them. They do say,' she added, her voice dropping to a confiding whisper, 'that such a spell, if it can be achieved, multiplies the power of the original curse sevenfold, although I dare say that's an exaggeration.'

Josse felt a shiver of dread. Sevenfold. 'Do you think that's true?' he whispered back. She shrugged.

She slept for a while. When she woke again, he could see she was almost at the end of her strength. Quickly he got up, about to go and fetch a nun – Sister Liese herself perhaps – but she shook her head and said softly, 'Stay.'

He sat down again, leaning close so he could hear her. Sensing a movement behind him, he glanced over his shoulder. Sister Liese stood there. Caring as she did for those in her charge, able to sense, perhaps, when the moment was approaching, she hadn't needed to be summoned. She was staring at the dying woman with eyes full of compassion.

'He *is* waiting for me,' Aeleis said dreamily, 'just as I knew he would. Oh, I can see him quite clearly now!' She gave a little gasp, and it was as if a soft light illuminated her face. 'Oh, he's holding out his arms and telling me to hurry up.' She turned to look at Josse, grasping his hand. 'Bury us together, Josse,' she said urgently. 'We don't want to be apart.'

'I will,' he promised.

She seemed to be looking at something beyond him. She began to smile – a look of such joy, such luminous, serene beauty, that he gasped. She whispered, 'Parsifal . . .' and then her breath stopped.

A little later, Sister Liese stepped up to the bed, reached down and gently closed her eyes. Aeleis was dead.

Prayers were said over her, and a sweet, soft chant, sung by four nuns, each with a lighted candle in her hand. Abbess Caliste appeared at Josse's side, wordlessly supporting him by her calm presence. Time must have passed. He found himself outside, the weak sun of the February morning shining down on the wooden bench he was sitting on, set against the infirmary wall.

And Abbess Caliste said softly, 'Sir Josse, someone's here to see you.'

He couldn't think who he could possibly want to talk to just then. For courtesy's sake, he looked up, trying to force a polite smile.

Meggie said, 'Abbess Caliste told me you were at the abbey, Father, that something sad was about to happen and you might appreciate some company.'

He found he couldn't speak. Standing up, he took her in his arms and, for quite a while, simply held her. 'Of all the people I'd have conjured up if I could,' he muttered in her ear, 'I'd have asked for you.'

'Here I am,' she whispered back.

Letting her go and wiping his eyes, he said, 'But you've got your hands full working on your new dwelling, and the forge, and that's where you should be. Doesn't Jehan need you?'

She grinned. 'I should hope so, and I'm sure he does, but he can manage without me for a few days and he understands why I want to be with you.' She reached for his hand. 'I'm so sorry she's dead,' she said, the clear brown eyes looking up into his. 'I know you cared about her.'

Slowly he shook his head. 'Meggie, I hadn't seen her for twenty years, and even that was a rare meeting. Somehow, though, that wasn't important. We shared a part of our childhood, and it seems the imprint of such experiences goes deep.'

She nodded. 'And she was your cousin, Father. It makes a difference when people are of the same blood.'

'Aye,' he agreed absently. He was thinking of something she had just said: 'A few days?'

'What?'

'You said Jehan can manage without you for a few days.'

She smiled. 'Yes, that's right. I thought I'd ride back to Southfire Hall with you. I've packed a few things in a bag and borrowed Auban. He's Jehan's horse, as you probably recall, and he's over in the stables with Arthur.'

He turned to Abbess Caliste, who had tactfully walked a few paces away to give them privacy. 'Is it all right if I leave?'

'Of course, Sir Josse. You will naturally wish to give your family news of Aeleis's death.'

And I want to be with Helewise, he could have added.

'What about her body?' he said quietly. 'She asked to be buried with Parsifal. He was her husband, and he lies dead at Southfire. He—' But explanations were beyond him.

'Don't worry,' Abbess Caliste said. 'We will keep Aeleis with us for now, and she shall lie in the crypt beneath the church, and we shall pray for her. When you and the family are ready, let us know about the burials.'

He nodded. Then Meggie took his hand again, led him across to the stables, and, very soon afterwards, they were setting off on the track through the forest and heading south.

At Southfire Hall, Helewise watched as four of the servants, under the command of Isabelle and Herbert, took a hurdle out to the steep slope on the north side of the house and carefully placed the body on it. Isabelle stepped forward with a piece of clean white linen, which she draped over the still form from head to toes. Then the servants carried Cyrille's body into the house, putting it on the bed in the room she had shared with Herbert.

Herbert, Helewise observed, was white with shock. As his wife's corpse was brought back, he had stared at it with wide, unblinking eyes, as if he couldn't believe she was dead. Did he mourn her? Helewise wondered. Was he heartbroken, or did one small part of him already rejoice because the problems that she brought into his life had died with her?

Herbert, however, was not her concern. He had his mother, his sister and the rest of his family to support him. Helewise resolved that her responsibility would be to watch over Olivar. The child had lost his mother, and, although she had of late been a distant figure, more likely to seek him out to admonish and punish him than to suggest a game or give him a hug, all the same she was his mother, and the boy must surely be shocked and grieving. *Although you did not know it, Olivar*, Helewise thought sadly, *you were just beginning to learn what your life would become as soon as your little half-brother was born.*

She would help him all she could. Allow him to talk as much as he needed to about his mother, or, if it suited him better, let him be quiet. When the news of Cyrille's death had gently been broken to him by Isabelle, he hadn't said a word. His eyes had shot briefly to Helewise, and just for an instant she had thought he looked . . . furtive, was the word that came to mind. She guessed this might very well be because he could not summon the instant storm of grief that he might well suppose was expected of him.

If he did not love his mother as he might have done, though, she reflected, then that was Cyrille's fault for not being a more affectionate and attentive parent.

She sighed. It was very likely that the little boy was still too stunned to react to the news. She would make sure she stayed close for when the time came.

She turned her mind away from the sad topic of Olivar and on to the dreadful question that the household now faced: did Cyrille somehow fall out of the window, or did she jump?

The third possibility – that somebody pushed her – was too awful to contemplate.

Yet.

After a meal had been put on the board in the Old Hall – a meal that nobody seemed to want – Philomena took Olivar and the three little girls off for a long walk along the top of the downs, remarking to Isabelle that, despite the intermittent drizzle, they were better off out of the tense, brooding atmosphere in the house. As soon as the main door of the house banged shut, Isabelle addressed the family still sitting around the table in the Old Hall.

'Is it possible,' she asked, 'to fall by accident out of the north window in the solar?'

'Are we sure that's the one she fell from?' Editha asked.

'Yes,' Isabelle replied shortly. 'She was found directly beneath it.'

'And she was in the solar yesterday afternoon,' Jenna added. 'I saw her busy at her needlework.'

Isabelle glanced at Herbert, who sat staring down at his hands folded in front of him. Then she said, 'I'm sorry if this sounds callous or disrespectful, but I think we ought to check.' Herbert's head shot up. 'You can stay here if you like,' Isabelle said gently. 'Editha, Emma, you stay with him. It's no time for any of us to be alone,' she muttered.

She swept out of the hall, Helewise and Jenna behind her. Their footsteps echoing, they marched along the passage and into the solar, crossing over to the north window. Its base was a little over waist height, and in shape it was almost square, each side about the length of a forearm and extended hand.

Helewise tried to force her head and shoulders through the opening. 'I would have difficulty squeezing out, never mind falling by accident,' she said.

'Yes, but you're broad-shouldered, and so am I,' Isabelle said. 'Jenna, you're the smallest. You try.'

Jenna looked doubtful. 'Hold on to me, then.'

Isabelle gave a short, humourless laugh. 'Naturally.'

With Isabelle and Helewise clutching very firmly on to her legs, Jenna thrust her upper body out of the window. She managed to get right through the narrow space, and then, with a cry, begged them to pull her back inside.

'You weren't in any danger!' Isabelle scolded her as she sank down against the wall. 'What do you think? Could she have fallen?'

'Not accidentally,' Jenna said. 'Although Cyrille's quite fat, she's got narrow, sloping shoulders, so she'd have got out through the window more easily than I did, but she's shorter than me, so, in order to tip over the windowsill and fall out, her feet would have had to leave the ground. She's broad across the hips, though, although I suppose if she'd already been falling, then the impetus would have carried her on.' She stared at the window. 'To over-balance, she'd have to be leaning out a long way,' she concluded.

'Could she have been trying to see something on the ground below?' Isabelle suggested.

'Yes, quite possibly,' Jenna agreed. 'She was always spying on people, looking out for tasks not being done properly, or for the children getting up to mischief, or anyone coming into the house with muddy feet. Maybe she heard, or saw, something, and leaned out to get a better look.'

'That could have caused her to fall,' Isabelle agreed, looking pleased that they had come up with a possibility. 'Couldn't it?' Her smile faded. 'Although somehow I can't quite see how,' she went on, frowning as she tried to puzzle it out, 'since what on earth could have attracted her attention down there, on a day when the weather had kept us all indoors?'

Helewise thought suddenly, *Nobody's sad.* Here were the dead woman's mother-in-law and sister-in-law, calmly discussing her terrible death as if it didn't disturb them at all. But a woman had just died; quite a young woman, even if she was older than she said. Other than the pale, shocked Herbert, no-one was really affected at all. In fact – Helewise hated to admit it, even to herself – there was a palpable sense of relief that Cyrille was no longer there.

Isabelle looked at Helewise, then at Jenna. Then she said very quietly, 'I wouldn't want to raise this possibility in front of poor Herbert, but do either of you think she could have jumped?'

'No, I don't,' Jenna said instantly. 'She was self-satisfied and self-regarding, and she set far too high a value on her own life to want to throw it away.'

Isabelle glanced furtively at Helewise, then turned to her daughter. 'Jenna, I don't think you should—'

'It's all right, Isabelle,' Helewise said. 'I confess, I was thinking much the same thing myself.'

As if encouraged by her frankness, Jenna went on, 'She thought she was indispensable, and no doubt she believed we all thought so too. She's the last person to kill herself. She'd have imagined we'd all collapse into a hopeless muddle without her telling us what to do.'

'Er, quite so,' said her mother, with another glance at Helewise.

But a thought had just occurred to Helewise, and she had barely heard Jenna's last, angry words. Was now the moment to share what she knew? Helewise decided that it was.

'There's a further reason why she would not have jumped,' she said in a low voice. 'Cyrille was pregnant.'

'*What?*' both women exclaimed incredulously. 'She was too old!' Jenna protested, and 'Are you sure, Helewise?' Isabelle demanded.

'I can't be certain, and I agree, I too would have said she was too old.' She paused, weighing her words. 'In addition, it's been my observation that women of her nervous, anxious, highly strung disposition often conceive only with great difficulty, and after many years' marriage.'

Isabelle nodded her agreement. 'Go on.'

'However,' Helewise continued, 'I observed several things: she was unwell in the mornings, suffering from fatigue and nausea. She refused hare, which it's believed can lead to a baby with a harelip if eaten in pregnancy. She stopped drinking red wine, presumably to avoid the danger of the dark crimson discolouration of the skin. And, perhaps most significant of all, I observed her once in the chapel, holding some small object suspended on a thread over her stomach, presumably to see which way it turned.'

'It's usually your own wedding ring,' Jenna said softly. 'One way means a boy, the other, a girl.'

'Cyrille knew she was carrying a boy,' Helewise said. 'That's why she changed towards Olivar: she no longer needed her first husband's son since she had convinced herself she carried Herbert's in her womb.'

'But that business with the wedding ring is by no means certain!' Isabelle protested. 'It's just superstition, surely?'

'I agree,' Helewise said. 'Obviously, however, Cyrille believed it.'

Isabelle had paled. 'If you are right, Helewise – and I am sure you are,' she added with a quick smile, 'then it is indeed highly unlikely that Cyrille would kill herself.' She shook her head. 'Oh, no. To provide a son – a true male child of my son's, and not her child by William Crowburgh, whom Herbert was to adopt – would, in Cyrille's eyes, put her in a totally unassailable position here. Wife to my father's heir, mother of his child; can you imagine what life would have been like for the rest of us, especially me?'

Helewise could imagine perfectly well, and she was quite sure Jenna could, too; perhaps even more so.

She thought she might as well put into words what all three of them were surely thinking. 'If she didn't fall or jump,' she said slowly, 'then there remains only one possibility.' Two pairs of eyes shot to meet hers. 'I hope and pray that Josse will be back soon to help us in our deliberations,' she added, her voice a little shaky, 'but, in the meantime, if you will both excuse me, I shall go to my room.'

It was a relief to be alone. She closed the door firmly behind her, lay down on the bed and began to think. If Cyrille was deliberately pushed, then who, she wondered, had a motive?

Just about everybody, she decided ruefully.

Isabelle disliked her intensely. As she had just admitted, she was faced with the prospect of being ousted from her family home and sent off to live in some specially-constructed, poky dower house because Cyrille wanted to lord it alone at Southfire. Uncle Hugh didn't trust Cyrille; he had made that very clear. Helewise didn't think it likely that he could have got out of bed, left his room and found his way to the solar at the very moment Cyrille happened to be leaning out of the window, but could he have persuaded, or paid, a loyal servant to watch, wait and do the deed for him? It couldn't be discounted.

Editha, Helewise thought, resented Cyrille's infuriating habit of insisting on *looking after* her and treating her as if she was a feeble-minded invalid. Her angry reaction to Cyrille's flapping was all too understandable; Helewise would have loathed someone patronizing and humiliating her in that way.

Jenna was furious because Cyrille kept picking on the three little girls. She clearly hated her sister-in-law's fussy, picky ways, her lack of understanding of the young, her intolerance, her constant and untrue accusations of mischief the children had allegedly done, and her labelling of the children as liars when they denied them.

Emma, Helewise considered, might well nurse a secret grudge against Cyrille because she threatened to destroy Emma's one ambition, to be a nun, by self-righteously revealing to the Hawkenlye community that Emma had kissed a young man, this rendering herself unsuitable – in Cyrille's narrow-minded, loveless view – for the life of a nun.

Was there anybody else?

Then, horrified, Helewise thought, *I have just come up with five people who profoundly disliked Cyrille.* She was shocked at herself; did she really believe that one of those good, decent people – Josse's *kin*! – was capable of pushing someone out of a window, to their certain death, just because they disliked her?

But the someone in question was Cyrille de Picus. The trouble was, Helewise thought sadly, she could believe it only too well.

SEVENTEEN

Helewise was awakened by voices coming from the Old Hall. Disorientated – she hadn't meant to fall asleep, and was amazed that she had done so – she realized she wasn't alone on the bed. Olivar lay beside her, curled up like a puppy. He, too, had been woken by the sounds outside.

Voices . . . Josse's voice . . . He was back!

She leapt off the bed, trying to straighten her headdress and smooth out the creases in her gown all at the same time, but then it didn't matter because Josse was in the doorway, still in his heavy cloak and carrying the damp, cold smell of outdoors, and she flew across the room and into his arms.

'Are you all right?' she whispered, her face pressed against his chest. In the brief glimpse she'd had of his face, he looked pale, haggard and exhausted.

'Aye,' he whispered back. 'Much has happened, and I have many things to tell you, but I'm fine. Now,' he added, squeezing her hand as he let her go.

She felt a hand grab hold of a fold of her skirt. Olivar had crept up to stand beside her, and was looking up at Josse with wide-eyed amazement. 'It's the big, strong man!' he said with happy satisfaction. 'You've come back.'

Josse crouched down to him. 'Aye,' he agreed. He seemed at a loss as to what to say next. Someone must already have told him about Cyrille's death, Helewise thought, remembering those voices out in the hall, and presumably he was wondering what you said to a child of six whose mother had just died.

But then Josse said, 'I've brought someone to see you, Olivar. She's heard all about you, and she's looking forward to meeting you.'

Both Olivar and Helewise craned to see round Josse's bulky shape and into the passage. To Helewise's delight, Meggie stood there. She looked at Helewise briefly, and Helewise had the sudden, irrational thought: Meggie will help. The two women exchanged a deeply affectionate smile. Then Meggie knelt down beside Josse and said solemnly to Olivar, 'I've just ridden here on a large, friendly horse called Auban. He's very tired, and also really hungry, so would you like to come out to the stables with me to look after him?'

Olivar nodded eagerly. 'Can I get his feed ready? I know how to, she showed me.' He jerked his head towards Helewise.

'Oh, I was hoping you'd offer,' Meggie said with relief. 'I have no idea where everything's kept, since I've only just arrived, and now I won't need to ask. Come on, Olivar.'

Helewise and Josse watched them hurry away. 'There are grooms and stable lads out there to see to the horses,' Helewise murmured.

Josse sighed. 'Aye, I know. But they've just told me about Cyrille, and Meggie must have realized I need to speak to you alone.'

'She was found beneath the solar window,' Helewise said neutrally, 'and her body discovered on the edge of the flooded stream, although she was soaked through and it was quite clear she'd been under the water.'

Josse looked intently at her. Then – and it struck her as a strange question – he said, 'Are you sure the fall killed her and that she didn't drown?'

Taken by surprise, she said, 'I don't know.' She thought about it. 'Surely it must have been the fall. It's such a long drop.' She found she couldn't bear to dwell on it. 'Why do you ask that? Have you discovered something?'

'Aye, I have, although how it relates to what's just happened here, I can't begin to imagine.' He smiled at her. 'I was hoping you would have made a few discoveries of your own while I've been gone.'

'Oh, I have,' she said fervently. He guided her back inside the room and closed the door. 'But, Josse, shouldn't we wait till the family is gathered together? These matters are their concern far more than ours.'

'Aye, they are.' He sat down heavily on the bed and pulled off his boots. 'All the same, my instincts tell me that you and I should share what we know just with each other first. Will you agree to that?' He looked anxiously up at her.

She went to sit beside him, taking his hand. 'Yes.' There was nothing she'd welcome more, she reflected, than a quiet talk with Josse.

'Shall I start?' he asked.

'Go ahead.'

Some time later, Helewise sat frowning in concentration as she tried to absorb all that Josse had just said. She was so sorry to hear that Aeleis was dead. She had hoped very much to meet Josse's favourite cousin. As for Josse, she knew now why he had looked as he did when he came into the room. But it wasn't the time to dwell on that still-raw grief.

'So he wasn't Aeleis's son but her husband,' she said wonderingly. 'Oh, Josse, she was *old* enough to be his mother!'

'He wasn't as young as we imagined,' Josse replied. He smiled. 'Certainly, he wasn't the nineteen-year-old you thought he might be.'

'I always was a bit dubious,' she agreed. 'But you must admit, it was very difficult to work out *how* old he was, under all that damage to his poor face.'

'He was eighteen when he met Aeleis; old enough to know his own mind, and—'

'He was *thirty-eight*?' Helewise interrupted. 'Oh, surely not!'

Josse laughed. 'No, of course not! Think, Helewise: we conjectured that he'd have had to be only nineteen or so when we believed he was her son, because the year after I'd seen her at Yule was the first in which she could have conceived him. Only he wasn't her son but her husband, so that timescale becomes irrelevant. Do you see?'

She nodded slowly. 'Yes, I do. How long were they together?'

'I don't believe she told me,' he replied. 'She just said they were happier than anyone had the right to expect, or some such phrase.'

'They were lucky,' she murmured.

Josse broke the brief, reflective silence. 'She wants them to be buried together. Abbess Caliste promised to look after the – to look after Aeleis until the family have decided where that should be.'

'Peter's – that is, Parsifal's body has been moved down into the undercroft,' she said. 'Isabelle ordered that Cyrille be put in the chapel.' She glanced at him. 'Both the undercroft and the chapel are cold, and the weather is warmer than it has been,' she added. There was no need for further explanation.

'So,' he said heavily, 'what about Cyrille?'

Helewise stood up. 'Come with me, and I'll show you what I've been doing.'

She took him first to the chapel. He spared a quick glance for the shrouded body before the altar, then turned away and followed her. It was only with great difficulty that he managed to squeeze through the little gap beside the pillar in the north-east corner, but, once they were down among the foundations of Southfire, he admitted it was well worth the effort. She watched as, with delight in his face, he revisited his childhood playground. Then – for she had not brought him here to indulge in nostalgia – she showed him the other discoveries she had made beneath the ground, finishing in the undercroft beneath the Old Hall. They paused, standing silently side by side, to pay their respects to the body lying there. Josse went up to the bier, briefly putting his hand on the dome of the head. He murmured something, but Helewise couldn't make out the words.

A little later, pausing together in the passage leading past the family's quarters in the first extension, he turned to her. 'How on earth did you discover that secret passage?'

'I knew it had to be there,' she said. They heard voices, quite near at hand: it sounded like Philomena and the little girls. 'Not here,' Helewise whispered. 'Let's find somewhere we won't be overheard.'

He looked aghast. 'Not back the way we came?'

'No, dear Josse, I won't make you force yourself through that tiny gap in the chapel wall again!'

They hurried back to their room. 'You see,' she said even as he was closing the door, 'there were two occasions when someone just seemed to vanish. The first time was when we heard someone outside this room, when you told Isabelle we thought Peter Southey was Aeleis's son, and the second was when I encountered Olivar's monster.'

'And, being the logical and down-to-earth woman that you

are, you realized nobody can disappear, there are no such things as monsters, and so you went looking for another explanation,' he said approvingly.

'Well, it wasn't all that clever,' she admitted. 'You'd already told me there was a network of crypts and passages down below the house, and it seemed the obvious place to search. Now we've discovered for ourselves that it's easy to move from one part of the house to another without being seen.'

'So, now all we have to work out is who needs to do so, and why.'

She hesitated. 'I think I know that, too.'

They waited until after the family had finished supper before telling them. Josse realized he felt very nervous. He had said firmly to Helewise that he should be the one to reveal what the two of them had worked out, but, now that the moment was at hand, he was very reluctant to start.

Despite all that had happened, the mood in the Old Hall was serene. All the family were there except for the children, who had been put to bed, and Emma, who had retired with a headache. Looking round at the faces, Josse couldn't see any signs of profound grief for the woman who no longer sat in her accustomed place. Herbert was very quiet; he had barely said a word all evening. He was pale, and clearly suffering, but once or twice Josse had caught a hint of something in his expression that could almost have been relief.

Meggie sat beside Isabelle, and it warmed his heart to see his daughter and his cousin with their heads together, talking as if they had known each other all their lives. He would tell Isabelle about—

But he didn't finish the thought. Helewise jabbed him in the ribs with her elbow and hissed, 'Time to start!'

Josse got to his feet, cleared his throat and said, 'When Meggie and I got here earlier this evening, I promised I would tell you what I have found out. Since then I've had a chance to speak to Helewise, and between us we believe we have a version of what may be the truth. If I may, I will share it with you all.'

His family sat staring up expectantly. He had no choice but to begin.

'When the man we knew as Peter Southey was brought to the house we realized he must know Aeleis, because he had her precious Queen Eleanor chess piece, and she would never have given it away to anyone she didn't love very deeply. We wondered if he was her son, and, carelessly, we allowed someone to over-hear our speculations.' He paused, staring at Herbert. This part was going to be difficult. 'We believe it's possible that this someone was driven to an act of violence. Someone had staked a lot on what they believed would be the line of inheritance, and, on finding out that there was another claimant – a legitimate son born to Aeleis of whom nobody had previously been aware – this person acted in the only way they could to safeguard the present arrangement.'

Again, he stopped, taking a moment to prepare himself. 'Peter Southey wasn't Aeleis's son but her husband,' he said. 'He was killed – and aye, I'm afraid he *was* killed –' there had been several gasps – 'there is no doubt of that. He was murdered to get him out of the way; to stop him claiming what his killer desired.'

'But *how* was he killed?' Isabelle said, her voice choked with emotion.

'A pillow, or cushion, was put over his face while he lay deeply asleep,' Josse replied.

Her hands flew to cover her mouth. 'I gave him the sleeping draught!'

'Aye, for a very good reason,' Josse said instantly. 'His death is no fault of yours, Isabelle.'

'How do you know this?' Herbert asked shakily.

'It was his habit to press Queen Eleanor against his lips,' Josse said gently. 'He must have gone to sleep like that, and, when the pillow smothered him, the chess piece was pressed into his flesh, cutting his lip and bruising his chin. It's been checked,' he said, raising his voice against the outburst of objections, 'and there is no mistake. Furthermore, there was a small piece of fluff attached to Queen Eleanor when I found her under Peter's bed, and we now know where it came from.'

'Where?' Isabelle demanded.

He held up his hand. 'I will tell you very soon,' he said. 'First, we need to speak of Olivar's night terrors, and what – or, rather, who – caused them, and why we believe this person was driven to act so cruelly.'

'Is it – is it the same person?' Jenna asked, as if she couldn't bear to think two people capable of such acts could be present under Southfire's roof.

'Aye,' Josse said gently. 'Driven by one of the oldest instincts: the desire to protect an unborn child.'

Herbert shot to his feet. 'You're speaking of Cyrille, aren't you?' he cried. 'It's Cyrille you mean when you say all that stuff about not wanting anyone to interfere with the inheritance, because it'll come to me, and then to Olivar, once he's legally my ward. But she's not – she wasn't pregnant, Josse! She *wasn't*! I was her husband! Don't you think I would know?'

He stood panting with his hands resting on the table, supporting him.

'I think she was, Herbert,' Helewise said calmly. 'There were many little things she did that implied she was suffering the early effects of pregnancy, and taking the appropriate care to protect herself and the baby.'

'But – but she'd have *said*!' Herbert whispered, although his voice held less conviction now.

'Perhaps she was waiting to be absolutely sure before she told you,' Helewise suggested kindly. 'She wouldn't have wanted you to face the disappointment if she was wrong.'

Herbert sank back into his seat. 'I thought she was too old,' he said. Only desperation, Josse thought, aching for him, could have wrung that revealing confession out of him.

There was a short, awkward silence. Then Meggie spoke. 'If it would be appropriate,' she said diffidently, 'I could look at the lady. I'm a healer,' she added, 'and I am experienced in caring for pregnant women.' She turned to Herbert. 'I will treat her with the utmost respect,' she said earnestly.

Herbert stared at her for a moment. Then, waving a hand, he said, 'Oh, do what you like.' Then he stood up again and strode out of the hall.

Meggie looked at Josse, then at Isabelle. 'I think that's a good idea,' Isabelle said firmly. She got up. 'Come with me, Meggie. Everyone else, stay here. This is not a matter requiring witnesses.'

They were not gone for long. Quite soon, their footsteps could be heard coming back from the chapel. Josse glanced at Helewise. She looked anxious; nervous, even. With good reason, he reflected. This was her theory, after all.

Isabelle and Meggie sat down. Meggie looked up, around the intent faces. 'She wasn't pregnant,' she said, her voice low but clear.

'Then why would she—' Jenna began.

Isabelle held up her hand for silence.

'She was probably too old to conceive,' Meggie went on, 'and it's possible she confused the symptoms of the time of change in a woman's life with those of pregnancy. She certainly wouldn't be the first to do that.' She paused. 'There's something else, I'm afraid.'

Josse stared at her. What could be coming? He shot a glance at Isabelle, who was also staring at Meggie as if this was unexpected for her, too.

'Go on, Meggie,' Josse said.

Meggie looked at him, and he saw from her face that she was both embarrassed and distressed. 'I'm really sorry to have to say this, because I realize it's not what you all thought, and what you'd been told, but, all the same, it's true and there's absolutely no doubt.' She seemed to brace herself, then said, 'The woman lying dead in the chapel there has never borne a child.'

There was a stunned stillness in the Old Hall. Nobody seemed to know what to say. Helewise, watching Josse, thought he looked guilty, as if afraid that it was his determination to discover what had happened to Aeleis that had brought all this disruption, distress and tragedy. *It isn't your fault, dear heart*, she said silently to him.

Then, breaking the mood, there came the sound of footsteps. Two pairs: one firm and steady, the other, a dragging shuffle. Several pairs of eyes turned to the doorway leading to the family's quarters in the original extension, where, presently, Herbert appeared, his grandfather holding on to his arm and propping himself up with a stick held firmly in his other hand.

'Father!' Isabelle leapt to her feet. 'What are you doing out of bed?' She rounded on her son. 'And Herbert, you should know better than to risk him damaging his health and injuring himself – what were you *thinking* of?'

'Leave him be, daughter,' Hugh said, with a note of command in his voice. 'You, what's your name, Josse, give me a chair!'

Hastily Josse leapt up and, between them, he and Herbert installed Hugh in the seat he had just vacated.

Isabelle, still sending fuming glances at both Herbert and Hugh, stood impatiently tapping her foot.

'Well, this is nice!' Hugh said, staring round at his assembled family with a smile. 'I really should come along to the Old Hall more often. I can already feel it doing me good.' Carefully he laid his stick down beside his chair then, folding his hands, rested them on the table. 'My mind is clearer tonight than it has been for a long time,' he went on, 'although –' he glanced compassionately at Herbert – 'this may well be because this young man's distress touched me deeply, as did the fact that he chose to come to me for comfort.' He paused. 'Not quite so far into my dotage as you all thought, eh?'

'Father, that's not fair!' Editha protested. 'We've only treated you like a confused and forgetful old man because that's what you've been, for weeks and months!' She was almost in tears. Getting up, she ran to Hugh and took his hand. 'It's wonderful to see you back in your rightful place, and I don't know how you could even *think* we wouldn't all be delighted!'

'Peace, Editha,' Hugh said, patting her hand. 'I dare say you're right. I can't seem to tell – for a long time it's as if I was seeing you all through a darkness, a shadow, but now, all at once, it's gone.' His eyes roamed over his kinsmen and women, over his own hall, with an expression of wonder. Then, staring straight at Josse, he said, 'I gather you have been making some discoveries, nephew.'

'Er – aye, I—'

'Don't bother, Young Herbert here has already told me,' Hugh said. He turned to Meggie. 'You must be Josse's daughter, since yours is the only face I don't know.'

'I am,' Meggie agreed.

'And the lady wasn't pregnant, was she?' Hugh went on remorselessly.

Meggie met his hard eyes. 'No.'

'And I will hazard a guess that she had never before had a child.'

Meggie looked surprised. 'You are quite right.'

'How did you know?' Herbert demanded.

'What *is* all this?' Isabelle cried, loudly and angrily. 'Father, you must explain!'

'*Be quiet!*' Hugh roared. Silence fell. 'I have been wandering in my mind, as you are no doubt all aware, but there has been one thing that has haunted me all this time, so that, even when I permitted myself to be treated like a dying man, petted, pandered to and patronized, yet always something kept nagging at me. Something I knew it was up to me to put right.'

An image flashed into Josse's head: Uncle Hugh, very distressed, struggling to get out of bed, calling for his horse and saying, *I have to see to this and try to sort it out, for it's all a muddle and I don't understand.*

'I will tell you what it was, for, now that I appear to be in my right mind again, all is perfectly clear.' Hugh turned to Herbert. 'I'm sorry, my lad, for this will pain you, but your late wife misled you. She told you – or rather, let us be kind and say she allowed you to believe – that Olivar was her son; hers and William's.'

'Yes, because that's—'

'The truth?' Hugh interrupted him. 'No, Herbert, I'm afraid it isn't. William Crowburgh was married before, you see, to a very lovely woman whose name was Marthe de Withan. She bore William a son, but, very sadly and to William's great grief, she never fully recovered from the birth and she died a couple of years later.'

Herbert's face worked with emotion. 'It's a lie!' he shouted. 'She wouldn't have pretended Olivar was hers if he wasn't! You're mistaken, Grandfather, you're thinking of someone else and you've become confused again, and—'

'Do not treat me like an imbecile!' Hugh shouted. Then, more kindly, 'Herbert, you must face the truth. Besides the fact that Meggie here has just confirmed what I'm telling you, you are forgetting that William Crowburgh's late father was my close friend.' He paused. Then, touching Herbert's hand with an expression of deep tenderness, he said softly, 'Lad, I went to both the wedding and the baptism.'

Herbert looked imploringly at him. 'Didn't you also go to William's wedding to Cyrille?'

'No, Herbert. Harold de Crowburgh was dead by then, and I had lost touch with the younger family.'

Herbert sank down on to a seat. 'She—' He shook his head, a bemused expression on his face. 'Why did she lie?' he whispered. 'Surely she knew I'd fallen in love with her? It didn't matter to me one bit if Olivar wasn't her son – it was her I wanted.'

Nobody spoke. Josse, looking at Helewise's eyes on Herbert, guessed she wanted to go to him, to try to find words of comfort. But he didn't think there were any. As if Hugh, too, felt Herbert's pain and wanted to alleviate it, he reached out for his grandson's hand.

'I think that's enough, for now,' he said quietly. 'Take me back to bed, please, Herbert. I'm very tired.'

Josse and Herbert got him to his feet, and, all but carrying him, got him to his room. They helped him into his bed, where he lay back against the pillows with obvious relief. Presently Isabelle brought a soothing draught. 'Go,' she said to Josse and Herbert. 'I'll sit with him until he sleeps.'

'Why did Cyrille lie?' Josse demanded. He and Helewise were back in their own room – Isabelle had found Meggie a bed in a small room along the passage – and he was pacing to and fro.

'I would imagine, because she thought Herbert would be more likely both to marry her, and to adopt Olivar, if he believed the boy was her own son,' Helewise said. 'As it is – as it was, I suppose I should say – Olivar has no connection with Herbert at all, being neither his own nor his late wife's true child.'

'He's his old friend's child,' Josse said quietly. 'Knowing Herbert, I think that will matter rather a lot.'

'That's what Uncle Hugh kept trying to say!' Helewise exclaimed. 'When we thought he was saying *martyr*, he was actually saying *Marthe*.'

Josse grinned. 'I always thought it highly unlikely that he'd had a late conversion to religious fanaticism.' He looked at Helewise, an expression that was almost furtive in his eyes. 'I probably shouldn't say this, but I can't help being very pleased that Olivar isn't Cyrille's child. Hugh said his real mother was a lovely woman, and Cyrille—'

'Cyrille wasn't,' Helewise finished for him. It seemed to be the least unkind thing she could think of to say.

EIGHTEEN

Josse was awake very early the next morning, the one thought going round and round in his head making it impossible to sleep any more. As the welcome daylight paled the sky, he got out of bed, put on his outer garments, picked up his boots and tiptoed out of the room. He peered into the little place where Meggie had slept, but the bed had been tidied away and she wasn't there.

He found her in the Old Hall, sitting alone beside the great hearth, cross-legged on the floor with her eyes closed. He waited. Presently she opened her eyes, looked at him and said, 'There is such a sense of relief in this house, Father, that I should think even you can feel it.' She was smiling, as if wanting to make sure he knew she was teasing.

'Oh, I can,' he assured her. 'What strikes me as sad is that nobody's grieving for her.'

'For – yes, I see what you mean.' She hesitated. 'Actually, I meant the house itself is relieved, not the people in it.' Before he had time to comment, she hurried on, 'I don't know how Herbert feels. He has shut himself away, perhaps because he is trying to cope with overwhelming sorrow. As for everyone else . . .'

She didn't need to complete the observation.

After a moment, he said, 'It may surprise you, but in fact I know exactly what you mean about the house, because I've been coming here since I was a boy and I've long been aware that it wasn't quite like other houses.' He sought the right words. 'I think it's precisely *because* I first came here when I was too young to question it, but I've always felt its spirit very powerfully.' He stopped, embarrassed.

'I'm so glad,' she said. 'To me, it simply shouts out, and it's not only powerful but undoubtedly benign. Protective of its own,' she added thoughtfully. She shot him a questioning look.

'Er – aye,' he agreed. Then – for talking about such matters made him awkward – he said, 'Meggie, I would like you to do something for me, if you will.'

'Anything within my ability.' She stood up, a single easy, graceful movement.

'I'm afraid it involves going back to the body in the chapel.'

'I don't mind bodies, Father.'

He nodded. 'Come on, then.'

They stood either side of the corpse. Josse had folded back the linen sheet to waist level. Silently he watched as Meggie went about her task. After only a short time, she said, 'She has breathed in water. Her nose and her throat are saturated.'

'Does that—'

Meggie held up a hand and shook her head, indicating she wasn't ready to say any more yet. He watched as she worked on, checking in the ears, feeling all over the head. At one point, she laid the flats of both her hands on the chest, steadily increasing the pressure until she was leaning down with almost all her weight. A trickle of water and some regurgitated food trickled out of the body's partly open mouth.

Meggie nodded, then carefully rearranged the disturbed garments, pulled the sheet up over the face and, stepping away from the trestle, said, 'The fall didn't kill her, or, at least, not straight away. She had time to draw several breaths, and, as far as I can tell, she took in water until she could no longer breathe.'

'She drowned?' He had to hear her say it.

'Yes, Father.'

He went over to her and gave her a swift hug. 'Thank you. I have to go – there is something I must check.'

'Are you going outside?'

'Aye.'

She grinned. 'I'll come with you. Some good, fresh air is exactly what I need.'

He led the way out of the main door, through the gates and round beneath the front wall of the house. 'Be careful here,' he warned as they negotiated the narrow gap between the wall and the start of the steep slope that fell away to the valley. 'It's slippery, after all the snow.'

They went on, placing their feet carefully and sometimes

holding hands, until they were standing directly beneath the north wall of the solar. Then, turning sideways to the sloping ground, they edged their way downwards.

'Here,' Josse said, stopping. 'She was lying here, with her feet pointing towards the valley.'

Meggie took in the scene. 'From the evidence of the mud and the flattened grass, it looks as if the highest level that the stream waters reached was here.' She took a pace back up the slope.

'Aye,' he agreed. He was crouched down, studying the place where Cyrille had lain, staring intently at the ground.

'Father.'

'Hmm?' He didn't look up.

'*Father.*'

'What is it?'

'Come and look at this.'

There was something in her voice – some altered tone – that made him instantly comply. He scrambled up and went to stand beside her. Silently she pointed.

In the mud some two paces above the spot where the body landed were two clear booted footprints. They were small, no bigger than a boy's; a youth's at most.

'Do you think—?' Meggie cleared her throat and tried again. 'Did one of those who came out to bring in the body stand there?'

He shook his head. 'I don't believe these are the prints of any member of the recovery party. Whoever it was stayed still for some time,' he said. He spotted something else: over to the right of the footprints there was a narrow hole. 'Long enough to make quite deep impressions.'

'What about whoever first found her? They could have stood there trying to work out how to wade into the water and pull her out.'

'No,' he said. 'Helewise was the first to reach her, but the others weren't far behind. Apart from the fact that you and I both know Helewise wouldn't have wasted time deciding what to do but would have plunged straight in, the levels had already gone down a little by then, and Cyrille was clear of the water.'

'Then—' Again, Meggie hesitated to put her conclusion into words.

Josse did it for her. 'Somebody stood here and watched as

the waters rose up,' he said solemnly. 'He – or she – must have seen she was still alive; that, even if the fall had gravely injured her, she was still breathing.' He looked up, meeting Meggie's clear eyes. 'They left her to drown,' he murmured. 'Either she fell into the water, or else it rose up over her as she lay helpless on the grass.'

And, although he fought the memory, telling himself it could only be coincidence, he couldn't help but think of Aeleis, and her utter certainty that Parsifal de Chanteloup was perfectly capable of turning the curse that led to his beloved wife's death against its perpetrator.

Of making that perpetrator die just as Aeleis had done: with her lungs slowly filling with liquid until she could no longer draw breath.

But what did Cyrille de Picus have to do with Aeleis and Parsifal? Josse was fuming silently, frustrated. Oh, he could hazard a guess, but guessing was easy.

He had to find proof.

Helewise, waking to find herself alone, had swiftly dressed and gone out to greet the morning. She had a task to perform; one she didn't really want to do. *Better get on with it, then*, she told herself.

First she crept along into the heart of the family's quarters to the little open hall where Cyrille's work-basket had been put. There was the cushion on which she'd been working, and there, as Helewise had suspected, was the pulled, amber-coloured thread of wool that exactly matched the piece of fluffy fibre that Josse found adhering to Queen Eleanor.

Then she went back to the other side of the house.

She heard voices coming from the solar, and hurried along to see who it was. Editha sat on the seat beneath the south-facing window, with Jenna beside her and Emma sitting at her feet. All three looked up as Helewise approached.

'We were just remarking,' Editha said after they had exchanged greetings, 'that this lovely, light room will now serve the purpose for which Father had it built, now that—'

'*Editha!*' Jenna hissed, with a glance at Helewise.

Editha ignored her. 'Now that Cyrille is dead,' she went on

firmly. 'Jenna, it's no good pretending, and I for one don't intend to. I won't be as unchristian and unforgiving as to say I'm relieved she's dead, but she is, and, as far as we can tell, it was a terrible accident, so nobody has anything to feel guilty about.' A smile spread across her face. 'But we can use this room now, all of us, without the fear of being accosted by Cyrille as soon as we come in and, for politeness's sake, either joining in with whatever mindlessly mundane activity she's doing or having to listen to her ceaseless chatter.'

'I had noticed,' Helewise said carefully, 'that, more often than not, Cyrille would be in here by herself.'

'Yes, she was,' Emma agreed.

'Was she—' Oh, this was difficult. 'Was she on her own the day she fell?'

Jenna's eyes shot to meet hers. 'She was indeed,' she said coolly. 'If you're wondering if one of us could have crept up behind her and given her a push, we didn't.'

'I wasn't—'

'Yes, you were,' Editha said calmly, 'but don't worry, it's something that has already occurred to all of us, too.' She smiled. 'The only people whose whereabouts can't be verified by at least one witness are you and Isabelle, Helewise. So, you see, we might ask you the same question: did *you* push her?'

'No,' Helewise said.

'And neither did my mother,' Jenna said angrily.

There was an embarrassed silence.

'Since we have broached the subject,' Helewise said eventually, 'why don't we discuss it openly? Not in an accusing manner, but simply to demonstrate that no malice was done?'

'I think that's a good idea,' Editha said. 'So: Philomena and Emma were setting out the children's needlework, which they were going to get on with when they came back inside. They were playing—'

'Yes, I heard them,' Helewise interrupted, remembering. 'I was resting in my room, and I heard them giggling.'

'Jenna was with Father,' Editha continued, 'and you said, Jenna, that Agnes helped you bathe him?'

'Yes,' Jenna said curtly.

'Were you with him all that afternoon?' Helewise asked.

'No, we left him to sleep. But you're surely not suggesting he got out of bed, shuffled along to the solar, just happened to find Cyrille leaning out of the north window and gave her a shove?'

Helewise lifted her chin. Jenna's antipathy was affecting her. 'I'd have said it was unlikely until last night,' she replied. 'Now, we do at least realize he's capable of doing so.'

'He only managed to walk with Herbert's help, and propping himself up with his stick!' Jenna protested.

'But he might not be as weak as he's let us think,' Editha said with a frown, 'especially if he wanted us to believe him incapable of – er, of that.'

Emma was shaking her head. 'Great-grandfather Hugh wouldn't kill anybody,' she said in a tremulous whisper. 'He *wouldn't*!' she repeated, when nobody commented.

Helewise looked at her compassionately. 'People are capable of extreme acts when they feel there has been a grave injustice, or when their loved ones are threatened,' she said.

'But all he's accused her of is lying about being Olivar's mother!' Emma cried.

Helewise looked at Editha, then at Jenna. Like her, they knew; they had been in the Old Hall last night, when Emma had gone to bed. Would it be right to tell her now?

I don't care, she thought. 'Emma,' she began, turning back to the young woman, 'I'm afraid Cyrille was guilty of rather more than that. It can't be proved without any doubt, but it appears it was she who smothered Peter Southey, since the piece of fluff found on the chess piece matches one of the wools in the needle-point cushion she had just completed. But, perhaps even more unforgivable, she was trying to drive Olivar out of his mind by dressing up as some fearful fiend, or monster, and creeping into his room in the night.'

Emma was white-faced and shaking her head in disbelief. 'Why would she do something so horrible?' she whispered. 'To her own little boy! *Oh!*'

'But he wasn't her own,' Helewise said. 'As it appears you already know, that, too, was established last night, and it is, I believe, why she had to get rid of him. She married Herbert pretending to be Olivar's mother, and then presumably persuaded him that it would be best if he adopted the boy as his ward and, naturally, also his heir. She did that, I would guess, to ensure the security of her own position; she was Olivar's mother, he was the son and heir. But then she discovered she was pregnant; or, rather, she believed she was. And, with a true son of hers and Herbert's in her belly – she would have convinced herself it was a boy – suddenly Olivar was redundant.'

The harsh, cruel word echoed through the room.

'*Redundant*,' Editha whispered. 'What a thing to say about a child.'

'I'm sorry if it offends you, but—' Helewise began.

Editha looked at her. 'Oh, it doesn't offend me,' she said softly. 'It's exactly how Cyrille would have seen it.'

Editha and Jenna were talking quietly to Emma, comforting her, but Helewise barely heard. She was thinking about Hugh, and the startling return to sense and sanity, if not to physical strength, that he had demonstrated the previous evening.

She was thinking, too, about coincidence: the coincidence of his recovering his memory – and one particular, very relevant and highly condemning memory – a little over a day after Cyrille's death.

What she was trying very hard not to think was that, in an extraordinary way, Cyrille de Picus had been exerting some sort of power over the old man, ensuring that his fog of confusion steadily increased so that he would never manage to tell his family the damning fact he knew about her: that she wasn't Olivar's mother and had lied to them all.

But of course she wasn't doing that, Helewise told herself firmly. People couldn't control others in that way. Such a thing wasn't possible.

Was it?

Josse and Meggie were back at the gates, about to go through into the courtyard. But then Josse stopped, and Meggie did too.

'Go on in,' he said to her.

'Are you not coming?'

'No. There's something I want to check.'

'Shall I come?'

He thought about it. 'No, thank you. I'm better alone. I have to work out something in my mind.'

'Very well.' She went on into the yard.

'Will you tell Helewise I've gone to see Gregory?' he called after her.

'Gregory.'

'Aye. She'll know who I mean and where I've gone.'

Meggie raised her hand in acknowledgement and went up the steps to the door.

Josse strode on down the path, soon meeting the track that wound its way down the long slope towards Lewes. He couldn't get the image of those footprints out of his mind. When he added in the small hole in the grass beside the prints, it seemed to suggest one thing.

And there was another reason for visiting Gregory. Hadn't he promised to try to recall why the name Cyrille de Picus was familiar, and what it had to do with some distressing event? *It was something to do with a marriage or a betrothal*, Gregory said, *and I have the feeling that something very bad happened . . .*

As he had hoped, Gregory was on watch in his little booth beside the gate. He greeted Josse's approach with a friendly wave.

'I'm glad you came by,' he called out as Josse walked up to him. 'I've remembered, see.' Josse's spirits rose hopefully. 'I was going to come up to Southfire and seek you out,' Gregory continued before Josse could ask him to elucidate, 'but you know how it is when you're busy, you're trying to attend to half a dozen things all at once, and of late I've been fair rushed off my feet.'

'But you've got something to tell me?'

'Yes, yes, I just said so!' He shook his head in mock-reproof. 'Come on in and sit with me in my guard house – well, that's what the holy brethren call it, but it's just a hut, really.' He ushered Josse inside, pulling up a stool for him. 'It's not much, but we'll be out of the wind.' He glanced back out through the door and, verifying that no black-robed figures were watching, drew out a flask from a little shelf set low down in the wall. 'Drop of something to warm the blood?'

Josse accepted. The fire water almost took his throat out.

'Powerful stuff,' Gregory observed, taking a much larger swig and smacking his lips. Then, without preamble, he said,

'I knew I recognized the name, and it's all come back to me. Cyrille de Picus was betrothed to a young man – quite a bit younger than her, truth to tell, because she was hanging on hand a bit and well past the age when a pretty little girl gets snapped up by some keen lad of a suitor. Anyway, the man wouldn't have her – didn't even agree to meet her – and the gossips at the time said it was because he was already wildly in love with someone else, someone even older than Cyrille, if you'd credit that!' Gregory sat back, a satisfied smile on his face.

Aye, I can credit it only too well, Josse thought sadly.

'Anyway,' Gregory went on, 'she – Cyrille – took it very hard. Oh, of course it was very humiliating for her to be rejected in favour of someone else, but there was no need for her to do what she did.'

'What did she do?'

'Ah, now, sir, this is only rumour, you know, and I'm quite certain the lady did nothing of the kind. I'm the last man on God's good earth to go placing any credence in malicious gossip.' He sniffed, nose in the air, assuming the demeanour of someone who has just been unfairly accused.

'Aye, I'm sure you are,' Josse said, trying to hide his impatience. 'But why not tell me the rumour anyway?'

As if he couldn't wait to repeat it, and had only needed to be persuaded, instantly Gregory leaned closer and said, 'They say she was quite determined, and managed to find out eventually where her rival lived. She made a dolly, see, in the likeness of the lady who'd taken away her sweetheart – not that there could have been any of *that* between Cyrille and the young man, seeing as they never even met – and she *put a curse on the lady*!' He didn't so much speak the last six words as mouth them. 'That doll was found head-down in a bucket of water, so the story goes, because she – Cyrille – wanted her to die by drowning.' He paused dramatically. 'Goes without saying that I don't believe a word of it,' he said self-righteously. 'Far as I know, the lady's alive and well, and I pray the good Lord above will keep her that way.'

I only wish you were right, Josse thought sadly.

Gregory was muttering something about hoping Josse wouldn't

think the less of him for repeating such a scurrilous tale, and being sure Josse would appreciate that it would avoid distress if he were to refrain from telling any of the good monks what he'd just been told, but Josse shut him out.

He was reflecting on what struck him as a great irony: Cyrille didn't kill Peter Southey because she knew he was really Parsifal de Chanteloup, the man she was meant to marry and who rejected her. She couldn't have done so, because she didn't even recognize him. She killed him in the mistaken belief that he was Aeleis's son and would do the child she thought she was carrying out of the inheritance.

Parsifal, on the other hand, Josse's sad thought went on, had come for Cyrille. Somehow he had discovered where she was – perhaps a friend, or a friend of a friend, had mentioned having attended the marriage of Aeleis's nephew Herbert to the widow of William Crowburgh, and mentioned the bride's name. Perhaps Parsifal had been searching for her all this time, and finally been successful. Nobody would ever know, now, and how he had located Cyrille didn't really matter. But, blaming her as he did for Aeleis's sickness, because he believed she had put a curse on her, he would not have given up until he found her.

Had he set out to confront her, accuse her or kill her? Josse wondered. Surely not to kill her, for, when Parsifal had left Aeleis in the care of the Hawkenlye nuns, he had had no suspicion that she was going to die: Aeleis had made sure of that. Perhaps, Josse thought with a shiver, he simply came to do exactly what Aeleis said he'd do: conjure up an invisible reflecting glass, hold it up against the curse that Cyrille placed on Aeleis, and turn it back sevenfold on the originator.

Cyrille drowned, Josse mused. Perhaps Parsifal succeeded . . .

He couldn't bear to dwell on that. Instead, he turned his mind to the other reason he had come to the priory.

Breaking into Gregory's interminable chatter, he said, 'How's the leper getting on? Has he recovered a little strength under the monks' care?'

Gregory laughed. 'Oh, him! He's gone.'

'Gone? But I thought lepers were always detained, and—'

'Come with me, and you'll find out,' Gregory said.

He led the way over to the infirmary. The black-clad infirmarian whom Josse had seen on his previous visit looked up, recognized him and, smiling, came across to talk to him.

'I'm Brother Anselm,' he said. 'You're the man who brought the leper in to us.'

'I am,' Josse agreed. 'I hear he's left.'

Taking Josse a little apart, away from the many patients lying in their cots and straining to hear, Brother Anselm went on, 'You are surprised, I expect, that we should permit a leper to leave our care and protection and allow him to go back among the general population?'

'A little, aye, although it's not for me to question what you do, and I do know the sickness isn't as readily passed on as people believe.'

'Indeed not,' the infirmarian agreed, 'although we do have a policy of keeping sufferers isolated as much as we can. But your man wasn't a leper.'

'Not – but he was missing fingers and toes!'

Brother Anselm smiled. 'Yes, but not as a result of leprosy. He'd lost his toes to frostbite, which is sadly all too common among the destitute homeless who perpetually travel our roads, out in all weather, frequently with no shelter and no fire to warm them.' He shook his head, as if despairing of the ways of the world. 'We did what we could for him. By and large, he just needed some good, nourishing food and a few sound nights' sleep. We found a pair of boy's boots that more or less fitted him to protect his feet from further damage, got the blacksmith to re-tip his staff and sent him on his way.'

'When did he leave?'

Brother Anselm looked surprised at the question, but said mildly, 'The day before yesterday, as far as I recall. He ate a good meal in the morning, then, when I came back later to see how he was, Luke told me he'd left.'

Thanking him, trying to take a very hasty leave without causing offence, finally Josse escaped.

As he trudged back up hill towards Southfire Hall and the top of the downs, Josse went over it all. He knew now the identity of Cyrille's killer, or, rather, he knew who he was, if not his name. Did he hold her down under the water? Did he do no more than stand there and watch her die?

And why did he want her dead?

Josse walked on. He had no idea where he was going, for nobody at the priory had known where the beggar was heading. He'd been seen clambering up the slope leading to the higher ground to the south-west of the town, but that was all.

He will be lurking nearby, Josse told himself. He will not be satisfied with her death; he will want someone to know why she had to die.

Hoping that he was right, and that he might be that someone who received the explanation, he went on.

Presently he came to a stand of stunted hazel trees, all bending over as if bowing before an undetectable wind. Within their shelter, his staff by his side and his legs stretched out in front of him and casually crossed, sat the beggar.

He smiled at Josse, patting the grass beside him in invitation. 'Come and join me. It's quite dry under here,' he said.

Josse sat down. 'I've just come from Lewes Priory,' he said.

'Ah,' replied the beggar.

'Before that, I stood by a dead body and saw the proof that death was brought about by drowning.'

'Indeed?' the beggar said in a tone of polite interest.

'I'm wondering,' Josse went on, 'why someone might stand beside a woman in mortal danger, and do no more than watch as the water slowly rose up her body until she drowned.'

'I could think of a few reasons,' the beggar remarked.

'He would have to hate her very much, I'm thinking.'

'Oh, yes,' the beggar agreed. 'Perhaps she had done something almost as dreadful to him, would you imagine?'

'Possibly,' Josse agreed cautiously.

'Supposing I set out a possible scenario?' the beggar suggested.

'Go on.'

'Let us say,' said the beggar, making himself more comfortable, 'that he was related to her; her uncle, perhaps, for argument's sake. Her dead father's brother, asked by her father when he died to take care of her, for the father was a poor man with little in the way of wealth or possessions to leave to his only child.'

'Very well,' Josse said.

'There they are together, the uncle and the niece,' the beggar went on. 'The uncle, although childless and unmarried himself, with no desire whatsoever for either wife or offspring, nevertheless has assumed responsibility for a niece he doesn't even like very much. The niece, however, far from being grateful, makes up her mind that the uncle is far more trouble than he's worth, and decides she will rid herself of him as quickly as she can.'

'How could she hope to do that?' Josse asked, intrigued despite himself. 'Is she not a child still?'

'Oh, no. She's a woman now.'

'But how can she throw her uncle out of his own home?'

The beggar turned to him, face drawn into lines of mock-sorrow. 'Because he's not very well, this poor uncle. He suffers from episodes of madness. When these fits are upon him, he believes that the devil takes over his body, so that the whites of his eyes darken to red as Lucifer's unholy hellfire rips through his body, and his water turns scarlet as he tries to expel it.'

The beggar's voice had risen, and a faint flush had coloured his pale cheeks. 'It sounds most distressing,' Josse said, trying to keep his tone calm, interested. 'So what did the niece do?'

'She waited until he had another fit of madness, and she locked him in his room.' Once more in control, the beggar spoke dispassionately. 'Soon he was lost within himself, helpless, and, without anyone to ensure he ate and drank, soon he became enfeebled. After many days, the niece, coming at last to see how he was, found him lying on the floor, barely able to move. By dead of night, she dragged him outside, bundled him up into a cart and took him to a run-down, out-of-the-way monastery and dumped him there.' He paused, took one or two breaths, and then, still in the same calm tone, resumed his tale.

'The monks were unsophisticated and ignorant. The care was rudimentary, ignorant and brutal, with barely anything to eat and many beatings to expel the devil. The uncle – oh, poor uncle! – was incarcerated for months, and the months grew to years, and, while he was helpless and sick, the niece made off with whatever of his wealth was portable and deserted him. She'd suffered a grave disappointment, however, that niece, because the pleasant little house she believed would be hers was only rented.' He smiled, then chuckled softly. 'Ah, how unwise it is not to ask the right questions.' He looked up. 'Where was I?'

'The uncle was shut away with the ignorant monks and the niece had run away with all his possessions,' Josse supplied promptly.

'Thank you. When the uncle was at long, long last deemed well enough to be released, he found himself homeless, penniless, friendless, without family. Still in feeble health, he had no option but to take to the road as a beggar.'

He glanced down at his hands. 'He lost some fingers and some toes because of the white freeze that eats into flesh,' he said conversationally. 'That was the first, terrible winter, before he had any idea of how to cope with destitution. People who saw him thought he had leprosy and they shunned him, shut him out, threatened him with sticks and threw stones at him to drive him away.' He sighed, and fell silent.

Josse was thinking hard. The beggar had allowed him and Helewise – and, to begin with, the monks at Lewes Priory – to believe he was a leper, he recalled, and he had a good idea why. It was because, clever man, he wanted the outside world to believe that, from then on, he would be held in isolation by the monks at the priory, and therefore nobody could possibly suspect him of having stood by and watched Cyrille die.

Was it murder? Josse wondered now. The beggar hadn't so much as touched her. Possibly, too, she was already dying as a result of that terrible fall.

Then he thought about madness. About a sort of mania that came periodically, and that made men – and women – strangers to themselves, so that they performed wild, cruel, uncharacteristic acts. Was such an affliction in the blood, so that it was likely to run through a family and appear, for example, in both an uncle and a niece?

Cyrille de Picus had killed Peter Southey, and tried to drive her little stepson out of his mind, because she wanted no other claimants to the inheritance she believed belonged to the child she thought she was carrying. Before that, she had been driven to such fury by the man who rejected her in favour of another woman that she placed a terrible curse on her rival. She was ruthless and cruel, and, when crossed, her revenge knew no limits.

Perhaps, now, Josse understood why . . .

But, on the other hand, perhaps this beggar was merely passing the time by telling him a horror story, and there wasn't a word of truth in it, and it certainly didn't describe himself or Cyrille.

Perhaps Cyrille *had* no excuse. Perhaps she was simply evil.

Time had gone by. Josse didn't know how much; he had the strangest feeling that he had just passed a period of minutes, or hours, outside normal time.

He got to his feet, and started walking slowly away from the hazel trees and back to the track.

'Goodbye,' called the beggar softly. 'Go well, Josse d'Acquin.'

Josse raised a hand in farewell.

Helewise was with the children, kneeling on the floor of the solar and trying to interest them in a game. But neither the three little girls nor Olivar wanted to play. All of them were listless, and, as the afternoon went on, increasingly distressed. Finally Helewise said, 'Something's the matter with you all, isn't it?'

Brigida looked up at her out of wide, frightened eyes. Philippa began to cry.

'It's just us here, so there's only me to hear,' Helewise went on persuasively, 'and, whatever it is you're all so worried and upset about, I'll do my best to help.'

Cecily looked at her little cousins, then at Helewise. 'Promise?'

'Promise.'

And, at last, it came out. How the girls, led by Cecily, played a trick on Cyrille, wanting to get even with her because she was so horrid to Olivar. The little girls planned it. They were going to yell up from the ground below the solar to get Cyrille's attention, then throw snowballs at her.

They positioned themselves under the west wall, where the ground was much nearer to the level of the windows. 'We could *never* have thrown a snowball right up to the north window, it's far too high!' Cecily said, an expression on her lovely little face that said, *Everyone but a silly fool would have known that!*

But Cyrille looked out of the wrong window. Not seeing anyone down there, but still hearing the children's shouts, she leaned further out. And further. And still further, until there was no going back.

Shaken, Helewise forced herself to sound calm and reassuring. 'You didn't mean her to fall,' she said very firmly. 'It was *very* naughty to scheme to throw snowballs at her, and I'm afraid I'll have to tell your mothers, girls.' Three little faces fell. 'But I will tell them how very, very sorry you all are, and say that, in my opinion, your remorse and your distress are punishment enough. Although,' she added quickly, 'your mothers may not see it that way.'

'What are you going to do with us?' Brigida piped up.

'*I* am not going to do anything,' Helewise replied. 'But I suggest *you* three go and find your mothers, tell them what you've just told me, and, in a little while, I'll go and find them and speak up for you.'

'You're not going to beat us?' Cecily asked.

'No, of course not!' Helewise exclaimed, about to laugh when she realized Cecily was in earnest. 'You don't get beaten here, do you?'

Cecily hung her head, but Brigida whispered, '*We* don't. But Olivar does. His mother beats him a lot. That's why we—' A jab in the ribs from her cousin's elbow stopped her. '*Owww!*' she yelled, scowling ferociously at Cecily.

The little girls got up and hurried away. Olivar crept closer to Helewise. She thought he was going to make some comment about the girls' confession; tell her, perhaps, that he hadn't known what they were planning.

But when eventually he spoke – in a very small voice – it was something quite different.

'I saw her fall,' he whispered.

Oh, no! 'Did you, Olivar?'

He nodded. 'I knew Cecily and the others were going to do something, but I didn't dare get involved because I was afraid of what she'd do when she found out. So I stayed in here, hiding behind the hanging over there.' He pointed to the corner of the solar. 'I was going to run away but then *She* came in and got out her sewing, and it was too late and I had to go on standing there, or else she'd have seen me coming out of my hiding place and she'd have demanded to know what I thought I was doing and I'd have told her because I always do in the end and then the girls would have been in terrible trouble too.'

The frightened, tumbling words stopped. Olivar, panting, was trembling.

'It wasn't your fault,' Helewise began, but he wasn't listening.

He looked straight up at her. 'The house didn't like her,' he said. 'I know it can't have done, because I saw what it did.' He drew a shaky breath. 'She was leaning out of the window, trying to see who was calling, and I crept out to watch. I was standing right behind her.' Briefly he shut his eyes, screwing them up tight. Then, opening them wide and staring straight into hers, he said, 'The house didn't want her here any more. It gave a sort of a shake, as if to rid itself of her, and she fell.'

Helewise couldn't speak. She wouldn't have known what to say, even if she could. Part of her was shocked to hear such an extraordinary story; one, moreover, which Olivar had told with total conviction, clearly convinced that it was what had really happened.

It can't be true, her logical mind was insisting. Houses don't have likes and dislikes! They don't shake themselves so that nasty people fall out of their windows and drown!

This one does.

Who said that? Helewise looked wildly around, but nobody was there. Belatedly realizing that she had done nothing to comfort Olivar after his painful revelation, she knelt down beside him and took him in her arms, wrapping him in an enfolding hug. Instantly he responded, clinging on to her as if he would never let go.

A small boy, she thought, who had lost his mother and then his father, and been left to the cruel, manipulative, evil vicissitudes of a woman who had tried to terrify him into madness. A child who, deprived of the love that was his right, was silently crying out for it.

Surreptitiously, Helewise wiped her eyes. In that moment, as the hot fury and the fierce, protective love soared through her, she sympathized entirely with the house.

She could cheerfully have pushed Cyrille de Picus out of a window herself.

POSTSCRIPT

Aeleis and Parsifal were to be buried side by side at Hawkenlye Abbey.

A cart had been prepared to carry Parsifal's body up from Southfire Hall. The old groom had worked hard to turn the simple conveyance into something that was suitable for its grave purpose, scrubbing the boards and laying out a bed of clean straw, and he had groomed the sturdy horse that was to pull the cart till he shone like a thoroughbred. Parsifal lay in a pale oak coffin over which had been draped a banner bearing the family's crest: 'For he was a member of this family,' Hugh had decreed, 'married as he was to my youngest daughter.' Josse and Helewise escorted the cart to the abbey, where the body would be placed beside Aeleis's until the day of the interment.

Josse and Helewise rode on home.

Hugh, Isabelle, Editha, Jenna and Emma made the journey to Hawkenlye for the burial. They had organized a means of transport for Uncle Hugh, piling a palliasse, cushions, pelts and blankets on to a wagon so that he was able to travel in a degree of comfort. For Editha, a well-padded chair had been put up on the wagon beside him. Hugh's family rode beside him, as if he were a king on a progress. They arrived at the abbey late one afternoon; the interment would be carried out the following morning.

Aeleis and Parsifal were laid to rest, side by side as Aeleis had requested, in a plot out beyond the abbey's regular graveyard, on the fringes of the forest. There was no priest to speak the words over the grave. People said, probably with justification, that there weren't any priests left in England. Abbess Caliste led a simple service, speaking eloquently and movingly of the pair's great love for each other, and a small choir of nuns sang a soft, gentle chant into the bright morning.

When it was over, Josse invited his uncle and his kinswomen

to the House in the Woods, for funeral meats, drink, and to stay for a few days to get to know his side of the family.

'Not me, nephew, thank you just the same,' Uncle Hugh said. 'I shall head back to Southfire Hall, and Editha shall come with me. I appear to be my old self again, by some miracle I don't begin to understand, but the fact remains I'm an old man, and old men need their own hearths and their own beds. One night away from home is quite enough! No offence,' he added.

Josse grinned. 'None taken. Of course, uncle. You'll be back by nightfall if you leave now.' He took his uncle's hands. 'I'll come and see you soon, I promise.'

'Good,' Hugh replied. 'Bring that lovely wife of yours.'

'I promise that, too.'

As Josse and Helewise led Isabelle, Jenna and Emma through the forest to the House in the Woods, the mood among them was bright, with a lot of chatter and even some merriment. There was a palpable sense of relief, Helewise reflected, hearing Josse laugh at some remark of Jenna's, and, as so often happens after the sad solemnity of a funeral, the living were affected by the sheer joy of being alive. From what she knew of them, Parsifal and Aeleis were unlikely to be the sort of people who would resent others' appreciation of the good things in the beautiful world they had just left behind.

Back at the house, Josse was gratified to find a generous spread laid ready, and his entire household waiting to greet the guests. Busy with making the introductions, he observed Meggie approach Isabelle, and the women exchanged a warm embrace. *I was right about those two*, he thought with a private smile. *They are going to be friends.* Then Ninian made a short speech of welcome, Geoffroi carried around a tray bearing mugs of ale, and the whole group spread out into the hall, the visitors swiftly making themselves at home.

Later, after the food had been eaten and the lively, noisy hubbub of chatter had died down a little, Isabelle beckoned to Josse and took him outside into the sunshine for a private word. She informed him tonelessly that the body of Cyrille de Picus had been quietly buried in an out-of-the-way spot where, since the imposition of the interdict, most of the dead of Lewes had apparently ended up.

'Did many attend?' Josse asked.

She shook her head. 'Jenna and I went with Herbert, and one of the monks from the priory mumbled a few words.'

'How is he?' Josse said softly. 'Herbert, I mean.'

Isabelle smiled briefly. 'Yes, Josse, I realized that.' She paused, gazing into the distance. 'I can't say,' she admitted. 'He's shaken, shocked, but some part of him is relieved. The good thing,' she hurried on, as if speaking of her son's mood distressed her, 'is that he and Olivar have grown close. Herbert looks upon the boy as his true son now, and will go ahead with making him his heir. Both of them need somebody to love, I think.' Once again hurrying away from the painful ground of deep emotion, she said, 'Herbert has explained to him that Cyrille wasn't really his mother.'

'I imagine the lad was relieved to hear that.'

'Oh, yes,' Isabelle breathed. 'Poor boy. The things she did to him . . .' She shook her head. 'Enough of that: it's over, and she's gone. Herbert has vowed to seek out Marthe de Withan's family so that Olivar can meet his true kin,' she went on in a matter-of-fact tone, 'and, with any luck, find some kindly soul who'll be able to tell him all about his real mother. My father has already started to do so,' she added, her expression softening, 'and he's the best person to begin, because he obviously thought a lot of Marthe.'

'He never let her memory die,' Josse said quietly. 'He kept on trying to say her name, even when—'

He stopped abruptly. *Even when Cyrille was doing her utmost to cloud his mind and make him forget*, he had been about to say, but there was no proof of that.

'Why did she do it?' Isabelle mused aloud. 'Oh, I don't mean why did she try to fuddle poor Father's wits, if indeed that's what she did, because that's obvious: it was to stop him revealing that she wasn't really Olivar's mother. What I want to know is, what drove her to do something so dangerous and malicious to poor Aeleis, and then put a cushion over Parsifal's face and kill him?'

Josse thought about how to reply. 'I believe,' he said slowly, 'she was motivated by a great need for security.'

'But—'

He held up his hand, and Isabelle's angry protest subsided.

'Herbert told me she came from lowly stock,' Josse continued, 'and that her life hadn't been easy. Perhaps the main attraction of marriage to Parsifal de Chanteloup wasn't so much his looks and his youth but his wealth and position.'

'*Was* he wealthy?' Isabelle demanded.

'I assume so. Aeleis implied as much, although no doubt his family cut him off without the proverbial penny when he ran off with her.' He grinned. 'I'm quite sure he thought she was worth it.'

'So am I,' Isabelle agreed loyally. 'So, go back to what you were saying about Cyrille?'

'Aye. Well, she probably thought she'd found a safe haven when William Crowburgh married her, but, it proved less secure than she'd hoped. Herbert explained that William had come to grief and was close to ruin when he died, and so, yet again, someone in whom Cyrille had placed her trust had failed her.'

'I'm sure he didn't do it just to spite her!' Isabelle exclaimed angrily.

'No, I'm sure not. And then, when she was newly widowed, with no money and the imminent prospect of losing the roof over her head—'

'Along comes my big-hearted, chivalrous son, who conveniently falls for her, marries her, and sweeps her off to live in a grand and beautiful old house, where she is called upon to do nothing more arduous than work at her needlepoint,' Isabelle finished for him.

He didn't reply. In truth, there was nothing to say. 'What *was* she, Josse?' Isabelle said in an anxious whisper. 'A witch? An evil spirit in human form?'

Josse had no answer.

'Cyrille recognized the beggar when he came to the door, of course,' Helewise said to Josse as finally, with the household and the guests having retired for the night, they sat together beside the dying fire.

'Aye,' he agreed. He had been thinking the same thing.

'What I took for horror at having a leper so close to the house,' Helewise went on, 'was in fact horror of a different sort. She recognized the uncle she had treated so badly, and instinctively she hid her face with her veil, so he wouldn't know who she was. Only he did.'

'And made up his mind to do what?' Josse asked. 'There was obviously some plan in his head, when he let us take him down to the monks at Lewes Priory.'

'Well, for one thing, nobody believed that a leper would ever be coming out again, which would have given him a perfect alibi for – er, for whatever he decided to do.'

'Aye, I worked that out, too,' Josse agreed.

She looked at him. 'You listened to him tell his story, Josse. What do you think? Did he slip out of the priory with the express intention of going back to Southfire Hall to accuse her? To *kill* her?' she added in a whisper.

'To accuse her, aye, I'll believe that,' he said. 'As for killing . . . I just don't know.'

'I think I do,' Helewise said after quite a long time. 'I think he came to seek her out and, by some stroke of fortune – I don't know if it should be called good or bad fortune – he happened upon her just after the fall. And—' She stopped.

'And, seeing her lying there, helpless, in the most perilous situation, he decided to walk away,' he finished for her.

'Yes,' she whispered. 'Oh, Josse, do you think he stood and watched? Do you think he hated her that much?'

He looked at her for a long moment. The vision she conjured up was indeed frightful, and he could barely conceive of anyone doing something so dreadful to another human being.

Cyrille de Picus wasn't human, said a soft voice in his ear.

Helewise was looking at him expectantly, waiting for an answer. He reached out for her hand, drawing her close. 'Aye, I think he did,' he said.

The Southfire kinswomen stayed for another day and night, then set off for home. Josse and Helewise rode with them as far as Hawkenlye Abbey, where they would halt briefly so that Emma could have a look around the abbey, speak to some of the nuns about their life there and, most importantly, have a formal

audience with Abbess Caliste about the possibility of her entry
into the community as a postulant.

Emma emerged from the abbess's little room at the end of the
cloister with shining eyes and a joyful expression.

Observing her as, walking between her mother and her grand-
mother she went to fetch her horse and mounted up, Josse said
to Helewise, 'Do you think she'll enter the community?'

Helewise turned to him, smiling. 'We'll see.'

By an unspoken conspiracy, all the people touched by Cyrille de
Picus's death resolved to regard it as a sad accident. The forces
of law and order were not put on the trail of the beggar; as Josse
remarked to Helewise, what would be the point? The man had
not been responsible for her fall out of the solar window, and
even the wisest in the land could not now say whether, had the
water not killed her, she would have survived the devastating
damage of the accident.

Josse wondered what had become of the beggar. Was he still
out there, treading his lonely path? The awful thing was, as fair-
minded, law-respecting Josse was forced to admit, he had a
sneaking sympathy for the poor man. Although he sincerely hoped
he would have done his utmost to drag Cyrille to safety as she
lay there helpless, the water rising, he found he just couldn't find
it in his heart to condemn the beggar. He confessed the sin, did
penance, sincerely apologized for his lack of charity, prayed to
God to give him the grace to mourn her as he should. But nothing
seemed to work.

Whatever he tried, he just couldn't help feeling that, with
Cyrille de Picus no longer in it, the world was a better place.

Helewise told nobody, not even Josse, what Olivar had said to
her. Indeed, as the days and the weeks went by, she was increasingly inclined to dismiss it; to put it down to the effects of severe
shock on a small child.

But it wouldn't quite *be* dismissed . . .

She knew one thing: she had to go back to Southfire Hall one
day. It both attracted and scared her, a little, but the attraction
outweighed the fear, and she knew she had to return and find
out more.

Not that it was going to be difficult.

Josse had fallen in love all over again with the house he knew in childhood. *The house of my ancestors*, he mused, sitting by the fire in the House in the Woods, his thoughts far away. Into his mind flitted an image of the strong, matriarchal women who tended the sacred fire up on the downs and, in the end, commemorated the spot by building the first dwelling there, still inhabited by descendants of the same blood. *I need the house, and perhaps it needs me*, he thought, although he wasn't sure what put the idea into his head. *I will never leave it so long again without going back.*

Meggie, too, resolved to return to the house on top of the downs. She had grown up knowing all about her inheritance from her mother; nobody had made any secret of it. This, though, this strong call from the ancient home of her forebears on her father's side, was something totally different. It was powerful and thrilling; she intended to get all the information she could from Josse, and Isabelle too. *It's my place too*, she thought with proprietorial pride. *It opened its soul to me, and I am accepted.*

Southfire Hall was calm again.

Evil had come, cleverly disguised, as evil so often is. Now it had gone away again; all vestiges of it had been removed; burned, buried or destroyed.

The house itself had got rid of the dark cloak made of the strange, clammy fabric, which once a woman had worn to scare a little boy out of his mind. It had been left where she had hidden it, under a pile of stones beneath the north wall of the ancient undercroft. Melt water had loosened some of the old stonework; the house had shifted a little on its deep foundations, and the breach had widened. The water found the weakness, as water always does, and quite soon a little streamlet was flowing through.

Just before the damage was discovered, and workmen hastily sent for to repair it before more harm was done, the water lapped up to the rolled-up cloak. The water lifted it, spread under and through it, supporting it up so that it floated like some frightening, repellent, dead thing. Slowly it began to move, carried on the weak current; under the wall, on, on, moving faster now as the waters gathered together and picked up pace. Down the long slope to the stream in the valley; borne along by the stream until it emptied into the river that ran through the town. On, on, tumbled and twisted now by the swollen river waters, till, at last, fresh water met salt and the cloak flowed out into the sea.

And, up there on the top of the downs, Southfire Hall settled back into its habitual tranquillity.

The spirit of the house was content.